"He can't make you marry me."

"We might not have much choice if we want to have a chance at the dreams we both want."

"All I want is to work on the ranch with my father, and you want to raise your horses."

Jackson nodded, his jaw sore from the tension. "Despite you lying to me, we were friends, right?"

Sofia nodded.

"We talked about you working for me."

"But that is different than getting married."

"It doesn't have to be."

That got her attention. Moving back, she wiped her face clear of the tears. "What do you mean?"

"We can treat it like a partnership. I didn't plan on ever marrying again."

"I know. I don't want a husband."

"Good. Because I don't want a wife. We could just stay friends. Have our own rooms, our own lives." He shrugged. "Just friends, business partners. But I'm not going to let your father force us into this. You have to agree."

A seventh-generation Texan, **Jolene Navarro** fills her life with family, faith and life's beautiful messiness. She knows that as much as the world changes, people stay the same: vow-keepers and heartbreakers. Jolene married a vow-keeper who shows her holding hands never gets old. When not writing, Jolene teaches art to inner-city teens and hangs out with her own four almost-grown kids. Find Jolene on Facebook or her blog, jolenenavarrowriter.com.

Books by Jolene Navarro

Love Inspired Historical

Lone Star Bride

Love Inspired

Lone Star Holiday
Lone Star Hero
A Texas Christmas Wish
The Soldier's Surprise Family
Texas Daddy

Visit the Author Profile page at Harlequin.com for more titles.

JOLENE NAVARRO

Lone Star Bride

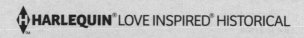
HARLEQUIN® LOVE INSPIRED® HISTORICAL

Recycling programs
for this product may
not exist in your area.

 LOVE INSPIRED BOOKS

ISBN-13: 978-0-373-42533-4

Lone Star Bride

Copyright © 2017 by Jolene Navarro

www.Harlequin.com

Printed in U.S.A.

Be still, and know that I am God.
—*Psalms* 46:10

Dedicated to my grandmother, Jo Ann Crawford.
She gave me the spark to tell stories and to
pass down stories from our own family.
Thank you for inspiring me and allowing me to
read all your Zane Grey books. This one is for you
and the women in our family who made Texas
their home before it was Texas.

Acknowledgments

Some say that writing is a solitary endeavor,
but I find I'm surrounded by many people
who help me along the way.

First, to my amazing brainstorming team,
Storm Navarro, Sasha Summers and Willa Blair
and the SARA to SARA Sundays.

Special thanks to the family of the late historian
W. T. Block. His article on the Opelousas Trail
inspired my pirates on a cattle drive.

To editor extraordinaire Emily Rodmell.
Thank you for your insight and eye for detail.
To executive editor Tina James for giving
Jackson and Sofia a home beyond my computer.
I discovered them six years ago. That they are
in the world is a dream come true.

To the most wonderful agent, Pam Hopkins, for
being a mixture of kindness, support and honesty.
Thank you.

Chapter One

Blood raced through Sofia De Zavala's veins as she stepped to the edge of the spacious veranda. The native stone floor kept the area cool in the Texas heat. It was only April, and the sun had already become a relentless rival to the numerous layers of material she wore. Wearing pants would be so much easier.

The sounds of the vaqueros and American cowboys filled the area near the horse barns.

Ignoring her father's orders, she planned on going to the stables today. Rumors of a new stallion that had come all the way from Ireland were impossible to ignore.

"Señorita Sofia, wait!" Her mother's maid ran after her. "I have your bonnet and gloves."

Not wanting to upset the older woman, she bit back a sigh. "I left them behind on purpose." Rosita went ahead with her mission and started pulling the long white gloves onto Sofia's hands. "These will be ruined."

"Your mother never allowed you to leave the house without them." The large overly decorated bonnet went on next. Tears hovered on the edges of the maid's russet eyes. "I can't believe they are gone."

"I know." She still expected to hear her mother's voice in the house. A voice that she took for granted and now dearly missed. "We all miss her, but I can't see as well with the bonnet on. It completely blocks my side view." What she wanted was a flat wide-brimmed hat like the men wore. If it wouldn't upset her father so much, she'd go get one of her brother's hats.

Her father still refused to talk about their loss, and Rosita cried at the mention of her mother. There was no place for her own grief to be shared.

Head high, more so in order to see in front of her than pride, Sofia hurried to the pens.

There were more people than she had ever seen at the corrals. Many of the women who lived on the ranch stood on the railing, watching the activity that stirred the dust. She loved being around the horses and had missed them.

On most of the ranches she had visited with her father, there were women working alongside the vaqueros, but her mother had believed that women belonged in the home. So, on their ranch, the men worked the livestock, and the women stayed inside.

This was her chance to change that for the De Zavala ranch and her people.

Her gloves immediately lost their whiteness when she grabbed the top of the wood fence and stepped up.

As she looked over the railing, she felt as if her heart and lungs stopped working. The most magnificent animal she had ever seen loped on the opposite side of the corral. Tucking his tail, he stopped and turned in one quick motion.

The glossy black coat lay over sculpted muscles. Long solid legs covered the ground in fluid motion. The stallion tossed his head, sending his mane flying in the breeze.

She was in love. "He's gorgeous."

Maria, Rosita's granddaughter, leaned in close to her. "They say he's from Kentucky." The younger woman sighed. "I've never seen anything like him."

"Kentucky? I thought he was from Ireland." Maria had never shown an interest in horses before. Frowning, Sofia turned her head to get a better look at the man working the horse. *Oh, my.*

He stood a head above any of her father's men. Booted feet planted in a wide stance, he held his right arm out, commanding the horse without a lunge line or whip.

It was more than just his height that made it obvious he was not one of her father's men. Without a hat, his hair was tousled. Streaks of wheat ran through his sandy-brown locks. She had never been so fascinated by a man's hairstyle or color.

Now she understood why all the females loitered around the horse pen. Not many visitors made it out to the ranch, and never men of this caliber.

The clothes he wore didn't help, either. No baggy trousers or loose shirt like many of her father's workers. He wore a black fitted vest over a white button-up that showed off a trim middle and long legs. Not a sound came from his mouth as he communicated with the horse.

How was he getting the stallion to move the way he wanted? Narrowing her gaze, Sofia focused on the man's movements. The man slightly flicked his fingers, and the horse stopped and spun to face him.

Head lowered, the big black beast walked forward and set his forelock against the man's broad chest. Nimble fingers rubbed the big jaw. All the women sighed as one.

Sofia glanced at the men surrounding the corral, many of them sitting on the top rail. Admiration was visible on the faces of the vaqueros, people she considered the best horsemen in the world.

A hand clasped on her shoulder. "*Mija*, what are you doing? It's too hot and dusty out here for you."

Her father's quiet voice startled her from the sight of horse and man. "Papi, I wanted to see the new horse. I hear he's from Ireland. Why didn't you tell me about him?" She glanced back to the cowboy.

"There is nothing to tell. It's business between Jackson McCreed and myself."

"But I love these horses. You allowed me to ride all over the ra—"

"That was years ago. Now you have house responsibilities and should be preparing for your marriage."

It was as though a mule had delivered a kick to her gut, almost had her doubling over. *Marriage?*

"I thought with the new Texas Republic, our contracts with Mexico were canceled?" This couldn't be happening. She had escaped the arrangement her mother set up. Her dreams had nothing to do with being the perfect wife.

"Yes, we have severed our ties to the old country, but to secure our future and legacy, we need connections to the new government. We could still lose our land grants." His jaw flexed as he looked over his people who had gathered to watch the new stallion.

"There are many political issues that need to be settled, and I want to ensure our ownership of the land is not questioned."

"But you stayed loyal to Texas. You provided horses and supplies to our fight for independence." Her father had stood by their new neighbors against the unfairness of Santa Anna.

"When it comes to greed, you can't count on fairness." His ebony eyes cut back to her. "You're no longer a child. Your mother wanted you settled in society with a family of your own. I will ensure her wishes become reality. By the end of the year, you will have a husband. A husband who can anchor our legacy in the new republic."

"Papi! I can—"

"Maria, take Sofia to the house. Go now. There is no business out here for you." He turned his back to her. Dismissing her and her wishes. She watched as he joined the cowboy with the magnificent stallion. They led the horse back into the stables where she wouldn't be able to see him.

A tug of her hand caught her attention. "Señorita, we must go to the house as your father ordered." The younger girl looked around Sofia. "My *abuela* says he's trouble, but he might be worth a little trouble."

Sofia nodded. "The best horses are."

Maria giggled. "You are not a normal girl, señorita." She started walking toward the hacienda. "I was speaking of the man. All the women are talking of him. Wondering if he will be staying. What have you heard?"

"Nothing." Her father no longer talked to her as a partner. Following Maria, Sofia started making plans.

Sometimes a little trouble was needed to achieve a goal. Why would God give her a talent and desire to work with horses if she was just meant to live in town taking care of a home for some man she didn't even know? "I don't know anything. Father no longer talks to me about the ranch."

Eyes sad, Maria nodded. "He feels the heavy burden of taking care of you and all the people who have remained on the ranch. With your mother and brother gone, he has much to worry about."

"You're right. We need to help him ease the burden." The cooler air under the veranda calmed Sofia a bit. Getting angry and arguing wouldn't convince her father of anything. He was too stubborn. She had been accused of being much like her father once too often for her to ignore.

Arguing would not get her anywhere. Her mother taught her that. She needed to show him how she could help.

Once alone, she made her way to the small crawl space upstairs, where the old trunks were stored. Dust and blankets covered everything. Digging through the piles, she found what she needed in the bottom of an old cedar chest—the clothes her brother had outgrown years before.

She ran her hand over the worn clothes. So many memories flooded her. Images of wonderful days with no worries, running free with the vaqueros and learning their skills. They grew up riding all over the ranch side by side. She could shoot a gun and hit a target, and lasso a steer faster and with more accuracy than her brother.

He would tease her and tell her she should have been born a boy. With a smirk, she would tell him she was too smart to be a boy.

She buried her face in a shirt and cried. She had lost her best friend, and no one would let her talk about it.

Wiping her face, she pulled out a pair of his riding boots. These would give her the freedom she needed. She was going to ride out to the cattle camp. If Santiago was there, he would encourage her, join her even.

With the right attire, she was one step closer to proving that she was just as capable as Santiago had been. Her brother's laughter rang in her heart. He would be the first one to point out that she was better with horses.

Tonight, the full moon would provide enough light. She was going to ride her father's new stallion.

Her mother had banned her from the stable a year ago, but tonight she was going to run free. Her blood was already racing. Yes, on the ranch, on the back of that great horse, that was where she belonged.

Her father needed riders for the drive to New Orleans. If she went to the camp and gathered and branded the cattle her father would see how much she could help. After hiding the new clothes and hat in her room, she headed to the kitchen.

It was hard to remain composed. She wanted to jump and laugh already. She could ride and rope with the best of the vaqueros, the same men who had taught her everything she knew. She would finally be putting those skills to the real test.

Now to keep busy until everyone went to bed. It was time to take her life into her own hands. She refused to be trapped in a marriage with a stranger who might not even love the land.

Glancing out the window, Sofia studied the sky. It would be hours until the moon was out. Then that black giant would be hers.

She was tired of waiting for life to happen. Tonight would be the first step in claiming her destiny.

Jackson McCreed sat up in his narrow bed, breathing hard. Goose bumps tightened his skin. A clammy sweat covered his body. One fast movement and his stocking feet touched the dirt-packed floor. The air hung heavy on his shoulders.

He reached for his silver pocketwatch and ran his thumb over the engravings. Not sleeping had become the only way to stop reliving the nightmare that haunted him every time he closed his eyes.

On the other side of the door, he heard his stallion Dughall give a low rumbling whistle. Jackson had been invited to stay in the hacienda, but he preferred to stay close to his horse.

The old tack room was better than some of the places he had slept the last couple of years. Hopefully that would change if the negotiations with Señor De Zavala produced the business deal he wanted.

The sound of a hinge opening, followed by another soft whistle from Dughall, brought his attention back to the stalls. Someone was messing with his stallion. Again.

There had been attempts to steal the horse in Galveston and San Antonio. His jaw locked. Anger turned his gut. He was sick and tired of people taking from him.

Jackson slipped on his shirt, pulling it over his shoulders. He didn't waste time with the buttons or tucking it into his pants. Not bothering with his boots, he picked up his Colt, checking to make sure the chambers were loaded as he headed out of the tack room.

Slipping through the door, he scanned the area. The wide corridor was better lit than his windowless room. He stayed close to the wall. At the opposite end, he saw Dughall's door open. The great stallion tossed his head as he stepped out.

To Jackson's shock, a boy sat on the brute's back. *It's just a kid.*

At best, the stallion tolerated strangers around him. The boy looked to be about twelve years old, maybe thirteen. He didn't recall seeing him on the ranch earlier today. The boy leaned over the black's neck. His small hand patted the quivering muscles ready to run. The kid had no idea how much power waited under him.

"Stop right there." Jackson kept his voice low and firm.

The horse and boy swung their heads toward him. Wide eyes stared at him from under the rim of the oversize battered hat. The boy wore quality clothes, but they were worn and ill fitted. The scuffed boots looked to be a size too big, going all the way up to his knees.

"Where do you think you're going?" He lowered the gun, but scanned the stables to make sure the boy was alone.

No answer.

He took a couple of steps closer and switched to Spanish, asking the boy what he was doing. *"¿Qué estás haciendo?"*

The boy's eyes went wider, obviously surprised he spoke the native language. The kid's lips remained shut tight.

"¿Qué estás haciendo?" he asked him again.

"*El caballo quiere correr.*" The voice was so low it was hard for Jackson to hear.

Was the kid trying to be funny? Jackson replied again in Spanish. "The horse told you he wanted to go for a run? Kid, that's still stealing. I should turn you over to the sheriff."

"No." The boy's hands fisted in the dark mane. He kept his head down, cleared his throat and coughed. "My... Señor De Zavala wouldn't mind."

"That's my horse. If Señor De Zavala gave his permission, why are you—" Jackson searched for the word he needed "—sneaking around in the dark?" Approaching the horse, Jackson slipped the gun into his waistband. "Should we go get your boss?" A quick jerk of the boy's head confirmed what Jackson already guessed. "Kid, do you even belong on the ranch?"

"I belong." Chin up, he looked so small on the big stallion. Patting the horse's neck, the boy relaxed his shoulders and turned away.

Jackson reached for the leather reins. "This stallion could have killed you. Don't think your ma would appreciate losing you over a ride."

"My mother is dead, señor." The youth tried to pull the reins from Jackson.

His hands looked too smooth to have ever done any real work. Jackson growled in frustration. The poor kid was an orphan doing what he had to do to survive. He continued in Spanish. "So who's waiting for you?"

"*Nadie.*"

Nobody. Such a simple word to describe a devastating existence for a child.

"Right." Jackson fought down the urge to offer the

kid a safe place. He didn't have the time or resources to take on a lost boy.

Helping people never worked out anyway. His hand felt huge circling the boy's upper arm as he pulled him off the horse. The warmth coming through the cloth surprised Jackson.

Once on the ground, the kid barely reached Jackson's chest. The youth's wide-eyed stare stayed glued on the front of his shirt he had left open. Turning red, the boy jerked his head down, then tried to yank his arm free. The underdeveloped muscles weren't much of a contest to Jackson's strength.

"When was the last time you ate?" For more times than he could count, Jackson was glad he had learned his grandmother's native tongue. She had been proud of her homeland of Spain.

"I am not your concern, señor." He tried to jerk his arm back again. "Release me."

The boy's Spanish sounded educated. "So you can steal something else?" With his hands wrapped around the small arm, Jackson pulled the boy closer. Just because he wasn't turning the youngster over to the law, didn't mean he couldn't scare him. "What's your name?"

The boy glared up at him with his lips pulled tight into a thin line. He had a fresh scrape across the left side of his face.

Jackson gave him a slight shake. The kid was going to end up in a bad way if he wasn't careful. "You want to dangle from a rope? They hang horse thieves. They won't care about your age. What's your name?"

The small jaw locked down and the muscle flexed, stubbornness written all over the soft face.

"Fine. You can tell the sheriff." He started pulling

the boy toward the old tack room. Jackson hoped the kid didn't call his bluff.

"Santiago! My name's Santiago." His voice cracked. The boy started coughing as he fought Jackson's grip.

Jackson stopped and stared down with one eyebrow raised, waiting for the rest of the name.

The kid shuffled his feet, looking at the ground. The narrow shoulders slumped. "Smith." The single mumbled word disappeared into the floor.

"Really? Smith?" The kid either didn't know his last name, or he lied. Knowing how harsh the world could be, Jackson figured it might be a bit of both.

"Listen kid, why don't we talk to the boss and see about getting you a job?"

Santiago's head shot up, his dark eyes large. With a short growl, the boy swung his leg back and kicked Jackson hard in the shin. Caught by surprise, he loosened his grip. The ragtag boy took the opportunity to run.

Straight to Dughall. The stallion still stood in the middle of the barn, ground tied when one of the reins dropped in a coil on the dirt-packed floor.

As if he did it all the time, the small body flew onto the bareback of the horse as he grasped the leather reins. With a kick the stallion bolted out the large barn door, past the corrals and into the moonlit pasture with the kid.

Jackson bit down the angry thoughts as he ran after them. The kid was going to get them both killed. At the door, he placed two fingers in his mouth and let out a loud whistle that covered the night sounds.

To Jackson's surprise, Dughall didn't stop right away. He whistled again.

At the edge of the tree line, the big black stopped and looked back at him. The boy's seat never wavered. The kid knew how to ride.

The stallion swung his head around, back to the trees. Santiago dug in the back of his heels and slapped the leather reins against Dughall's rump, urging him forward.

One last whistle pulled the horse's attention back to Jackson. As the big animal turned and moved toward the barn, he hung his head low.

The kid jumped from the stallion's back and ran into the trees. The big brute paused as if he wanted to join the little thief.

"Get over here!" Jackson scolded his horse.

A lit kerosene lamp came from the house, swinging as the carrier came closer to the barn. Jackson recognized Rafael De Zavala, the ranch owner.

"What is all the noise about? Is everything all right?" His smooth Spanish accent enriched his crisp English.

"There seems to be a little thief running wild."

"*Híjole*, more gangs have moved into the area. Is everyone safe? Did they take anything of value?"

"Tried to run off with Dughall." The horse stood next to him now and nudged him with his soft muzzle. Jackson wasn't sure if he was apologizing or asking to leave with the boy.

From the other side of the barn, a few of the ranch hands joined them, guns drawn.

"I'll send for the sheriff." De Zavala turned.

"No, don't worry about it. The kid was beat up and half starved. He didn't get away with anything. Everyone should go back to bed."

"Diego." De Zavala called out. "Stay in the barn

and stand guard. Estevan, make sure we have someone every night to watch the horses."

The men left. Jackson turned to De Zavala and held his hand to midchest. "He was about this tall. His name was Santiago. Do you know him?"

The older man's mouth fell open, then he shook his head. "No, it couldn't be. Are you sure? My son, who drowned during a storm, is Santiago." De Zavala gave him a tight smile and shook his head. "I'm being foolish. My son is gone, and he would be taller. He was a man, not a boy."

He walked over to Dughall and placed a hand on Jackson's horse. "You have a very fine stallion. Is it too late in the night to talk business? I'm unable to sleep, and I have an idea to give you."

That sounded promising. More so than anything else Rafael De Zavala had said since they started corresponding months ago. Jackson nodded.

"Settle your horse then, and come to the back of the house through the kitchen. We will meet in my study. Everyone is asleep, and we can finish our talk of business."

"I'll be there." His plans were falling into place.

"Good. I have given much thought to what you want, and I think you can take care of a problem I have. It will be a good partnership."

Jackson watched the man make his way back to the big hacienda. Arrogance and shrewdness radiated off him, much like Jackson imagined it did off the conquistadors of old.

Dughall looked with longing in the direction the boy had disappeared. "I know there was something about the kid, but we can't save them all, old man. Come on, we offered him a job and he ran. I'll take you out for a run tomorrow."

Jackson had one goal, and that was to get De Zavala to sell him a few of his broodmares. Their bloodlines were as old as those conquistadors. There was also a perfect property on the edge of town.

He brushed down Dughall and thought of the ranch he wanted to build. He visualized a place much like this one, but smaller. He wouldn't need such a big house for just him, and he wasn't going to marry. Not ever again.

He gave one last look out to the trees. Should he try to go after the kid? He had to be hungry. He sighed and threw the brush back in the bucket. Santiago would know the countryside better than he did. In the morning, he'd ask the ranch hands. Someone had to know the kid's story.

Chapter Two

Sofia leaned against the giant oak. Her hands trembled as she pressed them against her pounding heart. Eyes closed, she forced her lungs to relax.

Despite the horror of being caught, she had experienced pure joy for a moment. The big stallion's muscles flexing under her, all the raw power ready to be unleashed.

The imprudent man had to call him back. The American cowboy didn't even have the manners to button and tuck in his shirt.

Growing up on the ranch, she had been around plenty of men, but the man her father was doing business with made her uncomfortable in ways she didn't understand.

She never realized how sheltered her father had kept her even as she ran free over the ranch, or maybe she'd just been too young to notice the men. But she noticed him, and he was a distraction.

For a bit, she had forgotten she was supposed to be a boy. That would've been disastrous.

He had said the horse was his. That didn't make sense. She thought he was some cowhand delivering a new stallion for her father's stables. How did a poor cowboy get such a magnificent stallion?

Her breathing slowed to normal as she pushed herself off the rough tree bark. Her hands ran down the bottom of her oversize shirt. The ease of movement in her brother's old clothes was liberating. The thought of being trapped in a corset and dress again depressed her.

She could have her own clothes fashioned in such a way that gave her freedom of movement. Just because she was a female, her mother had convinced her father she needed to stay in the house, but she was different from her mother.

Sofia closed her eyes and bit hard on her lower lip, clearing her thoughts. The back of her head bumped the trunk. Above her, stars danced through the tree branches, winking at her.

Life was too short to live by someone else's expectations. She loved the land. Running the ranch with her father was all she wanted. She could be his partner.

He needed her. With her mother and brother gone, it was just the two of them. This was her legacy also.

The light was still coming from inside the barn. First, she needed to convince him to buy that stallion. She would find a way to go for a real ride on the horse the cowboy called Dughall. Maybe the man could stick around, too.

She would love telling him what to do. As his boss, he would have to follow her orders. She touched her arm where he left his handprint. The warmth of his touch lingered.

With slow steps, she moved back toward the hacienda. Inside the courtyard, she eased along the adobe wall. As she got closer to the window that provided her escape earlier, her father's voice drifted through the air.

She groaned. Getting back into the house would not be as easy as leaving now that he was awake. Sofia flattened against the wall as a light moved across the room.

Trapped.

She crossed her arms and slid down the rough side of her home. Her father's voice carried through the night. He didn't usually talk to himself. All the political upheaval had him more stressed than she thought.

"Thank you for taking my offer into consideration, Señor De Zavala." The rough baritone voice joined her father's.

Sofia's hand covered her mouth. The cowboy was having a late-night meeting with her father? Maybe he had seen through her disguise. Her heart jumped in her chest.

Staying low, she peeked over the windowsill and watched as the tall cowboy shook hands with her father.

A dark jacket covered his shoulders now, and leather boots had him standing taller than he was earlier in the barn. Her father was not a small man, but he lost some of his size next to the cowboy.

They turned, moving closer to her. She dropped to the ground, waiting to see if they were coming to the window to call her out. Instead, she heard the chairs at the small table scrape across the wood floor. They settled in and started talking about horses.

The cowboy wanted to buy some of their top broodmares? No way would her father sell his best mares to this man.

"Mr. McCreed, I have a trade in mind that would get us both what we want. With all the uncertainty of Texas winning its independence from Mexico, many of my people have fled back to our homeland."

A pause followed, as if her father needed to gather his thoughts.

"Texas is my home, and here is where I want to build my legacy. Losing my wife and son leaves me desperate to secure my land, my daughter's future and the future of her sons, my grandsons. I have a cousin in Galveston, and I need to send her to him in order to set my plans in motion to marry her to a well-connected American."

Sofia's stomach twisted. Her father intended to send her away, to marry her off. Not to Mexico this time, but it was just as far. She had hoped he changed his mind, but the only thing that changed was he no longer talked to her about his plans for the future.

"Sir, I completely understand the need to protect one's family. Especially a daughter, but what does this have to do with our deal?"

Her father gave a deep short laugh. It sounded as if he hit the cowboy on the arm or shoulder. "Forgive me. If you are ever burdened with a daughter, you will understand my worries. I love her, but she needs protection."

Burden? Slow tears trailed down her cheeks. She heard the familiar tapping her father did when he was thinking. "I have a buyer for cattle in New Orleans. With so many of my families leaving for Mexico, I'm shorthanded. I need a range boss I can trust to get them to that point. You have driven a herd to market, *sí*?"

There was a pause in the conversation. She tilted her head to see if she could get a visual of them.

Her father continued. "The cash will fund my daughter's trip to Galveston. I also have a small herd of geldings I'm selling. The sooner I get this done, the sooner I can settle her future and the future of the ranch."

A cold sweat on her skin battled with the burn in the pit of her stomach. She tightened her arms around her middle. Her father wasn't even considering her request to stay and help him on the ranch. He was in a rush to marry her off. *To get rid of his burden.*

Pressing the heels of her palms against her eyes, she tried to stop the tears. Crying wouldn't solve anything. It would just prove her father right. She was not weak.

The stranger's deep voice carried through the window again. Making sure to be silent, she leaned in to hear more of the conversation.

"We haven't been acquainted long, Señor De Zavala. I've been on a couple of drives, but never as the boss. What makes you think I can be trusted with your cattle, horse and cash?"

"You have more experience driving cattle than anyone else. I like to think I'm a good judge of character, and I know how important a man's dream can be to motivate him. You have one of the finest stallions I've ever seen. He will be well taken care of in my stables while you drive my herd to New Orleans."

Sofia heard the scraping of the chair. Her father was moving to his desk from the sound of it.

"Mr. McCreed, I have written out what I need in order for a trade to happen between us. As you can see, I'm being very generous. I have included five mares if you allow me two guaranteed breedings."

The men moved away from the window, so she couldn't hear the rest of their conversation.

Her stomach twisted. She had always thought of them as her horses, as well. How was she going to stop this?

* * *

Walking through the kitchen, Jackson picked up an apple from a wire basket. At the back door, he made a sharp turn to the left. The kid had been spying on them. Had he planned to steal something else, or was he sleeping in the courtyard at night?

Pausing at the edge of the rock fence, Jackson waited for his eyes to adjust to the darkness.

He spoke out in Spanish. "Santiago, I saw you at the window. I know you're here. Come out." He allowed silence to hang in the space between them. "I'm not leaving until I talk to you."

He leaned against the stone wall that enclosed the little bit of Spanish garden. The bright moon highlighted a fountain in the center, surrounded by exotic flowers and three giant oaks to sit under. It was a good place to hide. He tossed the apple up and caught it. Waiting.

Using his grandmother's language, he spoke loud enough for the boy to hear, but soft enough to not alert anyone in the household. "Does Señor De Zavala know you are sulking in his courtyard? Maybe I should go get him."

A few more minutes of silence, and the boy left his hiding place. Head down, he made his way to Jackson.

"What were you doing sneaking around the house so late at night? The last I saw of you, was you running to the trees."

"Pardon my bad manners, señor. I panicked. Your horse wanted to run."

"So it was Dughall's fault?"

The boy sighed and, after a heartbeat of silence, looked at the gate. "No, señor. I made a mistake, one I will not make again. He just wanted to go for a run.

In the morning, he would have been in his stall. I'm a hard worker, not a thief. I heard you will be driving a herd to New Orleans. You won't find anyone better with a lasso."

Jackson had to smile at the kid. "You mean you overheard."

The kid's body went rigid. From under the wide-brimmed hat, he looked Jackson in the eye. The big eyes looked too delicate to survive in this rough world.

"You know I'm good with horses."

"Here." Tossing the apple to Santiago, Jackson watched as the soft hands caught it effortlessly. "If you're going to do a man's job, you need to add some muscles. And no stealing or sneaking around." Jackson turned to make his way back to the barn.

The kid ran after him. "I don't steal."

"You want me to trust you? To give you a job? Why should I?" The boy kept his head down, but his spine remained stiff, and Jackson could hear the sharp hard breaths coming from the kid's nose. He got the impression little Santiago was angry. It reminded him of barn kittens whenever they hissed at him.

"The horse wanted to run. You keep such a fine animal in a small place. Maybe you don't deserve him."

Jackson suppressed a laugh. Despite his small size, the little guy had plenty of gumption. "So you were saving my horse. And I should thank you by giving you a job?"

Santiago followed him to the barn and through the doors.

"I'm sorry, señor. Sometimes my mouth gets ahead of my good manners. Hire me. You'll not regret it. I promise."

Walking into the dark barn, Jackson paused at Dughall's stall. "So you think you can handle a job on the trail?"

The kid didn't even look at him, but made a beeline to the gray mare a few doors down. One of the mares Jackson had wanted, but De Zavala had not included in the deal.

He leaned against the wall and studied the kid. Something was not right, but he couldn't identify the problem. The boy moved like he owned the place, and he sounded educated. He knew horses, how to handle them, how to ride. Not your typical lost orphan.

"Do you have a place to sleep, or were you sleeping in the courtyard?"

With a soft whistle, the kid moved to the next horse. They acted as if they knew him. Necks arched over the doors, trying to get the kid's attention. The boy laughed as he shared the apple with one of the mares. The small shoulders shrugged. "I like the quiet of the moon and horses."

Jackson understood the need to be alone. Dughall made a rumbling noise in his throat. He seemed to want the boy's attention also.

With a sigh, Jackson headed to his own small room. Maybe this time he could actually sleep. As he walked down the corridor, he yelled back to the kid. "I'm driving a herd east. I could use a helper for the cook."

That got the kid's attention. His head shot up. "Why can't I work with the horses and cattle? I don't want to cook." He ran a dirty sleeve across his nose and ran to catch up to Jackson's longer strides.

"You're too small." Jackson hoped he wasn't making a mistake. He avoided entanglements with people, but this kid pulled on all his protective strings. The kid was too small to handle the dangers of a cattle drive. He shouldn't have said anything.

In his room, he poured the fresh water into a bowl and removed his jacket.

"I know I'm going to regret this," he mumbled in English.

"No, señor, I'll be a great help for the cook. Please, I just want to go on the drive."

One of his eyebrows shot up as he gave the boy a pointed stare. The kid gasped and covered his mouth. He must have realized his mistake. "So you do speak English? Any other lies I need to know?"

"Oh, no, no. I understand little. I will…try to speak good."

He narrowed his eyes at the kid.

Santiago lowered his head. "I'm sorry. I'll do whatever you need."

"You sure find yourself apologizing a lot." He ran his hands over the stubble on his chin. "Be at the north bunkhouse Thursday morning. Can you do that?" Jackson untucked his shirt.

"Yes, yes. Thank you." Santiago's face turned red as he nodded. With a quick turn to leave, he ran hard into the wall next to the door. A loud yelp followed.

"Are you all right?" The kid didn't answer. Jackson reached for him, but Santiago bolted.

Jackson watched him run past the horses as if a bear chased him. That boy confused him. One minute he acted like the son of privilege, the next a scared gutter rat. And little Santiago knew English.

Normally, he had no tolerance for liars, but when someone was alone and fighting to survive, he could not really hold it against them. He turned and put as much mental distance as he could between himself and the kid. Once on the trail, he would be the cook's problem.

Sophia ran all the way back to the courtyard. Excitement roared through her body like the flooded Guadalupe River. She was going on a real cattle drive, and when she got back, her father would have to acknowledge her skills.

Nothing but riding all day, seeing the country and traveling to new places. Arms wide, she twirled under the full moon, laughing at the stars. She spent hours dreaming about this life, but never really thought she'd have the opportunity.

How would she leave without her father worrying about her or searching for her? Maybe she could trust him one more time. She could tell him, despite all his plans and his talk of burdens. Then, at least, she would not have to mask her true identity from the crew.

If she had to stay in disguise, she wouldn't be able to take one of her own horses. Mr. McCreed would think she stole it. It would be easier if her father allowed her to join the cattle drive as a De Zavala.

The wind caught her brother's hat, knocking it off. Her hair tumbled down. The long thick waves were hard to control on a good day. With a heavy sigh, she knew if her father was not open to her new goal, it would have to be cut.

She picked up the hat and put it back on. In the morning, she would talk to him. They were the only De Zavalas left.

Chapter Three

Sofia sat the plate of sweet breads on the edge of her father's desk. Next to the vase of roses and starburst she had cut from her mother's garden this morning.

"Father, it's nothing. I fell while cutting the fresh flowers for your study." She sat in the chair Jackson McCreed had occupied last night. "The bricks were wet from the morning shower. Distracted, thinking about ways to help on the ranch, I slipped."

Taking one of the large rolls with sugar and icing, her father shook his head. "You should not be concerned with matters of the ranch. You are twenty-two years old. Way past the time to be married and giving me grandsons."

"I can help you here on the ranch. I used to—"

"There are many things you used to do that are inappropriate for a young lady of good breeding. We have enough cattle gathered to drive to New Orleans."

He looked through some papers on his desk. "We will use the money to send you to Galveston. There, my cousin Perez has connections with good American families." He picked up a letter and handed it to her.

"We're making arrangements now. You, marrying into one of these families, will do more to secure our legacy here in Texas than working on the ranch. It will give us solid ground to stand on, no matter the vote from the new congress. I will allow you to marry the one of your choosing."

"That's very generous of you, Papi." He didn't seem to pick up on her sarcastic tone. Or ignored it. That had been his style since the flood that took her mother and brother—avoid any emotion. He expected the same from her.

He put the document down and sighed. "I don't want to lose the ranch. If congress votes not to honor our land grants, I want to have a plan to ensure we keep it in our family, for my grandchildren."

Reaching for his hand, she wanted him to understand she could ease some of his stress by staying. "Papi, you supported the new Texas, they will support you now. You know I can ride and rope better than some of the men out there. I don't want to leave to find a husband, a man who will be a stranger."

Desperation gripped her as she thought of ways for him to see her as a partner and not a burden.

"Your mother raised you to take your place in polite society and run a well-managed home. With the changes here in Texas, I'm not sure what our future holds. I want you protected and safe. This is what your mother wanted."

"My mother wanted me to marry a good family in Mexico. Now you want me to marry a good American." She stood. Taking a deep breath, she tried to remain calm. "I don't want either, Papi. I want to stay with you on our land. This is where I belong."

"No, it's too dangerous, and who would you marry? There are no proper suitors for you here." He looked at the family portrait that hung over the fireplace. "Politics have changed the country of origin, but not the intent. You will go to Galveston and find a proper husband."

"This canyon that holds our ranch is where I belong. This is the life I want, not city streets and walls. Papi, how can you send me away?" Tears threatened to fall. She couldn't believe he was doing this. She moved around his massive dark oak desk, which anchored the room. "Please, I'm all you have left. You're all I have left. I can help at the cattle station."

He looked at her. In the depths of his eyes, she still saw the clouds of sadness that formed the moment they found her mother's body in the swollen river.

"*Mija, you* are my future. My life. If something happens to me, you would be all alone with no protection. If anything happened to you? I would have no reason to live."

"We can't live in fear. In Galveston, I'll be alone. Please, Papi." She moved closer to him, reaching out to touch his hand.

His body went rigid. "You can help by doing what your mother wanted. You, to have your own beautiful home, a family, children and a proper place in society. I would be pleased with grandsons to carry on our family legacy, and little granddaughters as beautiful as their mother." His hand came up and cupped her face. "Your tears will not change my mind. When you hold your firstborn in your arms, you will thank me."

Sofia stepped back, away from his touch. She knew without a doubt his mind was set. Unless she did something drastic, she would be sent to Galveston to marry.

She looked at the shelves with its books all in neat and tidy rows, all in their place. She did not want to be put in place. She made a decision.

Jackson McCreed was taking their cattle to market, and he had offered her a job. Her father might be stubborn, but she could match him. She would show him she brought more to the ranch than just social graces and babies. By the time she returned home, he would welcome her by his side.

"Papi, the Schmitts have invited me to go to Galveston with them for some spring shopping. I had told them no, thinking you needed me here, but maybe I should go. I could meet my cousins and look at the list of potential husbands."

She touched the soft petal of a yellow rose. "They plan to be gone for a few weeks. If I'm going into Galveston society, I could use new gowns."

With a few steps, he was next to her. He kissed her on the forehead as if she were still a little girl. "That's a fine idea. You can become familiar with the city before we start going to socials. When are they leaving?"

"At the end of this week. I can go into town with Juanita." And by the end of next month, her reputation might be ruined, but she didn't enjoy town anyway. Here on the ranch, it wouldn't matter.

She didn't need or want a husband who cared more about social graces than daily life on the ranch. An image of the tall cowboy rubbing the jaw of his stallion popped into her mind, but she shook her head. She would not allow the cowboy to distract her, either.

A few days later, Sofia made her way through the tree line in the dark, an old work saddle on her hip.

She had to move slowly in order not to trip. The boots were a size or two too big and made moving awkward.

A few shirts and a pair of pants, along with extra strips of cloth to keep everything hidden, were stuffed into a worn leather saddlebag. The bag came from a raid of her brother's room. With a rolled-up blanket, a hunting knife and his prized Hawken rifle she had everything a cowboy would need to survive.

From her own closet, she pulled out the rawhide rope she'd made herself a few years ago. The vaqueros who helped her make it taught her that it was even more important than the horse under a person. It was an extension of the vaquero's arm.

She loved working with the rope. Her brother got mad whenever her skill outdid his.

Her left hand went to the back of her neck, bare of the long braid she had since her earliest memories. Now it was gone. In the bottom of her brother's drawer along with a note to her father. She had heard him in there late at night. It seemed once a month her father had developed the habit of going through every corner of her brother's room. What if he didn't?

Maybe if he found it with her cut braid, he would understand how important this was to her.

A shiver ran down her spine at the memory of the cold metal scissors pressed to the base of her neck.

The thick hair had fought the destruction. In chunks, the braid came loose in her hand. Soft curls sprang around her face, choppy and uneven until she ran a handful of hair grease through it.

She could imagine her brother teasing her about still looking like a girl. Choking back tears, she buried her thoughts of him. At times, she still expected him to walk into the room, make a joke about her being a girl and hug her until she was laughing. He would have loved this adventure.

A moment of sadness overcame her as she rubbed her bare neck.

Then anticipation rolled in her stomach. She was about to start a whole new adventure on the open range.

Sofia stopped at the edge of the trees. The sun wasn't up yet, but a group of American cowboys moved around the old shed, getting ready for the day. She was about to live with them on a daily basis. Could she do this?

Yes! If she started doubting herself now, she might as well go back to the house.

Connected to the building was a covered cooking area, open on two sides. The smell of bacon and beans made her stomach rumble. Between her nerves and getting out of the house without being caught, she had missed the last two meals.

She still couldn't eat anything at this point. Fear tangled her in its net. Air had a hard time finding its way to her lungs.

Would she be able to pull this off? She was relieved to find none of the men were from around the area. It would have been hard to hide her identity from someone who knew Sofia De Zavala, the rancher's daughter. What would the trail boss do if he found out?

Boots that had been worn by her brother helped her take the first steps to this new journey. All she needed to do now was introduce herself to the cook and cowboys. She would be living with, working with and traveling with these rough men.

"Santiago?"

The sound of her brother's name caused her to jump.

Jackson stood behind her. "What are you doing hiding out here?"

"I'm here to join the drive."

For a few heartbeats, he stared at her. Not sure what to do, she studied her boots.

"You're early, but that's good. I'll introduce you to Francisco Luna. He's the cook." Jackson nodded at a man who walked out from the back of the building.

Not wanting to hear her brother's name over and over again, she had to come up with something else. She needed a nickname. "Call me Tiago."

His gaze narrowed. "You're changing your name?"

"No, it's what I want to be called. It's shorter, and this is a new adventure. I need a new name."

"Okay, Tiago. Follow me. By the way, your English greatly improved since I saw you last."

There was nothing to say to that, so she trailed behind Jackson, walking faster than she was used to in order to keep up with him. Stepping out from the protection of the trees, she took a deep breath and reminded herself she was a boy.

Cook was wider than he was tall, not that it was a difficult feat. Straight up on his toes, he might be five feet tall. Under a bushy mustache and white beard, he had a smile that stretched from ear to ear. He called out to the cowboys to come get their meal.

When Jackson introduced her, the little man lifted his chin and looked down at her. "You know how to work hard, *mijo*?"

"*Sí*, señor." She forced herself to nod with confidence she didn't feel. Sweat ran down her spine.

He looked apprehensive.

"Whatever you need, I'll do it. You won't know how you did it without me on all those other drives."

He laughed and reached up to pat Jackson on his shoulder. "I think I like our little Tiago."

"Yeah, he has that effect on people. I'm going to talk to the boys before we head out."

Without pausing, Cook handed her a knife. "Take care of the bacon." He moved quickly around her, getting several things done at once. All the while, making jokes she didn't understand.

He explained her job was to tend the mules and chickens along with hauling, fetching, cleaning and anything else he needed doing.

This was happening. She was part of the crew that would drive cattle to New Orleans for her father. She might be cooking right now, but she was cooking outside, not in the kitchen like a woman. She was ready to ride over the country and out of Texas. She wanted to sing and dance.

Head down, she flipped the bacon and whistled as she checked the pot of beans. She was a boy on a trail drive.

In front of the bunkhouse, her new trail boss talked to a few of the men. She forced herself to look away. He could be her biggest threat to this new life.

When he was around she'd have to keep her head down and make sure not to look like, talk like or act like a woman. Jackson McCreed might make that difficult.

Chapter Four

The sun started peeking over the hills and highlighted the details of the rugged camp. Several cowboys walked outside, their boots hitting the old wood of the porch. They gathered around Jackson. After a few minutes, they started heading directly toward her as a group.

She wanted to find a place to hide. She hadn't really thought what it would mean to live as a boy for the whole trip.

"It's a kid. Where'd you come from?" She had never heard that cowboy's accent before, and she wasn't sure what he looked like because she kept her eyes down, focused on the sizzling bacon.

"I could use someone to polish my boots." Laughter followed.

Someone pulled her hat off. "Not sure I'd trust him. He has the look of a scamp who would steal everything he could and sneak off in the night." The new one speaking had a very strong Southern accent.

"Give me back my hat." She grabbed for the black felt hat that belonged to her brother.

The cowboy laughed and held the hat high above his

head. Even if she jumped, she wouldn't be able to reach it. All she could do was glare.

"He looks more like two bit of nothing than a cowboy."

"Boss, we running an orphan camp now?"

"Hey, Two Bit, you gonna stare at your boots or actually pass out the bacon?"

All the excitement she felt earlier drowned under a wave of doubt. She had been stupid to think that putting on her brother's pants would immediately help her fit into the world of men. These cowboys would never talk to her like this if they knew she was a De Zavala. She was tempted to tell them, just to see the look on their faces.

The closest cowboy to her spat on the ground by her feet.

Jackson joined the group. "That's enough, Will. This is Santiago. He goes by Tiago. He'll be helping Cook and only answers to him." He took the hat from the man named Will and handed it to her. "You stay with Cook. We'll be heading out to the cattle station as soon as these yahoos finish eating."

Standing as straight as her spine allowed, she used the knife to pass the bacon onto their plates, along with a ladle full of gravy and a biscuit.

Under the mesquite trees, she made a resolution. No matter what they threw at her for the next few weeks, she would ride and learn with these men.

As they sat on the ground to eat, they joked and harassed each other. Jackson stood in front of her.

"You sure about this?"

She couldn't back out now, just because the cowboys teased her. That would only prove she didn't belong here, and she knew she did. "Why wouldn't I be?" She added a shrug to make sure he knew she could be one of the cowboys.

"Okay. Once you get everything packed, you and Cook will head out first thing in the morning. The horses, then cattle will follow the wagon." His eyes narrowed. "This is it. There is no way out once we start moving the cattle."

She hesitated. To the core of her soul, she knew the next step would decide the direction of her life. Independence she never dreamed possible would be hers, along with all of the dangers.

Could she move back into the safe world her father had created for her? Where he also had an unknown groom waiting.

The men who worked for him, the business, the family…everything would be better off with her being a true partner of the ranch. In order to prove it to her father, she had to first prove it to these men. And herself.

Looking around the bare bunkhouse and outside cooking area, she knew this was easy living compared to the trail. She'd be sleeping on the ground, surrounded by wild animals.

Jackson looked at her expecting an honest answer. He didn't rush her, just stood waiting. He didn't know it, but she just put her life in his hands.

With a quick nod, she ran to the spot she had dropped her things.

The minute she walked back to the wagon, carrying her saddle, rifle and lasso, laughter erupted from the wranglers on the porch.

"That there's some pretty fancy equipment for Two Bit of a cook's helper."

"Two Bit, you going to be riding the big stew pot over hills and hunting down our dinner?"

"Naw, he's going to use his papa's rope there and saddle the biggest bull. You going to lead us all the way to New Orleans." They laughed at their stupid jokes.

They weren't even funny.

Cook put dirt over the fire. "Toss your gear in the wagon. And start hooking up the mules."

If Cook ignored the cowboys, so would she.

Jackson grabbed a saddle off the porch railing. "We've got work to do." All the men went to the round pen and picked a horse to saddle.

The wagon was the biggest one she had ever seen. Usually, they used one with two wheels. This monster had four large wheels and siding that was taller than her. De Zavala was painted on the side. Leave it to her father to make a grand statement.

The mules for the wagon grazed nearby with long ropes attached to their leather hackamores. There were six. One of her jobs would be hitching them to the wagon that carried all the food supplies. Cook told her the placement was important to keep everything balanced.

She bit her lip and put her hands on her hips.

For years, she rode with her father, learning how to handle a horse, rope and brand cattle. Not once did she wonder how it all came to be. That had been someone else's job.

Now she was expected to harness mules that didn't look very cooperative. She could do this. Really, how difficult could it be? She knew tack and how to…she lifted the pieces of leather.

Long lines, straps, loops and the large collar with loose pieces that she didn't have any knowledge of.

When Jackson realized she didn't even know how to do her first job, he would leave her behind.

Maybe if she got the mules in line, the pieces would come together. The mules ignored her when she tried to move them. "Boys, this would be a great deal easier if you would stand in front of the wagon."

After pulling and pushing, coercing and urging, she stood with her hands on her hips. It appeared that figuring out how to arrange the tack was not her biggest problem.

The creaking of leather warned her she wasn't alone. "It helps if you attach the mules to the wagon."

At the sound of Jackson's deep voice, her shoulders sagged. She was caught. With a deep breath, she turned, making sure to stand tall.

Confidence was all about how the world saw you. Leaning across the saddle horn, the grim set of his mouth was at odds with the merriment in his eyes.

Everything about Jackson confused her.

He dismounted and let the reins drop to the ground. "Here." From his pocket, he pulled wedges of apples. "Make friends with them, and they will do whatever you want. A good wrangler can get his mules to line up in order with one signal. They like routine and treats." He laid his hand flat, and the dark gray mule followed him to the wagon.

"Cook wanted oxen, but the mules move out faster and are easier to train."

She approached the one closest to her. It reached for the apple with its large lips and nudged her. Taking the rope, she placed him next to the gray mule in front of the wagon.

As they moved the six mules, Jackson explained the importance of their order. Step by step, he walked her through attaching the collars and lines.

"Make sure to use the pads, and that all the straps are lying flat. If they develop sores, they can't pull and we can't move."

"How does this look?" She stepped back and watched him check her work.

Testing the cinches and traces, he nodded. "This is good. You want to make sure they don't get tangled. Once you get this down, it will go by much faster. You'll be doing this on your own from now on, so make sure to do it correctly." He went on to explain all the things that could go wrong if she messed up.

Not that she didn't already have enough to worry about. This was it. Now it was her responsibility.

Once the mules stood ready, Jackson leaped onto his horse with one swing of his leg. He tipped his hat and left for the cattle station.

Alone, she turned to the gray long-eared mule. "I can do this."

Chapter Five

Teams of cowboys gathered small groups of steers into holding pens to finish the last brandings. Jackson leaned over the saddle horn and watched the ranch's Mexican cowboys lasso and brand. They were doing two to three for every one steer his cowboys covered. The Americans were proficient. They just weren't as fast as the Mexicans.

One of his men, Rory Brosnen, went over to see how they were moving through the herd so quickly. The local men seemed to anticipate what the longhorns were going to do every step of the way.

From behind him, the boy yelled a warning. With a sharp movement, Jackson turned to see a two-thousand-pound bull charging at him.

He pulled on the reins to move his horse, but before he had time to do anything else, Tiago had his rope swinging over his head and caught the bull by both back legs, causing it to stumble. The vaquero who had been showing one of the American cowboys some tricks, had his rope around the bull's wide sharp horns.

The angry animal forgot his original target and

turned to the horseless vaquero. Jackson swung his rope and caught a front leg of the bull, bringing him down for a short time. The cowboy joined the vaquero and looped his rope over the horns.

Once the bull was down, the horses and men set back and kept the rope taut, the boy jumped from his horse and ran to the bull, ready to tie him. Worried about the kid's size, Jackson did the same and met the boy at the sharp hooves. "Give me the tie, and I'll do it." He held his hand out. Without hesitation, the kid dropped the short tie into his grasp.

While the others kept the dangerous horns out of the way, he tied the legs and stepped back. Turning to the newest member of his crew, he slapped him on his small shoulder. The kid's chest moved in double time, and his whole body had a slight tremor. He might have been scared, but he reacted quickly. He was stronger and faster than his height would indicate.

"Good work. You saved my horse and me from a tussle with an angry bull."

Head down, the boy took a step back and cleared his throat. "What's a full-grown bull doing here? I thought we were driving steers?"

"Good question."

"Don't worry, *jefe*." One of the vaqueros yelled over his shoulder. Jackson wasn't used to being called *boss*, in English or Spanish. "He'll be a steer before you leave mañana."

The boy was already back on his horse. Jackson watched him as he coiled his rope and left the work area. He narrowed his eyes and studied the boy's movements.

Something was off. If he didn't know better, he'd say the young Santiago moved like a girl.

He frowned and shook his head. There was no way, with those kinds of skills, that he was a female. He'd hardly seen grown men act so fast with such precision. It would be impossible for a young female.

The crews worked together, starting to mix and talk. He hoped his cowboys learned a few tricks before going on the drive.

He scanned the area and decided now was a good time to solve the Tiago mystery. He hated surprises.

They had a tendency to turn good days into bad ones in a blink of an eye, especially when the warning signs were ignored. He would not let his impulse to help someone override his instinct that something was wrong. Not again.

Making his way to the wagon, he planned an in-depth chat to get this feeling in his gut settled. The kid was hiding something, but he didn't have time to find a new assistant for the cook. He sighed. If it came down to it, he'd rather be shorthanded there than run into unforeseen trouble later.

Dismounting, he paused behind the wagon loaded with supplies. Jackson was sure the kid had come this way, but didn't see him.

A sweet giggle came from inside the wagon. Jackson looked for the cook. He knew the man had several daughters, but he said they were all back in Mexico with his wife.

Looking between the canvas flaps, he only saw Santiago. The kid's head was bent over a wood box, curls falling forward, hiding his face. Chirping noises mixed with soft girlish giggles floated through the warm air. It was Tiago.

The giggles came from Tiago.

Looking up, the youngster had a small chicken cupped in his hands. Jumping from his knees, he walked to the back of the wagon. With one hop, he stood next to Jackson. Without a hat, the kid barely reached Jackson's chest.

"Cook has a few hens and some half-grown chicks. I have to keep the crate clean." Lifting the awkward looking bird up for his inspection, the giggle came again. The chicken was half yellow chick fuzz, and half new red feathers. It looked like an experiment gone wrong.

"This one hopped on my shoulder and wanted to sit under my hair. I never knew chickens had personalities." Tiago brought the chicken to a rounded cheek, and it cooed as it rubbed against the soft skin.

Jackson's eyes narrowed and disbelief flooded his thoughts. How had he missed it? The orphaned boy he hired...was a female.

Sofia looked up at Jackson, and her heart slammed against her chest. The fire in his normally cool eyes warned her that she forgot who she was supposed to be.

This close, she could see the details in his irises. The green as bright as the new growth on the cypress trees. Now they burned with suspicion.

Stepping back, she tucked her head and locked down her lungs. If he discovered she was a girl now, he'd make her pack her saddlebag and send her back to the ranch, back to the plans her father had for her.

This adventure would end before it even began, and she'd be married to a stranger by the end of the year.

How could she be so stupid?

Turning to the wagon, she tried to climb inside and

hide, but he reached for her arm. His strong hand holding her in place without effort.

"I think you have some explaining to do. Remember, I don't do well with liars." He started walking away from the safety of the wagon, pulling her along behind him.

Boots planted, she tried to stop him, but he didn't seem to even notice.

"Please." Lowering her voice, she wasn't above begging. "Please, release me. I need to return the chick and finish my job."

He didn't slow. "You need to answer my questions. And think about your answers, because it's starting to look like you don't have a job."

The chick squirmed in distress. Relaxing her hold, she tried talking to him again. "Please, let me return the chicken to the wagon."

Halfway to the trees that lined the Frio River, Jackson stopped. He released her and crossed his arms. "Make it fast, and come straight back here. Don't even try to run…again."

With boots planted wide, and his forearms over his chest, he made an impressive sight. A sight she would be better off not appreciating.

Hurrying to the wagon, she talked to calm the chick. To be honest, it was more to calm herself. What could she say to convince Jackson she was a boy? Picking up her brother's hat, she scanned the interior of the wagon, searching for anything that would help her.

"Santiago!" The command made it clear time had run out.

She had nothing.

Hat back on her head, she stepped out of the wagon

and saw Jackson still standing the way she left him. She'd seen stone carvings softer than his face.

Taking her time to get out of the wagon, she was at a loss as to what to say to him. How could she convince him she was a boy?

The boots became heavy as she walked, each step a chore. She was more scared now than when she saw the bull charging. Dealing with Jackson was new territory. Being a boy was out of her experience.

A few feet from him, she stopped and looked at her boots. He was the one who wanted to talk, so she'd let him. It gave her a bit of time anyway.

"Follow me." Without waiting, he turned and walked past the trees to the riverbed. Away from the cattle station. No one would see them there. She didn't know if that was good or bad.

At the edge of the smooth rocks that made up the riverbed, he finally stopped. "What's your name?" His jaw was tight.

Threads hung loose where they began to unravel at the end of her long sleeves. All her attention now focused on them as she rolled them between her fingers. Not knowing what else to do, she shrugged. "Santiago. Tiago."

He snorted. Stepping closer, he cupped her jaw in one large hand and lifted her face, turning it to the right, then the left. His stare cut through her as if he saw right to her core. She had nowhere to hide.

One movement and he had the hat off her head. His eyes moved as he scanned her features. He shook his head. "How did I ever think you were a boy?"

Biting the inside of her cheek, she worked to keep her breath slow and steady. Showing fear was not an option.

"How old are you?" He moved in an inch closer.

"Twenty-two." Forcing herself to keep eye contact, she didn't blink. "Old enough to make my own decisions." There had to be a way to save her job. She refused to admit she was a woman.

He dropped his hands as if they were burned. "Are you married? Is there an angry husband who will run us down and shoot us?"

"No. I'm not running from anyone or anything. Returning to the ranch after the drive is the plan, so I can work there. That's all I want, and the only reason I'm here."

He didn't look convinced.

It was time to remind him what she had already done. "Just like I did when the bull was about to gore you. All that matters is I can handle the work. I'm fast at learning, too. One lesson, and I hitched the mules."

"The trail is not the same as the ranch. It's even more dangerous and unpredictable. It's no place for a female of any age."

"I didn't say I was a woman." She talked from the back of her throat, hoping it sounded rough and manly. "I have a dream for my life, and riding out across the country is part of that. What about your dreams? That's why you're here, right?"

"This isn't about me." Each word slipped between gritted teeth. He crossed his arms over his broad chest. "There's plenty of work on the ranch. Why do you need to leave to do that?"

"If I can go with the herd and come back, that'll prove how good I am at the work that needs to be done. I have to prove I can do this. I might be small, but I'm strong. The thought of being trapped inside all day for the rest of my life, planning meals and making sure the dust is gone, is a nightmare. It makes me sick."

"Some men don't come back from the trail."

She stood straighter. "I'll come back."

Confusion and bewilderment clouded his face. "You're a strange female."

She heard that already this week. Narrowing her eyes at him, she took a step back. "I'm just telling you why I want to ride with the herd."

A grim slant tightened his lip. He looked off to the river moving over the rocks and around the roots of the old cypress. "You're still claiming to be a male?" He cut his gaze back to her.

Her throat constricted. Life was so unfair. All the power to change the direction of her life was in his hands.

Closing her eyes, she prayed. She prayed for wisdom, for fortitude and for guidance.

Standing as tall as she could manage, she made sure to look him in the eye and hold his gaze. *Show no fear.* "You hired me to work with the cook. I'll be cleaning the chicken crate, taking care of the mules and starting fires. I have the safest job on the drive. Please, you don't have time to replace me. Let me do the job. You won't regret it."

Last year, during a father and son lesson, she overheard her father talk about tending to business. He said the best way to ruin a deal was to overtalk when you were nervous. State your requirements, then stay quiet. She bit down on the inside of her cheek, forcing herself to remain silent.

He crossed his arms, glanced at her, then went back

to studying the water. Moving his hands to his pockets, he sighed and looked down.

She held her breath.

"Okay, *Tiago*." Sarcasm coated his voice. "I think we'll stick with that name. It'll be easier if the rest of the crew continues to believe you're a boy. Less disruptive. Plus, I don't really know all of them, and I'm not sure we can trust them."

Her heart thumped against her chest. She was staying. "Thank you. I'll be the best cook assistant you've ever had."

"Just keep your head down and stay out of trouble." Jaw tight, he squinted at her. "You sure about this? There's still time to go back to the ranch. It's going to get rough out there, and you're not going to get any special treatment."

"I don't have anything to go back to right now." Her heart wanted to jump out of her chest. Holding her smile at bay the best she could, she gave him a nod. "I've been ready for this longer than I remember."

He dismissed her with a wave of his hand, and she ran to the wagon. It was official. Jackson knew she was a woman, and she still had a job. One less thing to worry about. Every moment from here on out was a gift from God. She was going across the country with a herd of cattle, all the way to New Orleans.

It was time to get her job done. Going through the crates and barrels and making a list of the supplies wasn't as fun as roping and herding, but it was what she had for now. With a glance, she checked the location of her boss. He stood with Cook.

Back there, he gave in so quickly. She mentioned dreams and his expression changed, but that couldn't be all. She wondered if her seeming to be of low status had anything to do with it. Would he be willing to give her this chance if he knew she was De Zavala's daughter?

Chapter Six

Jackson took a deep breath, drawing in the morning air. A light fog hugged the low ground between the hills. Sounds of soft rumblings from the cattle and calls from the cowboys assured him all was going well.

The herd looked good, and everything was going as scheduled. The six drovers were in place, guiding the steers.

Cook had done this trail several times and started earlier in order to stay in front. The wrangler, Estevan, had the horses following the wagon. Jackson had checked on Tiago at daybreak, and she had seemed eager to get started.

One night on the ground hadn't scared her off. He wondered if she would have the same smile by the end of the week. His wife had hated traveling. She had joked that if they went anywhere, he would need a wagon big enough for a bed and a tub.

His thoughts returned to the wagon's petite passenger. Had he made a mistake that would put the whole trip in jeopardy?

He needed to stay focused to make sure everyone got home safely.

A horse ran up behind him. He put his hand on the butt of his rifle and turned to face the newcomer head-on.

It was the woman. He had a hard time thinking of her as Tiago now that he knew the truth.

Her smile was wider than the Mississippi. "Cook said it would be easier on the mules if my saddle and I weren't in the wagon. I saw you up here and wanted to see the herd moving out."

"This is not a sightseeing excursion. You can't be running all over the place without—"

"Cook knows where I am, and I don't need a chaperone. I'm Tiago, remember." She pulled her horse up next to his as if she wasn't afraid of him one bit.

He allowed his gaze to take in her profile. Even with the short hair and baggy clothes, she was perfectly feminine.

"If I had any sense, I'd send you home now, before we get too far out."

The smile disappeared, and with one quick motion she pinned him with a hard stare. "No. We came to an agreement. You have to honor it."

"Yeah, you also agreed to stay close to the wagon. Less than twenty-four hours out, and you're running wild."

The hat wobbled with the panicked shake of her head. "I'm not close to the herd." The rawhide gloves tightened over the slacked reins. "You need me and I'm…"

Oh no, was she tearing up? He cleared his throat and turned away, not sure what to do or say.

"Look at this, Jackson. It's breathtaking. I want to

hold it close to my heart and never forget it. The sounds and the sights. An endless motion of animals moving as one over the land I love. How could I miss seeing this?"

She looked back to the never-ending line of moving longhorns. "This is what I dreamed about." Turning to him, her smile was faint, but making its way back. "Thank you."

He sighed and scanned the wide-open vista. Texas was a place where big dreams found a home. "No reason your dreams can't come true just because you're a woman." What kind of woman would his daughter have become?

Would he have allowed her to have plans outside of the roles set for women? She had been six when she was killed, so he'd never get to know.

That morning he rode out she had asked to go with him, but he thought she'd be safer at home with her mom and baby Jack. The anger that simmered in his gut flared.

If he had taken her with him, she'd still be alive and turning eleven soon. "If you're not with the wagon, stay close to me. I don't want the others figuring out you're a female."

She nodded, happiness back on her face. "Thank you."

"Come on." He nudged his horse down the hill toward the sea of cattle. "What we want is an uneventful trip. That takes awareness and anticipatory action." In order to make sure he did his job, he had to stay focused. Maybe keeping her close would be easier. Wondering where she was at any given moment was going to wear him out.

* * *

Sofia took in everything around her. Later tonight, she would write it all down. She wanted to burn every detail into her memory.

The future her mother had wanted for her was a pale watercolor compared to the real-life energy brushed across the valley they were passing through.

Jackson checked in with each of the drovers.

Will Redmond and Rory Brosnen covered the end of the herd. Rory, the one she learned was from Ireland, was the first rider they approached.

"You got a bodyguard now, boss?" He smiled at her. "So we have the honor of riding with the tiniest bullfighter in all of the country." He clicked a couple of times to the cattle before turning back to her. "Maybe we should trade places. I've been known to cook up a mean meal, and my ropin' skills don't touch yours." He followed that with a wink.

Sitting straight in the saddle and staring at the horizon, she didn't respond.

Jackson frowned. "Tiago will be staying with the cook or me. There will be no trading."

Rory laughed. "Easy, boss, I was kidding with Two Bit here. You Yanks are so serious."

"I'm not a Yank." Jackson grumbled something else under his breath, but she couldn't make it out.

"Where I'm from, you're all Yanks. Except for Two Bit here. What are you, kid?"

"I'm a Texan. Why did you leave your home and come all the way here?"

"Oh, you don't know the rules on the trail." He shook his head as if truly disappointed in her.

In a panic, she turned to Jackson. "Rules?"

Jackson sighed. "You don't ask a man about his past, ever. If he wants to tell you, he will, but you never ask."

"I'm sorry, Mr. Brosnen. I didn't mean to offend you." There was so much about being a boy she didn't know. Her brother would have known not to ask those questions.

"No worries. Call me Rory. I have a clean shirt, a clear conscience and enough coins in my pocket to buy a pint. Life is meant to be lived in the moment with no regrets. But I can tell you already know that." He winked again. Maybe he had a tick.

Jackson cleared his throat and urged his horse forward, cutting between her and Rory. "We're going to talk to the others. See you tonight, unless you run into trouble. Let me know."

"Yes, sir." His voice had a touch of laughter in it as he saluted them. "See you tonight, Two Bit."

Once they got out of hearing, Jackson looked at her. "You need to stay away from the men." He shook his head. "You don't look anything like a boy, you're too pretty. I'm not sure we can maintain your disguise."

Normally, that would be a compliment. Coming from a man like Jackson, it made her want to blush, but she knew he wasn't flattering her. To him, it was a problem.

"I'm not sure what else to do."

"It was a mistake to let you ride with me to the herd." He squinted at her.

"What?" She wiped at her cheeks. "What's wrong?"

"Maybe you could rub dirt on your face. That might help."

She already had an inch layer of dirt, and they weren't

even two full days out yet. "I don't see how that will help."

"Stay away from Will. Of all the men, he's the one I trust the least. I'm taking you back to Cook, and you need to stay there."

"He said I—"

"You don't have to ride in the wagon, but I want you right next to it. No wandering off. It's not just the longhorns that are dangerous. There are all sorts of hostiles that roam the area, two legged and four legged. With the herd, we'll probably draw their attention. I don't want you caught alone."

Her hands fisted around the reins. Arguing with him would make her look childish, so she locked her jaw and studied the countryside opposite him.

As they rode in silence for a bit, a wooden cross appeared on the top of the hill they were climbing. As they got closer, she saw a pair of worn boots that looked out of place sitting next to the cross.

Without thought, she stopped her horse. The name Hank Winfield was crudely carved into the wood. Grass and weeds had started growing over the mound of dirt. Jackson took off his hat and lowered his head. She followed suit and took the time to pray. To remember. To listen to God.

After a moment of silence, Jackson raised his head and turned his horse back to their path.

"Why do you think they left his boots there by the cross?" Whispering seemed appropriate, even though there was no one else around.

"Don't know. I've never seen the like before. It meant something to the men who rode with him and buried him."

"Jackson, I know the dangers. I have lived in this country all my life. I thought I had gained your respect enough for you to trust me."

"This has nothing to do with respect. I've also told the men not to wander off alone, but you're the only one I fear will actually ignore that order. I don't want to leave any of you in this ground."

There wasn't a thing she could say to that. "I'll go straight to Cook. You go on and check on Will. I promise I won't wander off."

He sighed. "We already have a small team, so don't do anything to make us smaller."

She smiled at him. He was a good leader, the kind who cared about all his people. She needed to stop thinking it was all about her.

"Si, jefe." She laughed at the expression on his face. He didn't seem to like the title "boss."

With a kick to her horse, she galloped away from him. For all her bravery, she knew she needed to be careful. She was all her father had left, and if something happened to her, he might not survive.

If she was a good daughter, she probably wouldn't be here. But on the other hand, when she returned from a successful cattle drive, he would know he had more than just a daughter to marry off. Not a burden to be dealt with, but a partner who could help run the ranch.

Maybe then they could think about a future where they both could have what they wanted.

She wanted to be part of the ranch. Did that mean she'd never have a family? New people were moving in all the time. Maybe there would be a way to get both.

For the first time, she had hope that her dream and her father's could be one and the same.

Chapter Seven

They had been on the trail for a week, and she found herself always looking for ways to spend time with Jackson. His mission seemed to be avoiding her.

He was so different from any man she met before. Sofia pulled up on the reins and straightened her legs. It wasn't midday yet and stiffness held every muscle hostage.

Her thought about Jackson confused her. For this trip, she needed to remember to be a boy, but it was hard around him.

The urge to giggle irritated her. Settling back into the saddle, she patted the withers of the mare she was riding today. "Life was a lot easier when all I cared about was horses." Her mount tossed her head and Sofia snorted. "So is there a male horse that is giving you serious self-doubt?"

With a sigh, she realized she missed the company of other women. That was a surprise. If she had been asked over a week ago, she'd claim boredom with the endless gossip and talk of fashion.

Right now, she'd love to talk about silly things. Well,

she wanted to talk about Jackson, but he was the only one she could talk to, so that was not possible.

The mare nickered. Sofia looked around. To the right, there was a water hole, more like a mud puddle, but she gave the mare her head and let her go to the muddy edge.

Dropping her head, the horse pawed, splashing the shallow water over both of them. Sofia laughed. Now mud joined all the dust layering her skin.

"Come on, girl. Jackson wants us with the wagon." The horse leaped to the other side of the small drop-off. "I think we can cut across here to meet Cook up ahead."

The mare stopped and lowered her head. Her ears pointed forward. She took a step back. Sofia kicked her. "Let's go!" The horse refused to move.

Raising her head high, ears pointed forward, the mare snorted. Three horses with half-dressed warriors approached from the top of the grassy slope. They stopped when they saw her.

She bit her lip so not to scream. Blood ran over her tongue. Her hands clutched the reins until they were numb. Did she go for her rifle or run? Her heartbeat throbbed in her head, leaving no room for a clear decision.

The ground dropped away a few feet to the right. How far would the fall be? *God, please help me.*

She didn't want to die here. Would they even find her body? What if they didn't kill her? What if they took her?

The horror tales shared in hushed voices clouded her brain. Her horse took another step back. Did she lift her hands in peace or pull the rifle? Her father taught her to never point a gun at someone unless she was ready to kill.

She could kill only one, and the others would be on her. If they were slow, she could get two, but there was no way to kill all three.

What if her life was over right here and now?

"Santiago."

For a moment, she thought someone had called out to her brother, but he was dead. Was she already dead and didn't know it?

"Back your horse to me." It was Jackson's low steady voice that offered sanctuary. One slow step at a time brought her even with Jackson. He was holding up a rifle.

Without thought, she pulled hers from the casing and rested it against her shoulder. It was two against three now. This was doable.

Lungs filled with sweet air. She might live to see home again. The three dark warriors stared at them.

"Go on to the wagon. I'll follow you."

Gulping down a few breaths so she could find her lost vocals, she cleared her throat. "I'm not leaving you here alone."

He growled. She held her weapon firm and steady despite the trembling of her heart. She couldn't help but think her father and brother would be proud.

Her mother? Horrified.

"Start backing straight out, keeping them in your sight." He lowered his gun, resting it across the saddle. She mimicked his action.

With a slight nod to the men across the water hole, he moved his horse back. She did the same.

The three painted horses stepped to the water and

started drinking. With Jackson by her side, she breathed a little easier. A quick glance, and she saw his jaw flex. Other than that small tick, his posture was relaxed.

"We are going to turn to the direction of the wagon, nice and easy. I need to tell the boys to keep an eye out. They might grab a steer or two."

"What do we do to stop them?"

"Nothing. Consider it cost of business. The one thing we don't want is a full-on attack. They take a couple of cows to their people, and we move on to the border."

"So we're just going to let them steal our cattle?"

He sighed. "Yes. You need to keep the mules in their harness tonight. They are more valuable than anything else we have here."

She looked over her shoulder. The warriors were gone. "Where did they go?" Chills ran down her spine as she scanned the hills. "Are they watching us?"

"Probably." He slid his rifle back into its leather scabbard.

"What do we do?" Forcing herself to look straight ahead was hard to do when her skin felt tight from the unseen men studying her movements.

"Nothing. Three don't travel far on their own. Stay close to the wagon and make it hard for them to get to the mules. Once we join Cook, I'll go warn the others. Stay vigilant."

With a nod, she looked over her shoulder again. "How long will they follow us?"

"A day or two. We don't want to make it easy for them to get into the camp." He looked over his shoulder. "If we allow them to take a couple of the steers, and make sure we have the wagon and horses covered, they should move on."

Nodding toward her rifle, his eyes narrowed. "You know how to use that? Ever shot a living thing?"

"Yes. My father taught me to shoot what I was aiming for. I never missed my target. Even the moving ones."

He chuckled and looked at her. She couldn't tell if the spark in his eyes was amusement or admiration.

"Good. I tell you what—you are one strange woman, and for once I'm very happy about that. Tie your horse to the wagon and sit with Cook. You can ride shotgun."

The pounding of her heart seemed to have changed directions. Instead of fear, something else jolted it.

A different kind of anxiety. Jackson trusted her to protect the wagon. She sat straighter. "I can do that. Thank you for trusting me."

"What's your real name?" A grim line replaced any smile he might have had.

"I thought we agreed I would be Tiago so there was no confusion." Was he going to get all manly and protective on her? Riding with Cook might not be about her protecting the wagon, but keeping her locked away.

She glared at him, trying to figure out his motive.

"You know I can help. You don't have to keep me in a safe place." She didn't want to admit that her heart had soared with relief when he had joined her.

"When I saw you across from the warriors, I wanted your real name. What if something does happen? My first thought was…if I have to bury her, I won't know the name to carve into the marker." There was an angry clip to the edge of his voice. "I want to know the real you. Not the fake name."

"I am Santiago. If I die on the trail, that is who you will bury." Pushing her hat lower, her hands trembled.

He reached across his horse. Under his large hand, hers disappeared. "I will not be burying you on this trail."

Chapter Eight

Sofia wrapped the colorful blanket tighter. Weak and tired, her body still refused to go to sleep. There were saddle sores on top of saddle sores.

Images of Rosita in the kitchen making tortillas appeared like a fantasy, a dream from a fairy tale that didn't really happen.

Now she ate more dust than chow. Unable to sleep, she studied the colors in the woven patterns.

It would be easier to think about the parts of her body that didn't hurt, maybe her head. That was it. Everything below her jaw ached. She thought she had worked hard before, but she had been a sheltered baby.

The woman who returned to her father would be different from the woman she was before she left.

A quick glace to the loaded rifle laying within reach was evidence of the change. She glanced at the mules, making sure they were still safe.

Still in the harness, they lay on the ground a few yards away from her. She scanned the edge of darkness for any threats.

Today, she had faced the possibility of her own death.

She had survived without much of an incident other than going numb with fear.

She hated that she hadn't known what to do. That Jackson had come to her rescue. Would she have made it back to the wagon if he hadn't shown up?

Sometime during the week, she started waking up looking forward to seeing him. The chores were done in fast order, and she got the wagon moving quickly so she could ride out and find him.

He sat a horse better than any man she had ever seen, but it was more than that. He was more than a good-looking man that knew how to ride well. At his core, deep in his eyes, he not only understood her, but he needed someone to understand him.

Not that it was where her mind should go. Rubbing her face, she hoped to scrub the thoughts of the quiet talking Kentucky man from her brain.

The sounds of campfire companionship drifted over the night. The men still sat around the low fire, laughing and playing music. The songs were all foreign, not the kind she was used to.

Jackson warned her to keep as much distance as possible from the cowboys. She never felt so alone around other people.

She licked her lips. That was a mistake. So, she hurt above her jaw, too. They had never been so dry and cracked before. The taste of dirt and dust came with every painful breath she took.

She dreamed of riding alongside the longhorns, but instead most of her days were spent sitting next to Cook or going into the wagon and doing prep work for him. The one time she rode off, she got in trouble.

She coughed again. All the dust was never going to clear her lungs.

"Here, drink this." Jackson stood above her and handed her a metal cup. He tossed something on the ground behind her, but she was more intrigued with the content of his gift. It looked like tea. It smelled like tea.

A small sip confirmed her guess. She sighed as the warm liquid slid down her sore throat.

She moaned. Tea. "Where did you get this? I would trade my kingdom for another cup."

He just smiled at her, then stared off into the velvet night sky.

"It's pure bliss." She closed her eyes and groaned again as she took a slow sip. It was bad manners, but she didn't care.

Digging in his vest pocket, he pulled out a small tin before lowering his long body on the ground next to her. He draped one arm over his knee and with the other offered the small box. "Here, coat your lips with this. It tastes bitter, but it'll soothe the skin."

Too tired to ask questions, she smothered the damaged skin.

Relief. Closing her eyes, she sighed and leaned against the large wagon wheel. "Thank you." She handed it back to him. As much as she wanted to stash it away, she didn't want to appear weak and needy.

"You keep it. I always bring two, and if you keep a light layer on during the day, you won't need as much at night. You should also cover your face. The sun will eat your skin right off your bones."

"Right now my bones are so sore they wouldn't notice." There was a heat to her skin she'd never experienced before. Another pesky insect made a buzzing noise before landing on her face. She slapped at it and got it, leaving a splatter of blood on her hand. *Gross.*

Taking her hand, he used a bandanna to wipe the bright red stain away. "I hear the closer we get to Louisiana the bigger the mosquitoes get. Soon enough we'll be able to saddle them and fly over the herd."

She couldn't help but laugh. "Now that would be a sight. Driving the herd from the air." She groaned. "Maybe we could even breathe some fresh air that isn't heavy with dust. I really don't know how the bugs are even finding my skin."

"Cook says we'll be getting rain soon, which will create a new mess of troubles."

A star fell from the sky, leaving a trail. "Did you see that?" She pointed. "A falling star. It looks different out here than it does from a porch."

Scooting down, she lay flat on the ground and studied the endless sky. "Do you think our loved ones are looking down on us?"

"Never really thought about it that way." A few feet away he stretched out on his back, his hands behind his bare head.

He sighed. Silence lingered between them. The music from the cowboys softened as some moved out to watch the herd. Cook rambled around in the wagon.

"Do you have family back in Kentucky?"

"Not anymore."

The gruff reply reminded her about the code she had learned earlier today.

Man, she was a slow learner. "Oh look, Leo is out." Maybe he'd let her blunder slide if she changed the subject. Scanning the sky like her father taught her, she found the Big Dipper. "Ursa Major is really clear tonight. You can see all seven hunters."

"You know the constellations?"

"Not as well as my brother. No matter how hard I tried, he always found more and could remember all their names. He would even beat our father."

"You have a brother?"

The stars blurred, and moisture hovered over her bottom eyelashes. "I had a brother. I lost him when I lost my mother."

"So you're completely alone in the world?"

Her father came to mind. "What happened to the rule of not asking about someone's past?" Today she thought of her father as the three fierce warriors had stared at her. Somehow Papi had become a stranger who wouldn't even talk to her or listen. Had he found her braid and her letter yet? Guilt burned her insides. "Is there a way to get a telegram to someone? I've never sent one before."

"You're pretty educated to know about sending telegrams. Little Tiago, there seems to be a great deal you haven't told me. The code does not apply to you because you lied to me. And you're a woman. The code is a man's code." He turned and leaned on his left arm. "Who do you want to send a message to?"

"That's not fair. But then again that wouldn't surprise me. Women have always had to deal with uneven scales." With a shrug, she tried to keep it uneventful. "It's no big deal. Just someone back at the ranch who might be worried. What about you? Is there someone waiting for you?"

The silence settled hard and heavy. She glanced at his profile. The shadow of his beard lined a strong jaw.

A jaw that flexed with tension. Much like her father's when she tried to talk about her mother and brother. She could take a hint. Jackson could question her, but his life was not on the table.

There was so much she needed to learn. Lessons about dealing with men was something her mother would be teaching her. She wiped her nose. She didn't want to think about her mother right now. "Do you know the story of the Big Bear?"

As he turned his head to look at her, she was struck by the greenness of his eyes. She smiled to let him know it was okay not to talk if he didn't want to. The idea that her question upset him laid more guilt at her door.

"The Big Bear?" His low voice sounded raw.

The sky was less dangerous to look at. She pointed to Ursa Major in the center of the velvet backdrop. "In the spring, a giant bear comes out of her den. Seven hunters follow her. As the weather cools, four of the hunters fall away, leaving only three." As the words filled the empty space between them, she pointed at the stars.

"See those three?" He moved closer to her as his gaze followed her pointing finger. With a nod from him, she continued.

"Chickadee is carrying the pot they'll use to cook the bear. As the winds come in from the north, Robin shoots his arrow and wounds the now standing bear. Blood sprays across the sky and covers the trees, turning them red."

He chuckled. "That's a clever story."

She tilted her head and smiled at him. "That's not the end."

He raised an eyebrow. "No?"

"Nope." Looking back to the sky, she raised her

hands. "The bear is eaten by the hunters and travels across the sky as a skeleton until spring. Another bear leaves the den and the hunt is on again. That's the story my father told me anyway."

"Emily would have liked that story."

Jealousy snapped at her. No reason for that, so she pushed it away. "Emily?"

It didn't seem he was going to tell her who Emily was. He rubbed his face. "My daughter. Every night she wanted one more story. At six, she was already able to read. Her ma was having a hard time keeping her busy with work. She was so clever."

He had a wife and daughter? "Where is she now?"

The muscle in his jaw flexed. He had told her he didn't have any... "Oh Jackson. I'm sor—" His family was dead. He had lost them all.

"Don't." He stood and dusted the dirt and grass from his pants.

Standing, she pulled the blanket tight around her shoulders. "I hate those words, too. But people say them because there are no words to make things better. So, I am sorry."

The mules stirred close by. In order to protect them, they still wore the heavy harnesses. It was the same thing Jackson was doing with her.

It had been one of the best nights she had since losing her mother and brother. Now she managed to ruin it.

"Jackson." She reached out and placed a hand on his arm. The need to comfort him was strong. She wanted to hold him close and tell him that it was going to be all right, even if it wasn't true. "Please forgive me. I can't even imagine..."

He pulled away from her. "Nothing to forgive. I just

don't talk about them." He shook his head. "Good night. See you in the morning."

Moving to the back of the wagon, she watched him walk past the smoldering campfire and disappear into the night.

Where was her brain? She was here to prove she could do the work of a man, not fall in love with a rough rider.

"Mija."

Cook's voice made her jump. Then she realized he had called her *mija*, not *mijo*. He knew she was a woman? "No—"

"Shh. I've known since you joined us, but you work harder and faster than any boy I've had on the trip, so what's it to me if you want to run around acting as if you are a boy? I have eight daughters and know how strong they are." He shrugged his round shoulders. "But you need to be careful. As a father of daughters, I also know how easily they give their hearts."

"My heart is not going to anyone." She crossed her arms. Once they got back, Jackson would be taking his horses and starting his own place. Staying on her family ranch was all she wanted.

"Many good girls lost their way with much less. And I don't think you want the others to look too closely."

"No. I'll be keeping my distance." What would happen if the other men found out? "The hard work I've done should be enough to earn their respect."

He shook his head. "The world is not a fair place. You might want to guard the way you look at our boss. Could cause you both problems." He pulled himself back into the wagon. "It's late and you need to be asleep. No more stargazing with *jefe*, or we'll all regret it."

As he vanished behind the canvas, the last of the light went out. Alone, she stood there. Just the thought of sleeping on the ground again made her body ache. A blanket she had never seen was draped over the wagon wheel. She squinted into the darkness that Jackson had vanished into. He must have left it.

Moving closer, she scanned the area where the cowboys slept. Still no sign of Jackson. He must have joined the herd.

Returning to the wagon, she rolled out the blanket and ran her hand over the material. It was thicker and softer than her own blanket. Lying down and snuggling between them, she smiled.

Who would have ever guessed that an old trail blanket would be the most glorious gift she had ever received? Cook was right. Her heart was in danger.

Chapter Nine

An explosive crash caused Sofia to bolt straight up and reach for her rifle. A flash of light blinded her. In quick succession, it repeated the dance across the sky.

Standing, her heart racing, she tried to get her bearings. In the distance, the cowboys were yelling at each other. The mules were up. Cook poked his head out of the wagon. "Was that thunder?"

"Yes." She shouted above the ruckus. Everyone knew a lightning storm was dangerous on a cattle drive. For several reasons.

She ran to the other side of the wagon to see if the herd was calm.

The darkness swallowed the area whole. Not one thing was visible. Tossing the rifle to Cook, she slipped on her boots, grabbed the long whip and bridle and ran for her horse.

The ground started to rumble under her feet. Without taking the time to saddle the mare, she slipped the bridle on and swung up onto the animal's bare back.

If the cattle started stampeding, every man available

would be needed to mill them. If they lost control, they could lose everything.

Another flash of light exposed her worst fear. The cattle had panicked and were running. Leaning low, she dug her heels into the horse's ribs and raced to the front of the herd. Behind her, someone called her name.

Jackson rode up next to her, leaned in as close as he could and yelled over the terrified herd. "I'm going to the front. Stay behind me, use your whip and push them to the left." His voice carried above the chaos. "But keep your distance."

She nodded. He was trusting her to do this. To help mill the herd and get them back into control.

Her heart rate pounded against her ears, and her breathing became erratic. Taking a deep breath, she reined in her emotions. Her father's voice reminded her to stay calm.

The horns clashed as they ran into each other. Hooved bodies created a tidal wave that would swallow anyone who got in the way and spit out the pieces.

White eyed, crazy longhorns were heading straight to the edge of the canyon ridge. Up ahead someone shot a gun into the air. It was too dark to spot anyone, but firing a gun into the night sounded like a bad idea to her.

She flicked her whip over her head and popped it in the air. The sky opened, and the humidity gave way to heavy sheets of rain.

Rory rode past her, calling out to scared cattle, helping her force them to the left. If they could get the lead steers to turn, they could slow them.

She pushed her mare faster as she snapped the whip again, careful not to get too close. Her heart jumped to the top of her throat when she felt her mare stumble.

Leaning her weight against the reins, she worked to keep them both balanced.

The muscles in her thighs started quivering. Without a saddle, the pressure of her thighs was the only thing keeping her on the horse.

A long piece of deadwood was in front of them and the mare jumped it with ease, not missing a beat even though Sofia's heart might have missed two. On her left, a steer went down and was trampled by the others.

Another spiderweb of light crawled across the thick clouds. Will joined Rory ahead of her.

Jackson was in front of them. Will had cut into the herd. His horse was trying to stay up. He lifted his gun and took aim at one of the lead steers. What was he doing?

Rory yelled, but his words died under thunder and bellowing cattle. He followed Jackson's example and snapped a long whip over his head, trying to mill the scared herd into themselves.

The hard, dry ground became a slippery mess. Sofia's stomach rolled, but she didn't have time to think about that now.

Her hat flew off in a gust of wind. The rain pushed her hair into her eyes, and she didn't have a free hand to move it. Her mare was doing everything she asked of her without fear or hesitation. She needed to do the same. Jackson was trusting her. She was part of the team.

One of the larger steers swung his horns and jumped to the right, crashing into Will's horse.

Everything was moving too fast. Will took aim at the animal, but another hit sent his shot wild. Her heart and lungs froze when Rory jerked. His horse stumbled.

"No!" Will's shot had hit Rory.

Digging her heels into the heaving side of her mount, she leaned over her neck and pushed the mare to rush at Rory. His horse lost his footing. Screams from cattle and men mixed. Sounds that would haunt her dreams filled the valley.

Will and the horse he was on disappeared under a pack of crazed cattle. She reached for Rory as his horse went out from under him. Using all her strength, she launched herself backward hoping it was enough to pull him across her mare. She had miscalculated. His weight threw her off balance. She knew if she didn't jump to the right, they would all go down under the deadly hooves.

With as much force as her body could gather, she threw herself away from the herd. One moment she was flying, the next her body was jerked and pounded by the ground. Up and down, the world became a whirling blur of images. Tucking her head under her hands was the only protection she could control.

Sofia couldn't tell if it was rocks or hooves thrashing her body. Without warning, the ground disappeared and she was falling through air. Curling into herself, she waited for impact.

Jackson pushed the lead steer away from the ridge, forcing the herd to mill into itself. He glanced behind him. Clint, Eli and Red were riding alongside the herd, keeping the steers contained. Rory and Will had been right behind him with Santiago. All three were missing now.

He stood in his saddle and scanned the area, but it was too dark to really make out anything. At least the quick storm had already passed through, leaving a soggy mess.

He called out to them, but no reply came back. Will had been shooting into the air, trying to turn the herd. Idiot. That just made everything worse.

Estevan and Red rode up to him. Clint had stayed back, singing to the restless but now exhausted cattle.

"Did you see Rory or Tiago? Will is missing, too." Fear burned in his gut. "What about Sam and Eli? Where are they?" He had too many men missing. And Tiago. Where was she? He had told her to keep her distance.

He swallowed hard and used every aching muscle to chain down the fear and…nothing. To get his job done, he couldn't afford to feel. His stomach churned and his jaw burned.

Red nodded. "Sam and Eli are in the back keeping the herd calm." He looked around. "I haven't seen Will and Rory since we mounted. They were ahead of me."

Estevan was covered in mud, and blood dripped from a tear in his pants. "I saw Tiago ride in to help." He glanced over the herd. "Where is he now?"

He had to relax his jaw in order to talk. "We need to find them. Last I saw them, Will was waving a gun around and had gotten too close to the stampede. I think Rory was going in to help him. I had the herd turning at that time and lost track of them." He reined his horse to the right. "We need to find them." He called out their names again.

"Boss, it's dark. I don't think we'll be able to find a thing out there."

Spinning his horse to face Red, Jackson's face was

tight with anger. "We are not leaving till we have everyone!"

Red nodded. "Of course. Why don't you and Estevan start looking, and I'll start digging. It'll save us time in the morning."

Jackson pushed his horse into Red's mount. Fire burned in his gut. "We are *not* digging graves. We will find them."

Estevan moved in between the men. "*Jefe*, he didn't mean anything by that. You know the realities of the trail. If a horse goes down in the middle of a—"

Jackson cut him off with a glare. "No one is digging a grave. We will find them before the sun comes up. Alive." Water dripped from his hat.

Estevan cut his eyes to Red, and nodded. "*Sí, sí.* We will find them."

Taking a deep breath Jackson moved back. "They were over there the last time I saw them." He couldn't afford to lose it. He was the boss, and he knew the dangers of the trail. They all did.

"Red, go check on the others. Let them know to keep an eye out for them. Estevan, go check on Cook. Make sure he's good. They might have gone there if they were hurt." He moved his horse closer to the ridge. "I'm going to check to see if they went over and are now trapped."

He dismounted and walked to the edge. "It's not that far of a drop. As long as their horse didn't fall on them or any cattle jumped with them, they'll be fine." He knew he was lying to himself, so did the cowboys, but no one argued this time. As long as they didn't have a body, they had hope.

"Please God, I know I haven't been on good terms with you, but I need to find her whole and healthy. I

don't know how to ask other than I'm willing to beg."
His prayers had gone unanswered last time, but it had
been too late when he found his family. They had been
dead for hours.

There wasn't a prayer that could have brought them
back. Tiago was still out there. Hopefully, still alive.
Will and Rory also. He added them to his prayers.

He didn't know what else to do. The humidity was
heavy on his shoulders as he walked his horse up and
down the area. Every once in a while, he stopped to call
out to his missing crew.

There was no returned greeting. Just the night sounds
of cattle settling in and the swollen river below.

Tiago was so small. He couldn't leave her out there
by herself. Laying the reins against the horse's neck,
he turned and went in the other direction. If she was
unconscious, she wouldn't hear him.

"Jefe." Estevan rode up to him. The mud was gone,
and he had on a clean pair of pants. Well, as clean as
could be when a person was living out of a saddlebag.
All the blood was gone.

"How's the leg? We don't need you getting an infection."

"I'm good. Cook and the wagon were safe. Two Bit
wasn't there. No Rory or Will, either." Estevan moved
his horse in front of him, stopping his progress. *"Jefe*,
you need to go in and change your clothes. You won't
do anyone any good if you get sick."

He shook his head and moved his mount around the
wrangler. The shoulder of his big horse pushed the sorrel back. "I'm not going in until I find them."

"Sam and Clint have the herd. Red, Eli and I will
look for the others."

Horse hooves sounded behind them. Jackson's heart jumped in anticipation. They both turned. Hope that his prayers had been answered. He closed his eyes when he saw it was Red.

"Clint found Will." A grim face and one shake of his head confirmed what they feared. Shreds of ice stopped Jackson's heart.

"Is it okay if I start digging a grave for him?" Red's voice was low and hesitant.

Jackson nodded. "Do you know if he had family? Anyone we need to inform?"

Red shook his head. "I'll check his belongings to see if he had any letters or such."

"Okay. I'm going to keep looking." His mind was numb. He should have made her go back to the wagon when he saw her riding into the stampede, but he thought she was skilled enough and smart enough…

On the ground, he saw something. Rushing to it, he picked up the beaten felt hat. Not much was left. It was Tiago's. He scanned the area.

To his right, on the edge of a thick tree line, he spotted the outline of a horse. The mare Tiago rode.

Mounting, he kicked his horse and rushed to the scene. Head down, the mare stood over a body. Blood ran from a cut on the bay's shoulder.

Not waiting for his mount to come to a stop, he swung his leg over and ran to the form on the ground. The horse lifted its head, the reins dangling.

Falling to his knees in the mud, he found Rory. Blood puddled in the mud under his head. As careful as possible, Jackson turned him onto his back, checking for a heartbeat and breathing, anything to give hope for life.

Under his head was a rock, stained red. Rory

moaned, and relief flooded Jackson. Then he saw the blood on the young Irishman's shoulder.

A horse came thundering at him. Estevan pulled his horse to a sliding stop in the mud and dismounted in one smooth action. "Is it Tiago? Is he alive?"

The wrangler landed on his knees. "It's Rory." Then Estevan looked up at the horse. "That's Two Bit's horse."

"Yeah, I don't know what happened, but we found Rory so we'll find Tiago. I found his hat." Jackson spoke with more confidence than he felt. "We need to get Rory to the wagon."

Rory rolled toward Jackson, reaching for him. "Tiago…" He tried to sit up, then fell back, gripping his shoulder. "Pulled me off my horse when it went down, then disappeared." He closed his eyes and tilted his head back. "I think she jumped."

Estevan looked up, confusion on his face. "She?"

"He's talking about the horse. The horse went down." His heart wedged itself in his throat. Rory knew. "Where did Tiago go down?"

With a grimace, he nodded. "Yes, Tiago, fell somewhere in the herd. Just swallowed up. I tried to…" He fell back again. "Will shot me. It was an…accident. Where is he?"

Estevan shook his head, then turned to Jackson. "I'll take care of him. You look for our little Two Bit."

Rory sat up with Estevan's help and gripped Jackson's arm. "Find…him."

"I will." He prayed God let him find a living breathing Tiago, not a cold battered body, but it didn't look good.

Standing, Jackson went to his horse. He couldn't give in to the possibility that she was gone. He'd be on the back of this horse until he found her. He went south for a bit, then turned back to the cattle. When she didn't turn up, he started all over. She would be safe in camp by the time the sun came up.

The tightness in his chest threatened to strangle his breathing with each step he took without her in his sight.

His throat was raw from calling, praying and begging. Begging Tiago to respond. Begging God for intervention and making deals.

His father taught him that God didn't negotiate. Praying to live in peace with God's will was the only thing one could do. But he hadn't known a seed of peace for five years now.

After hours of searching the ridge and walking through the now quiet herd, Jackson turned his horse to the wagon. She didn't have a horse, so maybe she made her way back on foot.

The sun was edging its way over the distant hills. The morning air was still and heavy after the storm of last night.

The chill from his damp clothes caused him to shiver. He needed a new horse to continue the search, and now that the sun was joining them, he could get the others to cover more ground.

The smell of breakfast reached him before he was close enough to see it. Scanning the area, he couldn't find any sign of Tiago. The first thing he was going to do when he found her was force her to tell him her real name.

Estevan rushed to him, a question he hesitated to ask burned in his eyes.

Jackson, shook his head. "I haven't found him. Yet."

He was going to find her if it took the rest of his life. "I was hoping he made it back to the wagon."

"Nope. Rory wants to go lookin' for him, but he's got a bullet hole right under his collarbone."

Clint and Sam rode up to the campfire. "The herd is settled. There were a few that ran off into the trees. We gathered most of 'em. Red has Will in the ground. You want to lead us in a prayer at his grave site?"

Tired, cold and numb, Jackson wanted to yell no. He wanted to find Tiago and hold her. His gaze darted over the men who looked at him.

They waited. For what, he wasn't sure. Maybe words of encouragement? They would have to keep waiting. He had none.

He looked off to the newborn sunrise. "I'm getting a fresh horse, and I'm looking for Tiago."

"If we stay too long, we'll be late getting to New Orleans." Sam looked at Cook and Estevan. All three turned to Clint.

Clint shrugged and spit. "Sir, with all due respect, the kid's gone. He came off a horse in the middle of a stampede. We'll be fortunate to find enough to bury him."

Jackson had him by the collar of his shirt, pushed up against the wagon. Jaw locked down, he held back the desire to slam his fist into Clint's face.

"Tiago, is out there." He lifted Clint, the terror on the man's face didn't slow Jackson, but the pressure on both arms did. Sam and Estevan were on either side of him, pulling at his arms.

"*Jefe*, we'll find him." The younger man hooked his arm around his waist with the other on Jackson's arm. "You're wasting time if you beat up Clint."

His chest expanded hard and heavy, Jackson relaxed

his hands and stepped back. Clint wiped his sleeve over his face. "I didn't mean nothing by it, boss. Just the reality of the trail. You're actin' as if that kid was your own. He's just some orphan who ain't got no family to miss him."

Jackson growled and pulled back his fist. Before he could knock the callous idiot flat, Estevan stopped the lurch of his arm. "*Jefe*, keep focused on the mission. Go find the kid. We're already two men down." He turned to Clint. "Go get a fresh horse."

Without hesitation, the cowboy ran to the horses.

Rory stood. "I need a horse, too. The kid risked his life to save mine, and I couldn't hang on to him. He slipped right out of my grip. He has to be out there, alive."

Bloody and bruised, the charming Irishman looked like an ogre. Jackson looked at the other cowboys. Even Cook returned his stare with a deep sadness.

It was the same look everyone back home had given him when he went into town after the death of his family.

He had wanted to start over. Had wanted to escape the pity and guilt. There was no escape.

God, I don't get it. Did I do something so wrong that everyone I care about dies?

The men stared at him. They all knew the truth. She was gone.

He made her a promise that he wouldn't put her in the ground. Now he didn't even have a body to bury. Clint brought a black-and-white paint to him. "Boss, I'm going to check the herd. I'll keep an eye out for Two Bit."

Jackson made sure to smile and nod a thanks to

the nervous man. It wasn't Clint's fault he lost her. He rested his hand on the neck of the new mount. Estevan switched saddles for him.

"You might still find him."

"We both know the chances of that are slim to none." With nothing else to say, Estevan left. Cook disappeared, leaving Rory to watch him fall apart.

Behind him, Jackson heard the Irishman trying to move. "Stay here. We don't have enough hands to save your sorry hide again."

"But—"

"Stay." With one hand on the horn, Jackson heaved himself into the saddle, but he didn't get high enough. Back on the ground, he slammed his forehead into the hard leather. The gelding sidestepped away from him.

Once again, he put his foot back in the stirrup, hopping to follow the now nervous animal.

His body felt as if molasses surrounded him. He lifted his eyes and looked to the daybreak.

A blurry form wavered on the horizon. Squinting his eyes, he stopped breathing. It was a small human. A tiny form limped toward him. Hope surged his heavy limbs.

Dropping the reins, he took a step toward the emerging figure. Wary to believe what he was seeing. Another step toward the small muddy figure and adrenaline surged through his limbs. New energy woke up every tired defeated cell in his body.

Without the hat, the walking figure stumbled. Jackson let it all go and ran to her. Each breath heaved from his lungs. It was her. She was here. Not only alive, but on her feet. Before he could reach her, she fell.

Without thought of who was watching, he dropped next to her, sliding in the wet ground. She lay curled on her side, her black hair plastered to her head. The soft skin was livid with cuts and bruises.

Rips shredded parts of her pants. Her left arm supported her, and her right was wrapped tight around her middle as she tried to push herself back up.

"Easy. I have you." He tried to lift her, but his legs gave out. He went back down with her cradled in his arms. Sitting in the mud, he held her close. His head bent over her.

She coughed.

Thank You, God. Thank You. Pressing his forehead against hers, he wept.

He waited for her to make another sound, leaning closer just to hear her breathing. One of the sweetest sounds he'd heard in a long time.

Kneeling with her in his arms, he battled the urge to lay his head against her chest to hear the proof of the life-giving beat of her heart. She was alive. God had answered his prayers.

He threaded his big fingers through her smaller ones and gently squeezed. Tiago shifted and tightened her own hand against his.

One of his tears fell on their linked knuckles, washing dirt and grit from her delicate skin. He needed to get hold of his emotions. His crying like a newborn wouldn't help any of them.

Her face was half hidden by clumps of dark hair. With his free hand, he smoothed back the muddy, matted hair. He needed to see the life in her eyes. With a quick scan, he ran his hand down her arm and checked her legs. "Are you harmed?"

Her inky black eyelashes fluttered against her abused

skin. Shaking her head, she raised her chin, large brown eyes searing him to the core. She was alive and well.

He pulled her against his heart. A heart that had become too big for the small place in his chest.

One hand in her hair, the other pressed her against him. He leaned into her until his lips touched the edge of her ear. "Tell me your name."

She shook her head.

"Please. I thought you were dead."

"Rory? Will?" She pushed against him, trying to sit up on her own. He glanced behind him. Rory was the only one who could see them, and he was gone.

Reality dumped cold water over him. He needed to remember Tiago was supposed to be a boy. The others could return at any time.

One hop, he was standing and putting her feet on the ground. He didn't want to let go. "Can you stand? How bad are your injuries?"

"I'm good. Cold and sore, but…what about Rory and Will?" Her voice, low and ragged, tore at him.

She had risked her life for theirs. He clenched his jaw, stopping the angry words from spewing all over her. "Rory was shot, but he's well."

Her eyes closed, and she almost fell as her knees gave. He pulled her next to him with one arm around her waist.

"Thanks to your foolishness, he didn't fall into the stampede."

She sagged against him. "I saw his horse going down, and I knew he was a goner if I didn't do something." She closed her eyes and smiled. "Will?"

He shook his head. "We found him. Red dug his grave this morning."

Tears filled her eyes and slipped over her lashes. Trails formed in the mud on her face.

Turning from her, he scanned the area. "Don't waste your sorrow on him. He risked your life and Rory's with his senselessness."

He knew he sounded cold, but Will's stupidity put the others in danger. The thought of what could have happened ate at his gut. He'd have to get his emotions under control and quick.

It would be dangerous for everyone if he couldn't keep his thoughts on the job. He also needed to keep his hands in his pockets. Touching her was dangerous. For so many reasons.

But right now, she needed him. When they got to the wagon, he'd make sure to keep at least two steps between them and keep his hands off. In this moment, he couldn't keep his distance. "We need to get you to the wagon."

Head down, she bit her bottom lip and pulled away from him. "I don't need your help." She straightened her back and started walking. At least she tried. She stumbled, and he gathered her in his left arm again.

"What happened after you fell from the horse? Where'd you go?"

She took a deep breath before answering him. "When I pulled Rory over to my horse, the weight threw my mare off her stride, so I thought if I threw my body to the opposite side we'd all stay up. I misjudged and went too far. I rolled away from the herd."

The pit of his stomach heaved. The image of her going under the ocean of hooves and horns branded his brain. "But where were you? I rode all along the ridge and area."

"I knew the hooves were deadly. When I realized I was on the ground, there was no sense of direction. I kept rolling, hoping to stay out of the herd's way. Suddenly ground disappeared. A tangle of roots slowed my fall, and from there I went into the water. The current carried me a while before I could—"

For the first time, she heaved and started crying. Pulling her into his arms, he surrounded her. "It's okay. You're here. I have you."

She sobbed, burying her face into his vest. All he could do was hold her and stroke her back. Every once in a while, he smoothed her hair until her breathing was normal.

"That's how my mom and brother died. They…" A giant sob shuddered her tiny body. "They were swept away in a flash flood and never…"

"I've got you." For a moment, he pulled her closer, her heartbeat reassuring him she was in good health. Leaning back, he put his finger under her chin and lifted her face.

He leaned in until his lips were a whispered width of a dream from her full rose-colored mouth.

The desire to touch her, to kiss her soft skin overwhelmed him. He took his gaze from her mouth to her eyes. The morning sun kissed the valley and highlighted the curves of Tiago's battered face.

No. He closed his eyes. He couldn't do this again, not after Lilly. He needed the anger back. It protected them both.

The subdued rumbling of the calmed longhorns carried across the valley on a soft breeze, and the early sun gently caressed the green valley.

It was as if the events of the last night never happened. Other than the hole in the ground. The final stop for one of his cowboys.

One, two, three. The distance between them left him cold, but he needed that.

He couldn't afford to touch her again. Not only would it give her identity away to the others, it threatened his stability.

She started walking. A limp made her gait uneven. He thought about picking her up and carrying her the rest of the way. But one, it would put her back in his arms, and two, she wanted to be a cowhand.

Cowhands didn't get carried back to camp. She'd earned the right to walk back on her own two feet.

He growled and followed close.

"Tiago!" Estevan ran his horse straight at them. "God be praised!" He swung off the still-moving horse. He came up to her other side and put his arm under hers.

Not a good idea to let the cowboys get too close. Jackson got on her other side. "You get your horse. I'll make sure Tiago gets to Cook."

Estevan nodded, a big grin on his face. "I'll tell the others. This turned into a good day."

By the time Jackson got her to the wagon, she was breathing heavily. What if there were internal injuries they couldn't see?

Rory had reappeared. Clean from a dip in the river. He let out a shout and rushed them.

Cook came running from the back side of the wagon, a long meat cleaver raised over his head. His round body moved faster than Jackson thought possible. "*Mija*, you live." His dark eyes glistened.

One flick of his wrist and the blade was buried into the side board before he took the petite girl from Jackson's arms and took over the care of Tiago. Cook looked up at him, seeming to remember others were there. "I've got our boy. I'll make sure he is all clean and healthy."

And in a blink, Jackson's arms were empty. Cook vanished with Tiago.

Rory rested his back against the side of the wagon and cut a harsh frown. Displeasure stamped across his face. "If you don't want the others to know Tiago's secret, you might want to watch the way you're looking at *him*." He adjusted the sling holding his arm in place. "I take it Cook knows."

Jackson glared at the wounded cowboy. "I don't know what you're talking about."

Rory snorted. "Yeah, okay. I'm going to see if I can help the others.

"You sure you won't be in the way?"

"My good arm is still working. I'll take it easy, but I can't just sit here. Maybe I'll check on Tiago instead. We're going to need every cowboy riding the herd."

"Leave Tiago alone. He is not leaving the wagon for the rest of the trip."

"Boss, the kid's strong. Sh…" He grinned. "He saved my worthless hide last night, and managed to get back to the camp without help from any of us." Rory stared at him for a silent minute. "Tiago might be the best cowboy you've got. Don't punish *him* based on a social standard." Without waiting for a reply, he turned and left.

Jackson sighed. Did the Irishman have an interest in Tiago?

His fists clenched at his sides as he fought the urge to hit something or someone. He hated the way it overwhelmed him. He had never been a violent man, not until losing his family.

That time in his life was a fiery blur. He had gone on a blind rampage, tracking down the men who had taken everything from him. Watching as the law took care of them.

Nothing changed. His family was still dead. Everything was still lost, at times even his desire to live.

It was easier to stay numb. To keep his plan on a day-by-day journey.

On the edge of the river, Cook helped Tiago take off the outer shirt. The small figure was beaten and covered in mud.

Jackson's emotions came too close to the surface with her. His skin tightened over his bones, like he didn't fit in his own body. Not good.

He spun away from the sight and marched to his gear. He needed distance.

Tiago brought out the worst in him. Pausing, he tilted his head back and looked to the sky. It felt ridiculous calling her Tiago. She never did answer his question. She still didn't trust him with her real name. Then again, he didn't trust himself.

He shook his head. They would put Will to rest, then gather the last of the cattle that had gotten lost last night. He didn't even have a bible to say some verses over Will's grave.

Pushing his hat up, he rubbed the top of his forehead. Tiago read from a bible every night. Retracing his steps, he stopped next to the mules. "Tiago! When you're clean and ready, bring your bible over to Will's grave site. We'll be burying him at the base of the hill."

"Okay!"

Turn. Go to the cowboys. Instead, he stood there. "Are you healthy?" He'd heard of cowboys taking a fall, getting up, acting just fine, then dropping dead. "You need to be careful." His voice sounded gruff to his own ears.

"*You*—" she pointed at his chest "—need to stop worrying about me. We'll be there in just a bit."

He couldn't think of another reason to stay. Turning, he focused his gaze on the horizon ahead of him. The boys needed his help. Standing around like an idiot, waiting for Tiago, was not helping anyone.

What they all needed was a day of rest, but there was no such thing on the trail. They deserved to take it a bit slow today. Tomorrow would be time enough to move out again. He was determined to keep Tiago in the wagon. He'd take Will's place on the drive.

What he needed to do most was keep his distance from the cook's little hardheaded assistant.

Chapter Ten

Sofia joined the cowboys around Will's resting place. He'd be forever on the drive. Still a bit wobbly on her feet, she handed Jackson her leather bible. The need to stand close to him was denied when he took her offering, then hightailed it to the opposite side of Will's grave. If she wanted to stand next to him, she'd have to push Red and Sam out of the way.

With a sigh, she closed her eyes and reminded herself this was not about her. Looking down into the hole, she could see the outline of Will's body. No coffin, just his blanket. That could have been her and Rory.

She glanced up at the men standing around her. It could have been any of them.

No one knew what the day would hold, and who would make it to another. When her mother and brother were washed away, she was at home tucked in bed. She had been relieved when her mother didn't make her go to town with them that morning. She was under thick warm quilts while they were washed away and died. She should have been with them on their way to church.

Jackson cleared his throat and spoke of the darkest valley and the shadow of death.

The shadow of death. *God, why am I still here? Is Your will leading me on this path, or am I being stubborn? Is this a rebellion against You, or against people blocking me from being true to Your will?*

Wrapping her arms around her still damp middle, she settled in next to Rory. His hat in his hand, he put his good arm around her shoulder. She appreciated the warmth of another human being, but she longed for Jackson's comfort.

The men all mumbled an amen. Clint pulled a harmonica from his shirt pocket and started playing "Amazing Grace." Each man joined, with every voice becoming one. Sofia wiped her eyes, biting her lip. Head down, Jackson didn't sing. Once the last verse was sung, he stepped back a few feet.

With a small shovel, Red started filling the hole he had dug early that morning. The other cowboys joined in and covered Will's body with the loose dirt. He would remain young and on the trail, forever. Did he have family who would miss him? A mother or father?

She looked at Jackson, hoping to make eye contact, but he turned on his heel and left the grave site when the first shovel full of dirt hit the blanket.

In silence, the others started covering Will's body. Even Rory planted his hat low and used his boot to shove the dirt over the edge.

Her gaze darted from the six men to the retreating back of her boss. She wanted to chase after him, but staying with the men seemed like the right thing to do.

She filled her hands with earth and threw it into the

grave. The soft thud of hard dirt echoed in her heart. Life was over so fast.

Cook laid his hand on her arm. "Go check on *jefe*. Your body also needs rest, or you'll not be able to move tomorrow."

She glanced at the others, who all nodded, with the exception of Rory. His nostrils flared, each heavy breath moving his chest. He looked angry. Was it her?

Cook nudged her. "Go."

Looking toward Rory one last time, she found him stiff and staring into the grave. Jackson had made her a promise that he would not have to bury her. He took the burial of his people seriously. She ran to catch up to him. The bruises and injuries made movement difficult, but the last thing she wanted was for her boss to think she couldn't handle the hardships.

Reaching out to him, she touched his back. Hard muscles tensed, and he turned. A fire burned in his eyes, causing her to take a step back.

"What's wrong?" She tried not to stumble over the words, but he looked fierce. All traces of his easygoing nature gone.

"We buried someone I was responsible for. We could have easily had two other graves. What do you think is wrong?"

"You can't protect people from their own foolishness."

"We almost lost you." He closed his eyes and rubbed the center of his chest. "And Rory. I should have told y'all to stay back. Every decision I make has consequences."

"You wouldn't have been able to mill the herd by yourself. You needed us there."

He pinned her with a hard stare. She took another step back. His intensity scared her a bit. Swallowing the thickness in her throat, she tried to come up with words. All of them were blocked. Not a single word formed.

"I would rather lose every stinking cow than one man...or woman." After a moment of silence, his eyes soften.

His hand came up and stopped mere inches from her face. Callused fingers of a working man, so close she leaned forward wanting his warmth. What took her by surprise was the impulse to curl up against him and nip at the work tough skin with her teeth. She wasn't sure where that thought came from, heat climbing up her neck.

Waiting, her heart rate accelerated as his hand hovered. Her eyes went from his hand to his face. She watched as his gaze shifted from her to over her shoulder.

A guttural growl, his only response, was followed by his hand dropping. Weeping from disappointment was the only thing she wanted to do.

That wouldn't be wise. He had done the right thing. The cowboys could see them.

Jackson protected her from her own foolishness. Stepping back, head down, she mumbled an apology. Wanting the comfort his warmth offered, she had forgotten others watched them.

He crossed his arms. "Why are you here?"

"You hired me to—"

"That's not what I meant, and you know it. Why are you following me like an abandoned puppy?"

The words stung like a scorpion's tail. "I think you shouldn't be alone right now."

"Here." He yanked her bible from the inside of his vest and shoved it into her hands.

"Go rest. We'll be riding out early." Without another word, he turned and headed to the river.

Standing alone, she looked at the men, then at Jackson's stiff and strong back. She didn't really belong anywhere. Jackson was the boss. He shouldn't be hanging out with the cook's assistant.

She understood the need to be alone. After her mother's and brother's deaths, there were times it was just easier not to deal with people. Tomorrow, she'd ride with him. Hopefully, tonight he'd visit and she could tell him another story.

With a sigh, she headed to the wagon. There were times she wanted to be alone, but not now. She wanted to spend time with Jackson.

She'd get some rest and wait for him. He would talk to her soon, even if she had to hunt him down.

Chapter Eleven

Hawken rifle in hand, Sofia jumped from the wagon. A new level of pain surged through her body with every movement. Areas of her body she had always ignored were sore and stiff. The stampede had happened three days ago, and her body ached more now than it had when she fell. She'd never admit it to Jackson though.

He was being ridiculous about her staying in the wagon, and he refused to talk to her.

Cooked called from the driver's perch. "Do you have enough branches for the back wheels?"

In less than two days, the terrain had gone through a drastic change. The hills and rocks gave way to wet soggy ground. Cook said it was a good sign they were getting closer to New Orleans.

All she knew was that the wagon kept getting stuck. She had gotten good at throwing branches under the wagon and using her brother's rifle to help the mules pull wheels out of the bogs.

"What are you doing?" Jackson's sudden appearance caused her to jump.

When she realized it was him, anger surged through

her tired limbs, rejuvenating them with energy. After being so caring and sweet when she came back to camp, he had turned into a grumpy stranger. It was rare she saw him, and when she did, he just fussed like an old woman.

"I'm doing my job." She made a point not to look at him as she layered branches.

"You're to stay in the wagon. There are snakes and alligators out here. You're still bruised from your fall. Are you having a hard time walking? Does it hurt?"

She sighed. "Rory was shot, and he's riding with the herd. You need me out there, but since you won't let me, I'm helping Cook." Going to the other side, she wedged the butt of her brother's rifle under the wheel.

He just growled at her, like some wild animal.

She put her weight into the rifle to hold it steady. "Go, Cook!" She cut her gaze back to the infuriating man. He'd become worse than her father. All her weight went onto moving the wheel. He made another guttural disapproving grunt.

With a sigh, she shook her head. "You know, verbal skills help when two people are communicating." Each word came through gritted teeth.

"We are not communicating. I told you to stay in the wagon, and you're ignoring me."

The mules pulled the cart free. Sprinting, she ran to the front, tossed the rifle on the footboard and pulled herself up into the moving wagon. "You hired me to do a job. That's what I'm doing." Picking up the weapon, she wiped the mud onto her pants. At this point, more dirt on her didn't matter, but her brother's rifle needed to stay clean. She gave in and glanced at Jackson.

He sat in the saddle with ease, as if he and the horse

were one. His profile gave the impression that he was just along for the ride, but she knew what the miniscule flexing of his jaw meant. Good, she wasn't happy, either.

The wagon lurched over a fallen log. She grabbed the side with one hand and gripped the rifle tighter with the other. She was going to be tossed over the side.

Twisting in his saddle, Jackson caught her. His wide palm pressed flat against her shoulder. Arm braced, she looked straight at him. Heat ran through her limbs to her stomach. It all radiated from his hand. Another bump, and she remembered where she was. With a sigh, she looked down before righting her seat.

The warmth of his hand vanished as he pulled it away in a quick motion. Raising her eyelids, she found he went back to staring at the horizon before them. Was she the only one who reacted to their contact?

He rubbed his open hand on his chaps as if he touched something undesirable. An unforgiving line formed on his full mouth.

Heat lingered at the spot where his hand had rested. She missed the nightly conversations before the stampede. How did she get his friendship back?

"*Mija*, are you okay?" Cook glanced at her as he snapped the long reins. His normally friendly face formed hostile lines, tight and grim.

Jackson shot a glare at Cook. "Your assistant is a boy, not a *mija*. You need to remember that."

"*Jefe*, I'm not the one with the problem remembering."

Not knowing what else to do to relieve the tension, she laid her hand on Cook's arm. "It's okay."

A harsh throaty sound came from her boss. "It's not

okay. *Santiago*—" sarcasm dripped from her pretend name "—fell into the river and was lost. Almost killed. *He's* not strong enough for this type of hardship."

Her mouth fell open. Any thought of peacemaking ripped its way out of her thoughts. "You pretended to be different, but you're just like all the other men in my life. I'm strong enough. More than strong enough. I not only saved Rory, but I got back to the camp without a horse. I did that all by myself."

Tears stung the bottom of her eyes. She bit down too hard, and the taste of blood hit her tongue. Relaxing her jaw, she made a vow to not cry. Not in front of him anyway. He would see tears as proof that he was right. They thought she was weak and needed to be kept indoors.

She was so much more. What did she have to do to make them see all she had already done? She was just as capable as the men, if not more so. "I can help. You need another drover. Right now, with you wasting time checking on me, who's in the back with Red?"

"He's covering the back from the center. He's got it under control." He sighed. "I do need to get back. In the next couple of days, we should reach the Neches River."

Cook made a clicking noise to the mules and nodded, making eye contact with Jackson. "Last time I rode with Señor Taylor White, we used the new Collier's Ferry. They have holding pens and places for the boys to wash and sleep. Our supplies are getting thin. It's five miles north from the old crossing."

Instead of responding to Cook, Jackson studied her with narrow eyes.

"What?" She glared back. He was just getting ridiculous. "What did I do now?"

"I hear the new ferry was established and run by

Sterling Duval. Not sure if it would be a good idea to camp there."

"Sterling Duval?" She sat up. "I've heard stories of him. He was one of Lafitte's pirates." Her heart rate pounded faster throughout her body. "A real-life pirate. I hear he stands six feet and six inches tall and can—"

"He's a pirate, a thief. We can cross at Ballew's."

Cook shook his head. "The edge of the crossing at Collier's is easier for the cattle to get in and out of the river. Less risk of losing them to drowning. Plus, everyone could really use a good night of rest. He has a nice station set up."

Jackson made that guttural growl of his when he was displeased. "Rest? In the company of a giant pirate? No, I think it's too much of a risk."

"It's because of me, right? Because I'm a woman, you think you need to keep me away from the notorious Sterling Duval?" Even his name sounded adventurous. "I've been a boy for weeks now, and I can stay a boy."

Jackson grunted. "I'm not sure anyone really believes you're a boy anymore."

She turned to Cook. "Who else knows I'm not a boy?"

He shrugged. "Rory knows. The others just see what they think they're supposed to see. Estevan might wonder, I can't tell. Red, Clint and Sam are good cowboys, but also a bit dense when it comes to things outside the usual."

She faced Jackson. The wagon jostled her to the side, reminded her of the beating her body took a few nights ago and still hurt. "You're risking the herd and the men because of some misplaced goal of protecting me from a retired pirate." Fire clashed with ice and battled throughout her limbs.

"Pirates don't retire. He's just found another way of being a pirate. I don't trust him whether on the water or settled on land trying to look respectable. He's a pirate."

He had to understand he endangered lives of men and cattle being so stubborn. "When you found out I was a woman, you told me that I wouldn't get any pampering. I would have to work as hard as everyone else."

His jaw started working in double-time, popping in and out.

"I've done that and more. What else do you need from me to prove I can do the work?"

"Need I remind you that in the process of doing the work, you almost got killed? And the mare you rode was injured. You can't ride her."

"We have more horses."

Cook snorted.

"It's too dangerous." He still didn't look at her.

"I. Survived. We need to take the fastest route to New Orleans. Let me saddle a horse and help. Let me do what you know I can do. Rory is out there with a bullet hole in his shoulder. Let me help."

One hard jerk brought his head around, and his green eyes smoldered. "Rory is fine. He doesn't need your help." Closing his eyes, he took a deep breath. Relaxing in the saddle, he sat back and let out a heavy sigh. "Get your gear and get a horse. I'll move Sam to the back and put you in the front."

"No. You know that's not right. I'll just join the herd in the back."

"It's the—"

"It's where the new guy goes. I know the trail rules."

She eased over the bench and went to the back. Finding her saddle, she tossed it out. From inside she yelled a little louder to make sure he heard. "Don't you dare move someone to the back just to give me a better spot." Throwing the bridle and rope over her shoulder, she went to the back and jumped from the rolling wagon.

Standing over her saddle, she planted her fists on her hips. "I can do this, and I want to do it right. No favors."

Not giving him time to argue, she gripped the pommel of her brother's work saddle. Well, it was hers now. A sadness washed over her. Her brother wouldn't use his saddle or his prized rifle again. Would he be happy that she was using them?

"Give it to me." Jackson had brought his mount up next to her, his hand stretched down.

Was he not listening to anything she said? "I can carry my own saddle."

"I'm well aware of that fact, but it would be faster if I took you to the horse so you can pick a mount. It would be easier for me to pull you up if you don't have the saddle."

"Oh." She narrowed her eyes. "Are you sure your horse can carry me and the saddle?"

"If you continue to question everything I suggest, we will never get anywhere."

"You mean like the way you doubt me even after I proved myself?" She might be pushing him, but she couldn't afford to let him go back to treating her like a porcelain doll. What if he took her saddle and forced her back into the wagon?

"You are too suspicious for your own good. I'll balance your saddle in front of me, and you can ride behind me."

Heat burned her cheeks. They would be sitting on the same horse.

He sat back and pulled on the reins of the restless horse. The gelding had been standing in one place too long. "Are you going to give me your saddle, or are you going to return to the wagon?"

Without answering him, she lifted the saddle and waited while he adjusted its bulk. Finished, he reached for her again. Taking his hand, she jumped and swung her legs over the back of his broad horse. Not knowing what else to do she placed her hands on his waist.

With a nudge of his knees, the horse lunged forward, forcing her to hold on a bit tighter than she had planned. He laid the reins over the horse's neck, and they made a sharp turn and headed to the drive.

She scanned the long line of cattle. They were almost to the market where they would sell the steers and most of the horses. Would Jackson be open to staying on the ranch? If her father liked him and trusted him, maybe she could convince him to stay.

He might have put up a little fight about her riding with the cowboys, but ultimately, he allowed her to do the job she was good at.

Working together at the ranch would help the others see her as more than the owner's daughter. The little girl that grew up with them. He knew what she could do and would make a good partner.

She pulled her bottom lip between her teeth. She really didn't want to look at her own motivation, how she felt about him as a man. That would just get in the way of her dreams.

Jackson nodded to Estevan as they rode up to the horses. Jackson let his horse mingle with the moving herd. A fluttering tickled her lower belly as she readied her lasso to pull a horse out of the herd. Today she was riding with the cowboys, working with the cattle from horseback.

"The little bay is good." Jackson eased farther into the moving body of horses.

"She's the slowest one here." Sofia shook her head. "I can't believe you suggested her. I would be better off on the injured mare. You've seen me ride. Please stop doubting me."

"I'm not doubting you, I just want… I want you to make it home, and sometimes slower is safer."

"Not always. If something happens and I get in trouble because my horse was too slow, you'd feel so guilty." She punched his shoulder. "I can't let that happen. I want the Appaloosa."

He laughed and weaved between the horses, changing direction. "Either way I'm not sure I'm going to survive knowing you are riding alone in the back of the herd."

"I'll be on the swiftest horse out there."

"And the most headstrong." He looked back at her and grinned. "Come to think of it, you'll make a perfect pair. The horse is all yours."

Getting close enough to drop the loop around the gelding's neck, Sofia couldn't help but smile. She had a new favorite horse.

Moving out of the mass of horseflesh, they got far enough away that Jackson finally stopped. She sat there for a moment, not wanting to dismount. She had missed Jackson the last few days. Being close to him, she didn't feel so alone. Resisting the urge to press her cheek against his back and linger in the warmth and scent of him was difficult. She needed to stay focused on her bigger dream.

He smelled of outdoors and leather. So much better than her own scent after weeks of not being able to wash off. It was just too risky with all the men around.

"Are you asleep?" He twisted in his saddle and studied her. "Are you all right?"

Sitting back, she realized how close she had gotten to him. With a sigh, she swung her leg over and dropped to the ground. *Oh, that hurt.*

Gripping the edge of his saddle blanket, she bit her lip, trying to remain stoic, but it didn't seem to work.

Jackson was on the ground next to her, his hand on her back. She wasn't sure if she could stand straight. Everything hurt so much, and a deep moan escaped. Taking a deep breath, she sucked in her gut and stood straight. "I'm good. Just stiff." To prove it to him, she took a step to her new mount.

She ran her hand over the short mane along the top of his neck. The horse had a good height on him and was wide in the chest. Jackson laid the blanket and saddle on the broad back. "He's a sound horse."

Nodding, she held the mouthpiece for a moment to warm it before slipping it between his teeth, then fastened the leather behind his ears. "I think he likes me. He didn't hesitate to take the bit."

"That's a good sign. Red gave up the other morning and just picked another horse." Jackson checked the cinch, then went back to his sorrel.

She loved the coloring of the Appaloosa. He was white with large red spots covering his whole body. The ones on his rounded rump were the biggest. He was not a regular cow horse, and that suited her just fine, because she was not a regular cowboy.

Swinging into the saddle, she smiled at Jackson, then kicked her horse into action. She ignored Jackson's warning to slow down. She knew where she was going, and she was ready.

For years, she dreamed about riding and working the cattle on the ranch, now God had given her this opportunity. She wasn't going to let anyone stop her.

Jackson forced himself to turn his horse away from the departing spitfire. He wanted to go after her and remind her of all the dangers.

It wasn't his concern if she knowingly put herself in harm's way. He looked to the sky and took in a heavy breath. If he said it enough times, maybe he'd start believing it.

He didn't care about her any more than he cared about the other cowboys. He didn't. He couldn't.

Having her ride behind him had been one of the worst decisions he had made this whole trip. Her small hands had left their imprint on him. The heat still emitted over his skin.

Rubbing the back of his neck, he made his way over to Estevan. The wrangler responsible for the horses knew each animal better than anyone else.

"Please tell me I didn't put the kid on a horse that can't be trusted."

White teeth flashing, the wrangler laughed. "Two Bit picked one of the more spirited animals we have, but I've seen the kid ride. I don't think you have anything to worry about. The horse is a handful, but he's smart.

With a skilled rider, he's one of the best we have. Tiago will do well with that gelding."

Reassured a bit, Jackson tipped his hat and moved to the other side of the herd to check on Sam, then he moved back and checked on Rory. The Irishman might need a break, and now that Tiago was riding, he could give Rory a chance to take it slow.

The day went by fast, but he had to fight the urge to check on her every half hour. He'd gotten close enough to make sure she had everything under her control.

The cowboys started teasing him about letting the kid have some room to make mistakes. He was torn between not wanting them to question why he was shadowing the kid, and the need to guard her against any further problems.

The sun settled behind the horizon, and Cook had already served supper when Jackson finally came into camp. With the herd settled for the night, and Clint standing watch, he could finally eat and hopefully get some sleep tonight. Not that he was holding out much hope on that one.

The cowboys had started playing music around a low campfire. He relaxed a bit when he didn't see Tiago. Maybe she had gone on to bed.

"Jackson."

Muscles tensed in defeat. He should have known he'd not be so fortunate as to avoid her. Grinding his teeth, he turned to her. "You should be resting."

"You have developed a very limited vocabulary." She lifted a tin plate. "Eat."

Taking the food from her, he looked for a place to go. He didn't want to have to talk to anyone, and he didn't want to deal with the unwanted feelings he was battling about his little orphan. Of course, if she was little, he wouldn't have this problem. No, she was a full grown woman, alone in the world.

And she was not his. Definitely not his.

"I kept the plate next to the fire to make sure it stayed warm. We're down to the last of the supplies, but it's warm and solid. Cook said we're going to hit the river late tomorrow." Her fingers went to her neck as if reaching for strands of hair that were no longer there. "Are we going to take the longer route north to the Collier's ferry crossing? I hope you're not endangering the herd just because you don't want me to meet the famous pirate." With a hard glare, she nudged his upper arm. "You need to eat before it gets cold."

She finally paused. He lifted an eyebrow. She never talked this much at once. "Have you finished?"

Crossing her arms, she took a step back. "Sorry."

"Don't worry about it." He made his way to the area where the cowboys slept. The music had faded, and it looked as if the men were settling in to sleep. He dropped in front of his saddle.

Tiago followed him.

"What are you doing?" Her being this close was not helping him to keep his thoughts off her.

"There was another story I wanted to tell you." She sat next to him without being invited. "Since you haven't been coming to check on me, I thought I'd come to you. I've decided not to wait for others to do what I want. I just…" Leaning close to him, she spoke in a hushed voice that caressed the skin below his neck. "I don't want to be alone."

"You need to get back to your place." He shut his eyes, bolting the parts of him that wanted to pull her close. Instead, he crammed a spoon full of beans into his mouth. He could not give in to her. "You can't stay here. It's where the cowboys sleep." His voice was louder and harsher than he intended.

It worked though, she moved back, taking the faint scent of cinnamon with her.

One of the cowboys yelled at him across the dim campfire. "Two Bit has worked hard and deserves to bed down with the cowboys."

Sam, who was closest to them, stood by the fire. "Yeah, boss, the kid's earned the right to sleep anywhere he wants."

Making sure his voice was low and no eye contact was made, Jackson told her what he didn't really want to tell her. "Go away. Your spot under the wagon is the best place for you."

This time she got up and, without a word, left the campfire.

"Boss, why are you so tough on the kid?"

Ignoring Red, he gulped down the last of his dinner and took the plate back to Cook. The biscuit was cold and dry. He thought of tossing it, but he might be hungry enough to eat it later, so he slipped it into his pocket.

Not far off, the river rushed over roots and rocks. A dunk in the cool water would clear his mind. His clothes could use a washing. Halfway he paused, a few feet from the wagon.

The sounds of soft crying reached him, and it wasn't Cook. His fist clenched around the hard piece of bread. He should keep walking. Stopping would only complicate matters.

Movement under the wagon got his attention. If he didn't move now, she'd see him. Standing in the dark like an idiot, one foot pointed toward the river, the other stayed planted.

"Jackson?"

He didn't say anything. Maybe she'd go back under the wagon.

"Why are you standing in the dark?"

Why? He had no clue.

"Okay, you need to say something because you are starting to scare me."

He sighed. Biscuit in hand, he twisted and threw it as hard into the night as he could. A plopping noise confirmed he hit the river.

"Did you just throw one of our biscuits into the river?" She now stood a few feet from him.

How did he even begin to explain that it was his heart he was trying to get rid of? "I was walking to the river and was wondering if you wanted to take a dip before we hit the cattle station tomorrow. All the men are either asleep or with the cattle, and I know you haven't had a chance to bath off like the men. I could stay on the ridge and make sure you're safe."

She leaped onto him and wrapped her arms around his neck. "Thank you. I must be stinking if you offered to be my lookout. I don't even notice anymore." She was gone before he could even push her away or return the hug.

That was the problem. Returning the hug shouldn't even be up for debate. What was wrong with him? She darted to the wagon and grabbed her saddlebag.

Dropping his head, he rubbed his eyes. Why did he do this? He might not deserve to be happy, but why the need to torture himself?

Following her to the edge of the river, he dropped

to the ground and rested against a giant tree. His boots propped up on a snake-like root, he settled in as she jumped into the water fully clothed.

He thought he heard words, but he wasn't sure. "Are you talking to me?"

Joyful and carefree laughter bubbled up from the river. "No, I was thanking God for His abundance. Water has never felt so good." A wistful edge to her voice made him smile. "Nothing like being deprived of something to make you appreciate it." Some splashing followed that statement. "Thank you, Jackson."

"You're welcome." Pulling his hat down, he crossed his arms and dropped his chin. He might as well get some rest. "Let me know when you're ready to get back to the wagon."

He tried to keep his mind blank, but images of his wife at the river popped into his brain. She had loved the water and would use any excuse to get him to take her. She insisted that Emily learn to swim. He sat up. "You know how to swim, right?"

"It's a little late to ask me that. What if I told you no?" Droplets of water landed on the edge of his shoulder.

"Did you just try to splash me?" He chuckled.

Her only answer was to laugh. He remembered the last time he truly enjoyed himself and laughed whole-heartedly.

It had been the day he brought the stranded travelers home for the night. Lilly had been busy cooking and tending their baby son, Jack. The little one had been fussy. Their daughter, Emily, had tried to braid her own hair, but it had been uneven. So to her mother's horror, her solution was to cut it until both sides matched. With her hair sticking out at weird angles she had the biggest smile, so proud of herself for helping her momma and being a big girl. He had laughed until his eyes watered.

His wife hadn't thought it was so funny. He had reassured her it would grow back, but it never got the chance. The next day they were murdered by men he had brought into their home. He used to laugh all the time, now there wasn't a reason.

Guilt and joy did not live in the same house. He pulled out his watch and opened the engraved cover. "It's getting late."

"Okay, I'm almost done with my extra clothes. I will never take clean clothes for granted again. Maria deserves more pay."

"Maria?" He frowned. Orphans didn't pay washer-women.

"Oh. Uh...she works on the ranch and washes the De Zavala's laundry. I don't know what they pay her, but it is not enough."

Tiago was a study in contradictions. But it was easier to take people at face value than ask questions and get involved. The last thing he needed was to tangle up his life with hers.

She darted past him. He frowned. Was she skipping?

Turning to walk backward, she faced him with a smile. The dark curls bounced around her face. She was about the prettiest girl he knew, and she was dressed as a boy. He suspected that she'd bring him to his knees if he ever saw her in a dress.

"So I thought of this great story my mom used to tell me."

Turning his gaze to the far tree line so he wouldn't

have to see her face, Jackson shook his head. "Not to-night."

She stopped abruptly in front of him, and he nearly ran her over. Her dark eyes were large as she looked up at him. "It's short. I thought it would help my brain focus on something else so I can go to sleep. Are you clear in your head? You seemed preoccupied all day, and I thought it would help us both."

She turned from him and crossed her arms. "When I was little I would get scared, and my mother would tell me stories. Her voice soothed me until I fell asleep."

Tilting her head back, she seemed to be studying the crescent moon hanging in a deep purple sky, stars scattered across like silver dust.

Her slender neck was working up and down. He hoped she wasn't going to cry. Her gaze left the Earth's ceiling and turned back to him. Pinning him to the spot. He let out a strong breath of air. He should have left when he had the chance. "I can't imagine you being scared of anything."

"It's a short story." She might as well have begged him on her knees with the look she gave him.

She took a step closer to him. He held his breath in anticipation. For what he wasn't sure.

Tilting her head again, she studied him. "Do you know a quick story? Whenever I close my eyes, dark thoughts bounce around in my head like buckshot. I know there are times we need to be alone, but tonight I just feel so isolated. Will you stay, just for a little bit?"

He nodded. He understood, he did, but she was asking him to help with her unruly thoughts when he was dealing with his own.

Rushing to a cluster of small bushes, she spread out

her extra clothes to dry. Finished with her chore, she turned and looked at him, arms crossed as if to ward off the cold, which didn't exist.

"Back home there's this woman, this family that comes to town every few months or so." She took a step toward him, but looked to the river. "I avoided her when I saw her at church, because I didn't want to get trapped talking to her. She talked about everything and barely paused to breathe. I don't think I've ever heard her husband or four sons mutter more than a word or two. I think if I ever see her again I'll smile and ask her how she's doing and just let her talk."

He glanced back to the campfire. It wasn't that far away. Why couldn't he start walking in that direction? "You need to go to sleep. Tomorrow will be a long day, and every man needs to be in his best form."

A chuckle shook her shoulders, but she did move to the wagon. That was a good sign. He followed to make sure she actually went to sleep.

Yeah, he was getting good at lying to himself.

She crawled under the wagon and rearranged the blankets. "Do you think our life is set before we're born?"

She sat on the makeshift bed and pulled her knees up to her chest and hugged them, resting her cheek on the top of her knees. She looked so young and lost. He kneeled by the big wheel. "I don't know."

"I know I've felt God. I've never felt abandoned by Him even when my mom and brother were swept away in the river. I had my faith, but I didn't understand. Why them? I was supposed to be with them that day. They were heading to church. My stomach hurt, so my mother wouldn't let me travel. Why was I home safe while they drowned?" Her speech stopped, and they stayed in the silence for a bit.

"Why were they taken while I'm still here? For a while I thought I was being punished. But Pastor Philips helped through that. I still don't understand. They had a lot of life to live."

She closed her eyes and released a sigh that carried guilt and pain. "When I visit the cemetery, I stop at the markers for so many children and young people. Will was too young. Rory and I were right there. We could have gone down, too."

"Will made a stupid decision, and you and Rory were smarter and faster. Even when you realized you were falling, you made sure to roll away from the herd."

She lifted her head and gave him the gift of her grin. Half-hearted as it was, it was still a sign of hope. "Are you saying I'm capable of taking care of myself?

He couldn't help but chuckle. Rubbing his chin, he squinted at her. "Hmm. If I am, I don't think it would serve me well to admit it."

"I wouldn't expect anything more. I mean, you have a job to do and your job is to tell me to stay in the wagon…stay safe…get rest." A serious expression clouded her face. "You need someone to tell you to rest."

"This is not my first drive."

"After we get to market and sell the cattle and horses, what are you doing with your share? Do you have plans to go back to Kentucky?"

"I'm never going back to Kentucky. Nothing there for me." He leaned against the wheel, giving up any pretense of leaving. There was something soothing about talking to someone in the dark. Someone who didn't look at you with pity or blame because they knew your story. "I have a deal in the works with De Zavala."

"To work on the ranch?" Her voice pitched in either excitement or horror. He couldn't tell which.

"Nope. He has property on the edge of town." He picked up a blade of grass crushed by the wagon. "I want to buy it."

She shot straight up, bumping her head on the floorboard. "Ouch." She rubbed the spot she had hit. "He'd never sell that place. That was my…" She coughed.

"You okay?"

Silence followed, and her lips tightened.

One eyebrow went up as he pegged her with a stare and waited. Nothing. "Your what?"

She covered her face and took a deep breath, letting it out before she answered. "My mom lived there before she died. Her parents had built the house on the land before De Zavala owned it."

"It's a nice piece of property with everything needed for a horse farm."

"It is, but it's small. Not big at all."

"Perfect size for horses and a few cattle. I figured I'd run a small herd. But I want to focus on the breeding and training my horses. We're close enough to San Antonio. Once Texas becomes part of the union, I think it'll grow and become a good hub. I also like the hill country. Big possibilities and not a lot of people."

"Why Texas?"

"Sometimes you need a new start." He shrugged and threw the blade of grass he'd been messing with. "A place clean of memories."

"Are your other memories that bad?"

He leaned his head back and closed his eyes. "The

memories were good. It was the lack of…it's not the memories. It's the lost promises and dreams, of all the things that will never happen. Of memories not made."

"Like what?"

"Like watching a daughter grow up to become a woman and a mother of her own. A wife holding a new baby and laughing as your son rides his first pony. It's seeing your son get old enough to ride with you." He swallowed back the burn in his throat. Why was he talking? Because he needed to remind himself why she was not a possibility. He couldn't allow himself to forget.

She moved closer, but didn't touch him. "Jackson, I'm so sorry. I know the word is lame. I can't even pretend to know the kind of hurt it is to lose a wife and children."

"This is why I came to Texas. I didn't want to think about it or talk about it."

"And I wasn't supposed to ask about your past. Sorry, but why did you tell me?"

"Death has a way of putting you in your place, reminding you how fragile life is no matter how strong or smart you think you are."

"But with Jesus, we conquered death. Do you believe they're with God?"

"There are times I hope so, but other times I just don't know."

"I do. I see the stars. I feel the breeze, and I know my mother is part of a bigger world than I can see. Her faith was strong, and she taught me to always trust God's plan. When *abuelita* died, I was devastated. She was my father's mother and my world. Her and my mother were best friends, too. She taught me that God's plans are not intended to harm us."

"But they do." Anger flared in his gut. "There was no way the murder of my family was for the good. My son was just learning to walk. Lilly had just told me she was expecting our third child." He stood. This was why he never talked about it. It was easier to remain numb. "They're dead. It was my fault, and I should have been buried with them. I'll never marry again." She needed to know that in case she was getting any ideas. Or maybe it was to remind himself.

She gasped. He hated the pity he knew he would see in her eyes if he looked down. Without thought he walked until a large tree stood in his path. At least she didn't know how they died. The blame and horror reflecting his own guilt would be too much.

Drained of energy, he leaned his forehead against the rough bark of the trunk. Yeah, it cut into his skin, but he didn't care.

Chapter Twelve

Sofia put her hand on his shoulder. The muscles tightened, but he didn't pull away. What words could comfort him?

His breaths came in long hard pulls from his lungs. Her father had changed drastically when he lost his wife and son. A new shell had formed around him, hard and distant. In a way, she had lost her father also.

Biting the corner of her mouth, she tried to stop the tears. "I'm so, so sorry. I can't even imagine. There are people who carry something really bad inside them. All I know is God is always here." She pressed her hand to her heart. "I know without a doubt He is with me and they are with Him. He promises to restore us no matter what this world does to destroy us."

He did nothing to acknowledge her words. Not knowing what else to do, she leaned against his back and wrapped her arms around him. She knew words had no meaning when pain gripped your core. With her cheek pressed between his shoulder blades, she could feel his heartbeat. The soft sounds of the night clashed with his breathing.

He moved his hand on her forearm and held her in place. Time slipped by, she closed her eyes and prayed for God's love to be stronger than his pain.

"Tiago!" Rory's harsh voice sliced through the silence, scattering pieces through the air. Sofia jumped back and Jackson turned, slowly. The cowboy had his rifle resting in his hands.

With her hand on her chest, Sofia focused on calming her rapid heart. "Rory, you frightened me."

"Good." He shifted the rifle. "I don't think it's a good idea for you to be out in the dark, alone with our boss here."

Behind her Jackson growled. A few steps and he was squaring off with Rory. "Are you threatening me?"

"Boss, I'm just saying it's time for our little wrangler here to go to bed. It's late, and you never know the dangers that might be lurking in the dark." He cut his glare around Jackson's shoulder. When he made eye contact with her, his expression softened. "Go on with ya. Cook will need you early in the morning. You need to get some sleep."

Sofia tilted her head back and groaned. Why did men keep telling her to rest? "Thank you, Rory, but there's no problem here."

"Easy to say when there isn't anyone making sure your boss is not taking advantage of a girl alone in the world." His glare went back to Jackson.

Jackson didn't seem to take that well. Shoulders back, his chest became wider as he closed the distance between him and Rory.

Not knowing what else to do, she stepped between the men. Men who were acting like children. She turned to Rory first. "What are you doing wandering around in the dark? With your wound, you should be resting, too." Oh, great. Now she sounded like them.

"I can only lie down for so long until it starts throbbing." He nudged his rifle in Jackson's direction. "I noticed boss man here was missing, and I knew he'd come in late from the herd, so I thought I'd check on you. Why don't you go on now and get to bed?"

"I'm not going to do anything to harm Tiago. She doesn't need protection from me. Go back to the campsite Rory."

The Irish cowboy stood his ground. "With all due respect, boss, I'm not leaving without you."

Sofia threw up her hands. "You can both stand here and see who can spit the farthest. I'm going to bed." With one last glare she stomped to the wagon. Men were so…ugh…just so childish.

Throwing her blanket around and adjusting her saddle, she burned off her anger. She sat with a hard thud. Leaning forward, she narrowed her gaze and tried to see what the men were doing.

Had they come to blows? After a few minutes they started walking back to camp. Wanting to hear what they talked about, she crawled to the far end of the wagon.

"No one. Sir, what are your intentions toward her?"

"What about you?" Rough and raw, Jackson's voice caused her skin to tingle.

Rory made a clicking noise. "I think she might be more than I could handle in a wife."

"Marriage is not in my future. Especially to a female who rushes headlong into danger without a thought in her head. My only goal is to get her home safe and in one piece."

"Then we're of the same accord."

Well, she wouldn't marry them either, even if they asked pretty please. Their voices faded as they started walking again. Flopping on the thick blanket Jackson had given her, she wrapped her other one over her shoulders and pulled it up to her chin, burying herself in the cocoon she created.

Her mother said there had been many men who had asked her father for her hand in marriage, of course they were in Mexico, but that didn't matter. Just because these two cowboys didn't see her as wife material didn't mean she'd make a bad wife.

She pushed her hair back and paused to look at her hand. The skin was red and rough. Her nails, once neat and clean, were now torn and dirty. Bruises ran along her arm.

Why was she even upset? Just wounded pride. Being a wife was not her dream. She wanted to be a cowboy. So why did their words hurt so much?

She should be hollering with glee. A life of a safe and cautious wife, sitting at home, planning meals and watching babies was not what she wanted.

If her dreams made her less of a woman so much so that no one, not even a cowboy, would want her as a wife, then so be it. Being alone was not the worst thing that could happen to her.

They'd all probably hate her anyway when they found out she was the rancher's daughter.

Jackson watched as Rory settled into sleep. Shifting his legs didn't help bring any comfort. Sleep would not be visiting him this night.

Was Tiago still upset? He hated that Rory was right.

Being alone with her was dangerous. He had no intention of marrying ever again.

He glanced over the burning embers to the Irishman. What was the kid's story? Was he interested in their little wrangler as a woman? Rory was a hard worker and smart. He seemed to be a man of honor. She could do worse.

The fire in his gut at the thought of her married to the charming cowboy didn't mean a thing. He just worried about her. He knew how vulnerable a woman alone in the world was, how easily she could be hurt.

Tiago didn't have anyone.

He pulled on a blade of grass and chewed on it. Well, she had him and Rory now. She and the Irishman would make a good couple. If everything went as expected the next few days, and they made it across the river with a good majority of the steers, he'd be set. With a place of his own and the horses he wanted, he'd need a couple of trusted ranch hands.

To his left Rory rolled over and pulled the blanket over his head. Yeah, they'd work well together.

He couldn't take sitting here, mucking through his own thoughts.

Hopping to his feet, he shook off dirt and grass, grabbing his saddle he headed to the horses. Might as well get some work done if he couldn't sleep.

"Boss?" Rory was pulling himself up. "Where ya going?"

He kept walking, pretending not to hear the cowboy. Unfortunately, Rory wasn't deterred. He caught up with him, a worn saddle in his good hand.

"You heading to the cattle? I can't sleep, so I'll join ya."

Apparently he took Jackson's silence as encouragement.

"I can't believe we are so close to delivering the cattle. There were days I didn't think we'd ever make it."

With his gaze focused on the horse, Jackson tried to ignore the Irish cowboy. The kid was getting under his skin. He knew he hadn't done anything wrong other than protect Tiago.

"You should be resting. Go back to bed." Maybe he'd get the hint.

"*Jefe*? What are you doing with the horses this time of night?" Estevan approached, rubbing his eyes. "Rory?"

Jackson groaned. Leather creaked as the horse shifted his weight. Had the wrangler heard what they were talking about? It was getting harder to keep Tiago's identity a secret. "We're just going to check the cattle and relieve Clint from night duty. Go back to sleep. Thanks for checking on the horses."

Jackson mounted his gelding and pulled him around to face the cowboy.

"Sure. See y'all in the morning." He yawned and headed back to his sleeping area.

Jackson realized how close Estevan was to the wagon. "Do you think he knows about her?"

"No. I think he might think something is off, but no he doesn't know we have a woman with us." Throwing his saddle on a sorrel and started looping the cinch, Rory shook his head.

"How did you know?" Jackson asked.

Swinging up into his saddle, he pulled the horse up as he started prancing. "I had a sister that preferred breeches to dresses, so seeing a woman dressed as a boy wasn't anything new."

"You got a problem with the way she dresses?"

"Nope. Just because she wears pants don't mean she can be disrespected."

"I agree." With a flick of the reins, he moved his horse to the area where the cattle bedded down. He needed to get past this anger over Rory's interest in Tiago. For his own sanity, he needed to encourage them to come together. He wouldn't have to worry about her. "Are you sure you're not interested in marrying Tiago?" It sounded ridiculous to use a boy's name.

Only the sounds of the horses, leather and soft bawling of the cattle filled the night. After a bit, he thought he'd not get an answer.

"Nope. I got problems chasing me, and the only thing to my name is this saddle. I ain't got no business taking a wife. Even one as tough as our Tiago."

Jackson narrowed his gaze. "You got the kind of trouble that will cause a problem for us?"

"Just the kind that keeps me from going home."

With a nod to acknowledge his trust in the man's word, Jackson kicked his horse into a trot. His attention heightened as Clint came into view. Something was wrong.

"Someone's with Clint?" Rory pulled up next to him.

"Yeah, I see that." Sitting back in his saddle, he slowed his horse. "Can you tell if it's a friend or trouble?

"All our boys are back at camp." Rory's horse went in a circle when he pulled him up.

Muscles strained under his shirt as he forced the horse to stand. He couldn't believe what he saw. "What is she doing out here?"

"Well, I'll be. It's Tiago. I thought we left her back under the wagon safe and sound."

Jackson grunted. "She apparently doesn't like safe."

Pressing his heels in the side of his horse, they lunged forward.

"Boss, remember Clint doesn't know."

Burying the urge to grab the reins of her mount and taking her back to camp, he growled.

"Howdy, boss. Rory. Man, this is a busy night. I've never had so much company. Everything all right?"

Jackson took his horse right to Tiago's Appaloosa. The white of her eyes grew bigger. Good, she knew she was in trouble. "Does Cook know you're running around in the dark by yourself?" Leaning as close as he could, he looked her right in those big beautiful brown eyes. "I told you to sleep."

"I couldn't. I thought you were going to bed." She glanced at Rory. "It appears none of us could sleep." Her gaze came back to him. "I'm not alone. I'm with Clint. I was lonely and thought he might be, too. We were talking about the stars."

"Boss, this kid knows the craziest stories about the stars."

He wanted to yell at her that those were his stories, not Clint's or even Rory's, but they weren't his. She wasn't his.

"It's dangerous riding around in the dark."

She crossed her arms with an unlady-like humph sound. Clint laughed. "Then we'd all be in trouble, boss."

Rory sighed. "How's it going out here, Clint? We thought we'd relieve you so you can get some sleep."

Clint nodded and looked as if everyone had gone a bit crazy. He might be right.

"Go on Clint. We'll keep watch."

"Don't have to ask me twice. There's some activity

over to the left of the hill. I've been keeping an eye on it. I think a momma wolf has her pups out. As long as I touch base with the steers, they seem fine."

Rory turned his restless horse in the direction Clint had pointed to. "Want to go with me, Tiago?"

"He doesn't need to go off with you." Jackson wished he could pull the words back as soon as Clint laughed.

"With three of you here, I'm leaving and letting you figure it out." With a tip of his hat he left.

Tiago threw her head back. "You two are going to drive me crazy. Are you really riding out together to check on me? What do you think I'm going to do?"

"We didn't know you were out here. We just couldn't sleep." Rory talked too much.

"If I'm not going to be able to make a step without both of you next to me, we will never get anything done."

They all turned to the area Clint pointed out.

"I want you on the wagon with Cook when we roll into the cattle station tomorrow."

"Grrrrrr." Did she just growl at him?

He narrowed his eyes and stared at her. She stared right back. Her top lip pulled up in a sneer. He glanced over to Rory. "Did she just growl at me?"

The only reply he got was a snort. He turned back to her. "Why are you growling at me?"

She sat and straightened her spine. "It seems to be the language you understand best, *jefe*."

Yeah, he chose to ignore the sarcasm dripping from the word *boss*. He shook his head. "You will not be riding into the cattle station on the back of a horse. I want you to stay out of sight and in the wagon. The plan is to get us across the river without incident."

"You're going to need me to get the cattle across."

"No. I'll be able to hire a couple of cowboys for the day. With the rains, the river is going to be up and moving fast. You'll stay with Cook."

Her graceful neck worked as she swallowed hard. "I can handle the river."

"I know you can, but you don't have to. Stay with Cook. He'll need help getting the wagon ready for the trip back." He hoped giving her a reason to stay away from a rushing river would make it easier for her.

She nodded. He relaxed. She wasn't going to fight him.

"I'll help Cook while you take the cattle across, but I'm going to help drive the cattle into the station. You can't afford to be down a man."

He opened his mouth, but Rory held his hand up. He pointed with his chin. Jackson followed.

Tiago gasped. Her hand went to her mouth.

On the edge of the trees a pair of newborn twin fawns with long wobbly legs were learning to stand. One leap from beside them, and the doe stood between them and her new babies. She stomped her front leg.

"We're upsetting her." Rory pulled on the reins and started backing his horse away from the mother and her offspring.

"They're precious. Hey, Momma, we aren't going to hurt your babies." She turned in the saddle and looked at him. "Jackson, do you think I could touch them?"

"No, we need to leave her alone. We're stressing her out. They can't run yet."

The doe snorted and stomped her delicate leg. "She doesn't have a chance against us, but she's willing to fight, isn't she?" A clicking sound to her mount and she had him moving backward.

His wife had fought, but it hadn't done any good. "Most mothers will give their lives and fight impossible foes to protect their little ones."

She nodded, she watching the mother. The doe took a couple steps forward she stomped again, head held high.

"My mother was like that. She was very proper and a true lady, but she would have fought a bear to protect me and my brother." With her sleeve, she wiped at her face.

He suspected she had shed tears. "You know she'd be happy you weren't with her the day you lost them."

Turning away from the momma and babies, she looked at him. "You're right. I never thought about that. She would have been happy I wasn't with them."

Their eyes locked as he leaned forward. Closer to her. Keeping thoughts of touching her lips out of his mind was a constant battle.

Rory walked his horse between them. Forcing them apart. "Hey, kids, why don't we circle the cattle? I heard some coyotes over yonder." He kept moving. Obviously expecting them to follow.

Jackson nodded and kept his focus on Rory's back. He didn't even want to think about how close he had come to kissing her. "You will be in the wagon tomorrow."

"We have over a thousand steers to move into the pens. You need me."

"I'm not arguing with you about this. In the morning you will be in the wagon."

Rory laughed.

"What are you laughing at?"

"Your expression in the morning when you have to

admit she's right." He clicked to his horse. "Come on, Tiago. Let's go to the far tree line and make sure none of our cattle have wondered off." Rory said something else Jackson couldn't hear.

They both laughed as they rode away. He growled. "Tiago, tomorrow you will be in the wagon."

Silence.

"You will be in the wagon." Was she ignoring him? He yelled louder. "Do you hear me?"

"Yes, *jefe*," she called over her shoulder.

He was starting to hate sarcasm, but he relaxed a bit at her agreement.

Until he realized all she had really said was she heard him, not that she was going to follow his orders. They would move the cattle into the pirate owned crossing station without her.

She needed to stay away for the infamous Sterling. Retired pirate or not, it was too dangerous.

They could move the cattle without her, and they would.

Chapter Thirteen

Sofia pulled the bandanna up over her nose. With the rains, they traded the dust for mud and mosquitoes. If the buggers got any bigger and meaner, they could brand them and sell them at market along with the cattle and horses.

But not even the bloodsucking critters and the red welts they left behind smothered the excitement of approaching the cattle station. They were one day away from getting the cattle to market. She had done it. A bit bruised and banged up, but she was an experienced cowboy.

A cowboy who might get to meet the notorious Sterling Duval. Stories of his escapades had fed her childish imagination.

When she had turned twelve, her mother had taken her to visit friends and family in Galveston. Standing on the edge of the sandy beach, she had been fascinated by the endless horizon of water. The tall ships with bellowing sails coming into port. Imageries of being aboard one of the ships and sailing into the unknown stirred her heart for adventure.

Her mother had quickly put all that nonsense away with stories of ships lost at sea. Hundreds of people drowning with no way to get help. Her mother was very practical that way.

Stopping the thoughts of the past, she focused on the building and pens that grew larger as they plodded along, one step at a time.

The lead drovers had already started penning the cattle. Checking behind her, she noticed a few had wandered off. She spun Domino around on his hindquarters and went after the stragglers.

As she swung her lasso over her head, most of the stray cattle jogged back into line. Their long horns clashed as they jostled for positions. The Bar DZ marked them as her father's cattle. She glanced over the herd, all the way to the front. The steers looked good, and they had lost very few. Of course the river would be the final challenge, but still her father would have to acknowledge her ability.

Not only could she help him and be a partner in managing the ranch, but she had proved she thrived at the dirty work, too.

"It's time for you to get in the wagon." Jackson's deep gravelly voice startled her, and she yelped.

With a glare, she twisted in the saddle and looked at him. "Why are you sneaking up on me?" Back stiff, she focused on keeping the cattle in formation. "Shouldn't you be making arrangements with the station manager?"

He got closer, and she noticed he had a new hat on his pommel.

He handed it to her. "Here. I got you this so you don't have to wear that overly large flashy thing you and Cook call a hat." The short flat brim was sharp looking. The headband was tooled leather with silver rings.

"That's for me?" Heat climbed up her neck. She pushed her tongue against the back of her teeth. Why did she get so awkward around him when they weren't disagreeing? "Thank you. It's beautiful."

In one motion she took off the old sombrero Cook gave her after the stampede and planted the new hat on her head. It was a perfect fit.

A grunt was the only acknowledgment she received before his horse pushed a few distracted cattle toward her. "I was afraid the other one would draw unwanted attention to you."

"And I thought you were being nice. I'll pay you back."

Without making eye contact, he shook his head. "Don't. It's a gift. I'm heading to the headquarters to finish up the arrangement as soon as you are safely in the wagon."

She might have rolled her eyes. Her mother would have had a fit at her disrespect, but she'd earned her right to ride in with the other cowboys.

"Santiago, I'm serious. There are dangerous characters around here that I have no control over. I don't want to be worrying over you."

She hated it when he used her brother's name.

"No one asked you to. How many times are we going to have this conversation?" Focusing on her gelding, she patted Domino on the withers.

"As many times as it takes. I know you've proved yourself more than capable, but if someone recognized you as a female, it might cause real problems for all of us."

"I look like a boy, and it shouldn't cause problems just because I'm a woman."

"That's true, but that's not the world we live in. I'm the boss. You helped get the herd in the holding pens. Now I need you to help Cook."

"You mean hide." She sighed. What if she told him she was a De Zavala? Would she win the argument? Probably not. He'd be even angrier. "I'm not trying to be difficult, Jackson. Don't bury me away in the back of the wagon. I'm here to see and do all the things a real cowboy would."

His horse came up next to hers. Their knees brushed. "As much as you want to be a cowboy, even as skilled as you are, you're still a woman in a man's world and you need to be careful."

Ready to argue, she turned to him. The concern and warmth in his eyes stopped her. He wasn't being mean, he was worried. So she just managed to mutter. "The world isn't fair."

His gaze moved over her face, taking in the details she had tried to hide. She could get lost in the green of his eyes.

Clearing his throat, he sat straighter and looked to the front of the herd. "I reckon there are many people that would agree with you, including me. But it doesn't change the truth. If you're discovered, all sorts of problems will follow. Do us all a favor and keep your head down and stay close to Cook."

Rory galloped his horse toward them. "Don't you need to be getting to the wagon?"

She threw her head back, a few soft puffs of white floating across a brilliant blue sky. Eyes closed she prayed. "Please God, grant me patience."

Rory nodded. "Pain and patience would bring a snail to America."

Crossing her eyes at him, she shook her head. "I don't even know what that means."

He shrugged. "My mum said it all the time. She also said asking God for patience was a dangerous thing."

"Rory, you take over here. I'll escort Tiago to the wagon so *he* can start helping Cook."

"Sounds good, boss."

They had almost reached the wagon when a trio of riders cut them off. Jackson put his big sorrel between her and the newcomers.

The man in the middle had to be the tallest she'd ever seen. The muscles in his arms strained the sleeves of the long black coat he wore over a crisp white shirt. There was nothing dirty or unwashed about him.

The high collar brushed against a black trimmed beard. Narrow hips went into long legs in tall black boots. He didn't even wear a hat. His raven black hair was swept from his face in a dramatic fashion. He looked like a man who walked right off the pages of a storybook. Pushing his horse past Jackson's, he came straight at her.

Surrounded by thick lashes, his eyes shined a brilliant blue. She might have gasped at the startling contrast between the black hair and stunning blue of his eyes, but she hoped not.

He held his hand out to her. "*Mademoiselle*, I'm Captain Sterling Duval. It's an honor to have the De Zavala ranch visit our ferry."

From years of her mother's training, Sofia reacted without thought and placed her hand in his as he bowed over her wrist.

As soon as she heard Jackson's groan, she pulled her hand back, pressing it against her tightly swathed chest. From the mischievous gleam in the ex-pirate's eyes, she was too late. Her stomach dropped.

He knew her secret, and there was no recovering. Jackson used his horse to push the big man back, blocking her view of Sterling Duval. The man was much younger than she imagined. And better looking.

A loud rumble vibrated the air around them. She had never heard such an all-consuming deep laugh. "No reason to get your guns cocked, cowboy. I assumed the girl was a De Zavala. I take it she belongs to you?"

"The *boy's* name is Santiago Smith. We don't want any trouble, just to move our cattle across the river."

"Smith?" A snort followed that question. "If that's what you want, then so be it."

She shifted her horse a little to the side so she could see what was happening, but she kept her hat low and her chin down. Had he recognized her as her father's daughter from the time she was in Galveston?

What if Jackson started questioning her about being a De Zavala. She thought back to the socials they had attended. She glanced at Jackson.

How would he react if he discovered her true name?

"He's my cook's assistant." The hard edge of Jackson's voice carried its own warning, but it didn't seem to bother the pirate captain.

The big man held his hands up, and he winked at her. "I understand. To show my good intentions, I invite you to my table for dinner tonight." His gaze moved back to Jackson. "Both of you of course."

"We'll be eating with our drovers tonight." Jackson's

horse bumped hers, causing him to move back. It looked like an accident, but she doubted it.

"Of course, of course. I have a large enough table for all of your men." He laughed as he emphasized the word *men*. He turned to the two that waited behind him. "Make sure they get the time and directions for dinner." He tipped his hat. "I look forward to sharing a meal with you and showing you how I treat a courageous woman. A woman who deserves the finer things in life."

He winked at her before kicking his horse into action and leaving them with his men.

The one on the left gave Jackson the information, but before they rode off the largest one, a bear of a man, grabbed her reins. "The captain would be insulted if you failed to accept his generous invitation."

The two men kicked their horses into a gallop and followed their boss.

Jackson took off his hat and slapped it against his leg. "You wanted to meet the pirate."

Slamming his hat back on his head, he flicked the reins over his horse's neck and turned it back to the wagon. "This is what I didn't want to happen. Come on. You need to get to the wagon. I'm not sure how he figured it out so fast."

She moved her horse into a trot. Jackson's reaction had her scared. If she didn't have her father's name to protect her, what could happen? "We're free citizens. He can't make us do something we don't want, right?"

"At times you are so naive." Arriving at the wagon, he dismounted. "We are in a no-man's-land right now. A strip of land between Texas and Louisiana. There is no law other than his. If he wants something, he can take it."

"Why would he want me? I'm dirty, beat up, wearing horrible clothes and my hair is hacked off."

He moved to her horse and looked up at her. The green of his eyes lightened. Swinging her leg over the saddle, she jumped to the ground. She should have stayed on her horse. It was easier to look down on him than feeling so small next to him.

He took a deep breath and put his knuckle under her chin. She stopped breathing and waited. For what, she wasn't sure.

"Some men are smart enough to see the truth, even when it's hidden."

They stood like that as the world disappeared around her. She licked her lips. It sounded like he took a sharp intake of his breath. "Jackson, I'm sorry I didn't get in the wagon sooner like you wanted. I didn't want to bring trouble to you or the boys."

"I know. I'm thinking he scouted us earlier and saw through your disguise. He knew you were female before he rode up to us. He was watching us."

Goose bumps tightened her skin. The thought of strange eyes on her when she thought she was going about her daily chores would give her bad dreams tonight.

He dropped his hand and went to the back of the wagon. "Cook!"

Stunned by the sudden change, she stood alone for a moment. She needed to tell him the truth about her name. But the thought of his reaction burned her stomach.

Following him, she found Cook and Jackson discussing her. "She'll need to have a weapon on her at all times."

Jackson nodded. They both turned to her. "You aren't going to clean up or change clothes. Hopefully that will kill his interest. Also, stay with me and Rory every moment from the front steps until we lock the door to your room."

He turned back to Cook. "I'll finalize our lodgings and take care of some other business. I'll meet you back here before we head to dinner." Taking off his hat he pointed it to her. "Don't leave Cook's side. While we are here, make sure you are always with someone and you're armed. Understand?"

She nodded. "Don't worry. I'll stay with Cook." The encounter with Sterling and his man had scared her more than she wanted to admit. She had gotten so used to being a cowboy she forgot how dangerous it was being a woman.

"Do you have a weapon on you now?"

"Yes, and I have my Hawken on my saddle."

"Good. I'll see you soon." She was with Cook, so why did she suddenly feel alone? The desire to follow Jackson was strong. He made her feel safe. Touching the gun tucked into her trousers, she reminded herself to be strong and independent. Her stomach hurt. Being strong and independent was not always fun.

There were jobs that needed to be done. "I'll settle the mules."

"It's going to be good, *mija*. Señor Jackson and Rory will make sure you are safe. I'll be there with my knives." He grinned at her.

She nodded. What she hated was that they had to protect her. If anything happened to them because of her, she'd never forgive herself.

Please God, protect the men who are with me and get us all home safely.

As she pulled the heavy collar off the lead mule, she looked at her hands. These were not the hands of a lady. Her hair was a disgrace, and she didn't even want to look at the condition of her clothes. This was how she would be going into a grand house to eat dinner at their host's table.

Sorry, Momma.

Chapter Fourteen

Pressed between Rory and Jackson with Cook standing in front of her, Sofia couldn't see much as they were led to the parlor by the butler. At the sight of her, his nose went higher in the air.

Red's gaze darted around the hallway. His voice sounded small against the grandeur of the house. It was more like a palace. "Boss, shouldn't you have made Two Bit at least wash off? This is some fancy place. Maybe he should have stayed back." Red had his hat in his hands.

Sam, Clint, Eli and Estevan seemed just as unsettled.

With a short bow, the butler left them, closing the door behind them. She had been in many fine homes. This one outdid them all.

Clint looked at the velvet chair. "I've never seen such fancy furniture. Are you sure we were invited to dinner and not to clean out the barn?"

Estevan stood in front of the marble fireplace and went through the motions of warming his hands even though sweat dotted his brow. "I don't understand why we're here." He eyed her with judgment she had never before seen from the boys. "Perhaps they have some-where Two Bit can wash off. I was raised on a ranch, but even I know to wash the dirt off my hands and face before sitting at someone's table."

Lowering her head, she felt the heat climb up her neck. When Jackson told her to remain unwashed, she thought it was a good way to dissuade Captain Duval's interest in her. Now it was just humiliating.

Worse, she was embarrassing these hardworking cowboys.

Jackson pressed his hand on her shoulder. "Tiago was working hard, and if Duval wants the De Zavala team, then he gets all of us as we are."

Everyone looked a bit uneasy except for Rory. He had taken a seat by the door and stretched his legs out as if he were right at home.

He nodded to her and motioned for her to stand be-hind him. Jackson pushed her in his direction.

At this point, she might as well be hiding behind a giant potted palm. The knot in her stomach told her she would rather be hiding in the corner tonight.

The double doors opened, and their host walked into the room, his coat and tie putting the best dressed of them to shame. His tall leather boots were so polished they reflected the light.

"Welcome gentlemen and, well, the cook's assistant." He turned his head, scanning the room. "Where is the young Santiago Smith?"

Her heartbeat pounded so loud in her ears it had blocked out all other noise. The world was an easier and more exciting place when she was thought to be a boy. As brave as she wanted to be, she didn't want the big pirate to see past her disguise. Would he kidnap her and take her to his ship? She had heard those kind of stories about pirates.

Rory stood, shoulder to shoulder with Jackson. They were acting more like momma bears than cowboys. Their support lightened the knot in her stomach.

"Aw. Is that your little cook assistant hiding behind you there? The boy's not hiding from me, is he?" He stood with his feet planted wide.

Neither of her self-appointed guardians moved. She tried to move around Jackson, but he took a step to the side, blocking her.

"Boss? Everything all right?" Clint shifted his gaze to the others. They all stood now.

The two men from earlier walked into the room, and they were joined by three others. No women.

Straightening her spine, Sofia took a deep breath. She was one of the men tonight and needed to act accordingly. Jackson and Rory were making it worse with their behavior.

Suppressing the urge to pinch her boss was not easy. He was making this into a bigger deal than it had to be, and if they didn't stop being mountain men, real trouble was going to start brewing.

Putting her foot forward, she stepped around Jackson. Cook moved to stand next to her. The butler stood in the doorway. "Captain, dinner is served."

"Good. Good. Would you escort our young guest here to the washroom? I believe he would prefer to have clean hands and face before he sits at my table." He winked at her. "I know how to take care of my friends. We will not be eating off the ground, boy."

"Of course." The man looked as if he was holding

his breath when he moved toward her. Not that she blamed him.

Jackson stayed with her. "I need to wash off, too." He nodded to the others to follow their host. She realized the men, without understanding what was going on, were ready to defend her and back up Jackson. They were her family.

The captain took everyone down the hall, and she and Jackson went in the other direction. It took a bit of scrubbing to get the dirt out from under her nails. There was no helping her hair. Using the water, she pushed it off her face.

Everyone was sitting around a huge polished table. Gold-trimmed china and fancy cut glasses sat atop fine linen. There were only two empty chairs, next to each other on the right arm of their host. Jackson went to sit next to the pirate.

"No, I want to talk to the boy about his adventures. Sit boy." He laughed. "So they call you Two Bit. You're a little thing for such a big job."

Red who had been looking at the elaborate decorations with awe, laughed. "Oh, Captain Duval, don't let his size or age fool ya." Sam and Clint nodded.

Estevan stopped staring at the chandelier and looked down the excessive table, the finery sparkling in the light. "Never seen anyone ride like our kid here."

Servers set bowls in front of them. They were used to drinking soup straight from old tin cups and all looked a bit lost. Except for Rory, who made a big show of picking up the spoon on the outside of the lined silverware. The others followed his example.

Jackson hadn't touched his drink or soup.

Clint dripped soup and tried to clean it with the white

cloth folded next to his plate. "You want to see some fancy tricks with a lasso, watch our Two Bit. He's top-notch. Never seen any like him."

Jackson's scowl went deeper as he glared at his men.

Sterling Duval laughed and leaned forward on his elbow, his warm breath too close for her comfort. "So you're more than a cook's assistant?"

"No, sir. That's all I am."

"Is this your first drive, or you more experienced than you look?"

Jackson moved closer to her. "He's never been off the ranch. Once we get back, he'll stay there."

Leaning in, the pirate rested his chin on his knuckles. "Are you sure?" New dishes replaced the bowls with silent efficiency from several servants.

He looked straight at her, ignoring everyone else in the room. "In a couple of weeks I'm sailing south. Want to be my cabin boy? I'll make it worth your time, and you'll have my protection."

Stories of pirates kidnapping women and sailing off rushed all other thoughts from her head. She didn't want to be on this man's ship.

Rory moved to stand, but Jackson put his hand on his shoulder without taking his eyes off the captain. Sterling Duval kept his gaze on her. He smiled as if she wouldn't turn him down.

Red shook his head and laughed. "This kid don't belong on no boat. His ma must have brought him into the world while riding a wild mustang across the Texas Hills. Never seen nothing like him."

Sam nodded, swallowing a mouth full of steak. "Yes, sir. He could just about rope the river and bring it around to his way of thinking. Ain't none better than this kid."

Captain Sterling Duval sat back and raised one perfect eyebrow. He picked up a delicate long-stemmed glass and took a slow sip.

Jackson shot a glare to the others before turning to face their host. "They're making the stories bigger than they were. You know how cowboys love to tell tales. The bigger the better. Not much truth to them. The kid is nothing special, or he wouldn't be the cook's helper."

"Humph." He pressed his thumb against his chin, and his steel-blue eyes narrowed. The pirate's attention became more intense, and all of his men shifted to look at her. She could feel the heat climb her neck and along her arms. She wanted to defend herself. But she knew Jackson was just trying to get the focus off her and downplay the stories.

Sam didn't seem to understand the code though. "Oh, come on, boss. Two Bit saved your life taking down a four-thousand-pound bull all by himself, then he pulled Rory here out from under the pounding hooves of a stampede." Realizing he had the attention of the captain and his men, Sam went into full story mode.

Halfway into the story, the captain looked at her as if she were a treasure to collect. Keeping her head down, she focused on the food in front of her and tried to avoid eye contact with the man sitting next to her.

Just warming up, Sam went deeper into his story.

Jackson stood. "That's enough Sam. We have to be up early. Getting the herd across the river will not be an easy task. Thank you for the di—"

"Sit back down." Sterling waved his hand. "The evening has not even started yet. I have offered the extraordinary Santiago Smith a job on my ship. He doesn't belong to any of you, correct? He can join me if *he* so desires."

The De Zavala crew looked a bit confused, but ignoring the pirate, they all stood, ready to follow Jackson's orders.

The captain's men stood.

Sam, Red and Clint frowned and turned to Jackson. Rory and Cook stood taller, watching the men on the other side of the table as if they were ready to fight.

She slowed her breath and pressed her hand to her stomach. The pirate's friends looked as if they had killed men before breakfast. There had to be a way to stop the tension from building.

Bowing her head, she turned to the captain. "Thank you for your offer, but I have a job back at the ranch waiting for me. I'm with Mr. McCreed and De Zavala. That's where I want to stay."

"Shame. It's seems such a waste to give you over to the dust and sun of ranch work. I could offer you much finer things."

Across from her, the pirate's man narrowed his gaze, like she had done something to offend him. She stepped back and tried to make herself as small as possible. It went against her instinct, but pride had no place on this bundle of dynamite.

Clearing the sawdust that had gathered in her throat, she tried to defuse the tension. "It's like Jackson says, I hook up the mules and gather the wood. That's all I do."

"Captain, I don't understand the fascination of this dirty river rat." One of Sterling's men crossed his arms and snorted. "You don't look strong enough to rope a newborn calf let alone a full grown bull."

All of the pirate's men laughed. "There's no way this runt can outride any of our riders."

Clint and Red howled.

Sam leaned on the table with his fist. "Are you calling me a liar? That's funny. Because I know our kid can outride and out rope your best." He jammed his finger in her direction.

The pirate grinned and lowered his chin to stare at Jackson. "Sounds like a challenge to me."

Noise erupted in the dining room. She closed her eyes and prayed. God was the only way they were going to escape this mess unscathed. Why had she been excited to meet a famous pirate face-to-face?

Jackson stepped in front of a fuming Sam. "We did not issue a challenge. Sam was just telling a story. Your men are the best around these parts, and we have nothing to prove."

"Are you mocking us? You don't think we're worth the effort?"

The dark-haired man with the fancy mustache lifted his chin at Jackson. "You haven't even seen our best. Captain, I think we need to head out to the arena before the sun goes down and lay out a little challenge. The winner gets to call a favor."

She gasped, then quickly pulled her mouth tight when she noticed Duval studying her with an intensity that burned her stomach.

Jackson gripped her upper arm, then leaned low next to her ear. "You need to leave now. Cook will take you to the cabin."

She nodded.

Clint, Red and Sam turned to him. "Come on, boss.

You know our kid. He can take any of these yahoos when it comes to horse skills."

Jackson closed his eyes. This close she could see the details of his features. His jaw was so tight, it looked as if it were going to pop off its hinge. "We have nothing to prove to them." Straightening his spine, he looked to the pirate. "Gentlemen, it has been an enjoyable evening. Thank you for your hospitality."

Attempting to back out slowly so not to draw attention to her movement, she kept her gaze on Jackson. Cook was already there, waiting.

In a few steps the pirate was next to her, holding her arm. "Where are you going, little one? It would be rude to leave now. We are not finished."

Jackson was now behind her, his warmth surrounding her, chasing out the chill caused by the pirate.

"We don't want any trouble. Just let us leave. All of us."

"Oh, but there's no fun in that, and if nothing else, we like our fun. Right, men?"

His men laughed. "The day is young."

Duval moved a short foot away. "I have no problem if you leave now and don't accept the challenge my men have put down." He smirked. "But I'm not sure when your cattle will be allowed to cross, and I can tell you that none of my men will be available to help if I do open the crossing. What a shame to come all this way on the Opelousas trail only to lose all your profits."

"You can't do that." Red moved closer to the pirate.

A shrug was the only response the man gave. His stare stayed on her. He was making it clear who could end this standoff.

The first attempt to talk didn't work. She cleared her throat and managed to whisper. "What's the challenge?"

With his victory, Sterling Duval smiled. "Javier."

The lean man joined them. "Yes, sir." His perfect white teeth flashed with his obnoxious smile.

"Set up a course that includes running a horse and roping. Use the ring."

Sam spoke up. "One of us should go to make sure there ain't no cheating."

Everyone headed for the door behind Javier. She was going to be sick and lose the little bit of dinner she had managed to eat.

Jackson's hand pressed on her shoulder, and the warmth seeped into her muscles. She wanted to lean into him. There was no time for that kind of weakness, so she forced her feet to move. Jackson stayed with her in the back of the pack.

"You don't have to do this. One of us can take the challenge." His breath tickled the sensitive skin of her ear.

She shook her head. "I don't think he would allow a switch. What did I do to get his attention?" Looking down at her dirty clothes and ruined skin, she couldn't figure it out.

"You intrigued him. He sees what's beneath. I'll be right here the whole time. If something goes wrong, I'll get you out as soon as I can."

"I'm not worried about failing. I just don't want to get us in trouble. There is no doubt I can do whatever they throw at me."

He snorted. "Now that sounds like the Tiago I know. Except for staying out of trouble. You seem to thrive on that."

"That's not—"

"Are you coming, or are you going to stay huddled in the back until it gets dark?" Captain Duval came straight at them. "Where is your horse?"

"I'll get him for you." Red was gone before she could say anything. They knew she had taken to riding Domino every day. He had become her horse. One of the smartest horses she had ever ridden. What if something went wrong and she lost him?

"We've accepted the challenge in the name of sportsmanship." Sarcasm dropped like old molasses over his last word. "When she wins, we will have access to the river and help from your men."

"And if my man wins?"

She stood straighter. "He won't."

After a long minute, he laughed and nodded. "Then I will name my prize if my man manages to beat you."

"Here ya go, Tiago." Red interrupted and handed Domino to her. Then Javier, the rider from the pirate's camp, was in his saddle and smirking at her.

He was the one who had set up the course. He'd done this before.

Chapter Fifteen

Jackson followed the captain to the high platform raised above the sand-filled arena, which was surrounded by a tall fence. Behind them the sun hung low in the sky. The pirate stopped in front of a high-back chair in the center as if he were a king. He lifted his hand, and the ruffles at the end of his sleeve waved in the wind. He waited until everyone looked at him. It didn't take long.

"Javier will run the course once. Santiago Smith will watch him, then follow. Each challenge must be done until it is complete. The rider with the faster time will win.

He looked at the two on horseback. "Do you both agree?"

They nodded. Jackson wanted to offer himself up to the contest, but he knew it would be useless and cause more problems.

The pirate continued holding court. "Good. You will walk into the arena, and once you mount your horse the time will start."

A couple of cowboys ran to the center of the arena

and lit a wooden obstacle on fire. The pirate's men cheered.

Jackson made sure to keep his breath even. He should have forced her to stay in the wagon, but then again maybe his first mistake was allowing her on the trail drive at all. He had failed at protecting her.

He had put himself in the danger of caring for someone again. The feelings she stirred were not settling well with him. He popped each of his knuckles. He had to get her to safety, then make sure she was out of his reach in order to keep himself safe.

A cowboy at the entrance opened the gate and Javier led a large palomino mare through the deep sand. In one fast motion he swung up in the saddle, leaned forward and kicked his horse into a run. All of his fellow cowboys yelled and hollered as he rushed the first obstacle.

It was a tall pole with a couple of hooks on the side. Each held a ring. Javier reached for the higher one and took both rings. He left the lower one for Tiago to retrieve.

"Boss, he wasn't supposed to take both rings. That leaves the bottom hook. It's only a foot off the ground." Red leaned in, the anger in his voice hard to miss. "Our kid's going to have to get off his horse to get it."

With just a nod to Red, Jackson watched as Javier pulled a pistol from his jacket. He reached across his chest to hit a large glass bottle on the post opposite from them. From there his horse flew over the burning log as the man started spinning his lasso over his head.

A small steer without horns was released from a side pen and ran across the arena. Swinging the rope over his head, he brought down the steer. Setting back, his horse pulled the rope taut. Javier jumped from the saddle and ran down the rope, flipped the steer and had it tied in quick order.

Jackson knew Tiago could rope anything, but the thought of her bringing down a steer all on her own wasn't settling well. He leaned forward and gripped the wood railing.

As Javier released the rope from the saddle and re-mounted, Duval moved closer to Jackson. "What will it take for me to keep the girl here?"

Clinching his jaw, Jackson rummaged through his brain to find something to say that would not get them killed.

In a full-out run along the fence, Javier headed straight toward them. As he passed, he reached over and pulled a silk ribbon off the post directly in front of the captain. It fluttered to the ground, and Sterling called time.

Javier and his friends hooped and hollered at his success. That was going to be tough to beat. They definitely sent their best rider.

Red bumped him in the arm and pointed to the pens across the way. "Did you see the size of the steer they have for Two Bit to rope? That ain't the one we saw. They're cheating."

"Tiago can handle it." He started praying. Thinking of David and Goliath. He had to believe she could do this.

She was an amazing woman that could lasso his heart and good sense if he allowed it, but he'd made a vow to Lilly. A vow he could allow his heart to break.

Red grunted and moved back with the other men.

Jackson glanced to the grinning pirate. He leaned in close and kept his voice low. "Any of my men can take this challenge. You know the truth. Hurting or humiliating her won't change the fact that she is going home with me. There is nothing you can do to keep her here."

"You decided to claim her, have you?"

Jackson realized he would do whatever it took to keep her safe.

Red and the rest of his men started cheering. Tiago was walking into the arena, but they all went silent when she left her horse just inside the gate and went on without him.

Rory was behind him. "What's the kid doing? Is he forfeiting?"

Shaking his head, Jackson watched as she stopped and bowed her head and rested her hand on her chest. It was the pose she took whenever she prayed. His stomach tight, he joined his prayers with hers. She raised her head and whistled. The Appaloosa charged at her in a full run.

His stomach lurched into his throat when he realized what she was doing. She started running also, and as the horse passed without slowing, she grabbed the horn and hurled her body into the saddle. She had been practicing tricks when he wasn't looking.

She was moving fast, but she'd have to dismount to get the ring.

Leaning to the side, she disappeared behind the horse. With the horse still running, she had dropped to the other side of the saddle and vanished from view.

She wasn't on the ground, either. What was she doing? At that speed, she was going to get herself killed if she tried to dismount.

He was going to be sick. As the gelding passed the post, she came back into view and lifted the ring high.

Cheers filled the arena. Even Sterling's men were being pulled into the excitement she stirred.

The pirate laughed and slapped Jackson on the back. "Seems as if the stories about your little cook might not have been exaggerated much. You're a fortunate man."

A growl through his clenched teeth was all he could manage as Tiago pulled the gun from her holster on the saddle. Lifting the gun, she shot at the small bottle without slowing.

She had to be way ahead of Javier's time. Jumping over the fire, she put the gun away and started working her lasso.

A steer was turned loose and, as Red had pointed out, it was much bigger than the first one. It had to be well over one thousand pounds.

Her lasso went flying and roped the steer. Her horse did his job and pulled the rope tight.

Jackson gripped the railing ready to jump over and help her.

A big hand weighed on his shoulder. The pirate shook his head. "Don't. She's gotten this far. Don't humiliate her by running to the rescue now."

Pulling his shoulder away, Jackson was torn. He knew she could do it, but she'd always worked with a team.

She went for the steer's legs, but he kicked at her and swung his horns around. The horse moved back, causing the steer to switch his focus. She was spending too much time wrestling with the big animal.

The time she had gained was slipping away. At this rate, his biggest fear was her getting hurt. A few more seconds, and he was going in, no one was going to stop him.

The steer had become a deadly hunk of muscle on hooves. He twisted his horns at her and tossed her a couple of feet away, ripping her jacket.

Jackson jumped the railing, but when his boots landed in the sand a couple of Duval's men stopped him.

He could barely breathe.

She stood, undeterred, flung the ruined coat to the ground and charged at the steer. This time she took his legs out from under him and tied them before he could get back up. She worked as a team with the horse. But she was running out of time.

With one blur of motion, she turned, her knife lifted above her head, and threw it straight at them. All the men ducked to the side before realizing it had stuck in the post. The ribbon fell to the ground. "Time!" The pirate yelled. The arena erupted into cheers.

"Well done, my lady!" Sterling bellowed over the cheers.

Complete silence filled the space that had just been bursting with deafening shouts. It was the kind of silence that came from shock.

Breathing hard and without the jacket, she felt as if the pirate's words ripped off the mask she had been wearing and now she stood exposed with her shoulders back. The wind tossed the short curls around her face.

Anyone who hadn't known Tiago was a female, knew now.

The blood left her face as she stood before them all. Eyes wide, she crossed her arms as if cold. His warrior princess of just a minute ago was gone.

Without thought Jackson rushed to Tiago. Shrugging off his jacket, he wrapped it around her.

"My back hurts." The smallness of her voice hurt

him in ways he didn't want to explore. It wasn't too late to protect his heart. It couldn't be.

"Maybe the horn or hoof caught it. Are you hurt? You don't seem to be bleeding. We need to clean it to see the damage. Can you walk?"

She cut a glare at him. "Of course."

There she was. He smiled, reassured she would be fine. "Okay. Let's leave."

"My knife. I need to get my knife and horse." She looked behind her, but Rory was taking care of Domino.

Her breathing was starting to return to normal as he moved her to the platform where her knife was still embedded into the post.

Not wanting to cause more embarrassment, he stayed a close step behind her. She stopped in front of the post and reached for her knife. A sharp intake of breath was followed by a pause in her motion before she pulled out her knife.

It happened so fast he was sure he was the only one who noticed she was in pain.

"Congratulations, *cherie*. You were magnificent. Are you sure there is nothing that will convince you to stay with me? Adventure, wealth and all the things you desire could be yours."

"I desire my land and horses. Thank you, but I will be returning with Mr. McCreed."

Jackson put an arm around her waist to help her, and it had nothing to do with possessiveness or pride. He glanced at his men.

Red leaned forward. "Boss, you knew he was a girl?"

"Yes. Clint, go help Rory get her horse and things. She's been injured. I'm taking her back to our cabin. Cook, will you—"

"I'll warm some water and gather supplies." He was already down the steps. "How bad is it?"

She stepped away from him. "It's not—"

He cut her off. "We don't know yet."

Sterling came down the steps. "I'll send my doctor over to your quarters."

"That won't be necessary. What I do need is three of your men to meet us in the morning to get the cattle across the river."

"We will be serving breakfast at sunrise. I'll have my best there for you."

They kept walking, and the pirate stayed with them. Jackson tried to relax his jaw, but the man just annoyed him. "We are good. Thank you. I can take care of her from here."

The pirate stopped them, the tail of his long coat flapping in the wind. With his right hand, he gathered hers and kissed it, lingering a little longer than necessary. A growl rumbled low from Jackson's chest. He wanted the man away from Tiago.

Sterling chuckled. He raised his gaze from the girl to stare directly at him. "You are a most fortunate man to have such a woman. May peace travel with you." He looked back down at Tiago. "And grand adventure." With a nod, he was gone, his tall leather boots crushing the gravel with each step.

"He's a very strange man. What is it with you and the growling?"

"I have no idea what you are talking about." Making sure to gently take her elbow, he started walking again.

Glancing over her shoulder, she tripped. He caught her before she fell and held her for a moment to make sure she was steady.

Head down, she muttered something he couldn't hear. He hooked his finger under her chin. It was scraped and looked like a rope burn. "Are you all right?"

She nodded and looked back to the arena. "How did our men take it?" Her gaze swung back to him. The burned biscuit eyes just about did him in. "Are they mad at me?"

Distance. He needed distance, but for now she needed someone to care for her injury. "Keep walking. You don't need to worry about them."

They walked in silence. Cook was in the small common area, water, soap and bandages ready. "Do you think she'll be needing stitches?"

"Maybe."

"No." They answered at the same time, causing Cook to chuckle.

"Go get her a clean shirt, *jefe*. Or do you want to see if we can find you a dress now that everyone knows?"

"I'm still riding the trail. A dress would be foolish." Taking Jackson's jacket off, she rolled her shoulders to test them. She gritted her teeth against the pain. "Let me change, and if I need tending I'll let you know."

"You have a clean shirt, *sí*?"

She nodded, then took a deep breath and bit down hard on her lips. Yeah, it hurt. "I have one more shirt. I don't know how clean it is, but it's not torn or bloody. I'll go change."

Cook touched her arm. "Let me look at the shoulder first. We can clean off the blood before you put the other shirt on."

Jackson couldn't leave her yet, so he walked around to stand next to Cook. "Do I need to get the doctor?" He shouldn't have turned down the pirate's offer so quickly.

"No. I don't think it's that bad." She twisted her head to look at her shoulder.

It had started to discolor. Angry marks covered her skin, but those could have been old. The gash looked shallow. "Doesn't look like she needs stitches."

Cook wiped the blood away with the clean water, and she flinched. Jackson reached for her hand. She took his offering and squeezed. Hard.

She dropped his hand. "I'll take the water to my room and clean the rest of it."

Both men stepped back and let her go. She moved to disappear into the small windowless room that was her private space.

The front door opened before she went inside. The men eased into the small cabin one at a time. Red had her tattered jacket. Rory stepped past the men and put her gear against the wall. "Are you well?"

With a smile, she nodded.

Red cleared his throat. "So y'all knew the whole time Tiago was a girl?"

"I think we need to let her change then we can talk." He wanted to stand between her and the hostile stares. The need to comfort her had to be buried. He looked at the men. They were watching him in a new way, and it wasn't good.

"Go get your extra shirt." He was still the boss.

Eyes closed, she nodded. Red spots formed on her neck, climbing higher as he watched.

Turning away from her, he addressed his men. "I'll meet you outside. Let's give her some privacy."

Her secret was no longer a secret, and he wasn't sure how he felt about that, or how his men would react to his knowing but not telling. They had been working with a woman.

They hadn't understood why he had kept Tiago isolated. Now they knew. It had to be a good thing that everyone knew that Tiago was a female. So why did it feel as if he had lost something precious?

Chapter Sixteen

The rooster proclaimed it to be morning, but the sun was not up yet. Sofia tried to breathe softer and slower, but it didn't help the dull pain in her back and ribs. As delicious as the biscuit and bacon smelled, the food tasted like sawdust.

Sitting straighter, she tried to look alert and awake, even though it had been a sleepless night. Once all the cowboys came back inside, she thought they'd have questions or at least be mad. Instead, they treated her like she had an illness they could catch if they got too close or even looked at her. It was maddening.

On the cattle drive they had finally acknowledged her as one of them. Now she felt like it was her first day again, maybe even worse. They had at least teased her and given the new kid a hard time. Now they ignored her.

Before she had left the windowless storage room that morning, Jackson and Rory had already gone to organize the trip over the river. They had not returned yet.

Looking down the table that had been set up outside,

she tried to make eye contact. The men she thought of as friends all found seats as far from her as possible.

She refused to let them ignore her. "Red, do you know the plan today? I can still help."

"Crossing the cattle over the river takes tons of strength. I think it would be best for you to stay with Cook and out of trouble."

"You need my help more than Cook does." Holding her breath, she scooted closer to them.

They shifted and acted as if she were holding the back end of a skunk up to them. "What's wrong?"

Five sets of eyes looked away, avoiding any eye contact with her.

"I'm still Tiago. I worked alongside each of you on the trail."

Nothing.

"*Mija*, I need your help to get the wagon unloaded and sold. We need to sort and replace supplies you'll need for the return trip. Everything will have to be packed on the mules. You can help me get the wagon sold."

Her head jerked up. "You are selling the wagon? But how will you get back to the ranch? You told me you never rode on the back of a horse."

"I'm going by ship to Mexico. I've been gone from home too long."

"But I thought—"

She didn't have a good feeling about this. Blood touched her tongue when she bit down on the soft skin in her cheek. Loneliness swamped her, and she wanted to cry, but she knew if she gave in there would be no going back as one of the cowboys.

"You could come to the ranch and your wife could join you there. You don't have to go back to Mexico."

"No, *mija*. I'm getting on a boat that will take me home. It's time for me to return to my family. With just a few of you riding back to the De Zavala ranch, the wagon would slow you." He gave her another strip of bacon, as if that would make everything better.

She turned to the men who had become part of her family. She didn't want to lose any more family. "Are all of you leaving too?"

Red nodded. "I have a wife I hope is still waiting for me. I came along to make enough money to get us our own land back in Indiana."

"Clint? Sam and Eli? What about you?"

Sam spoke first. "Now that we got some cow experience, we want to hit more drives. Maybe work for some of the big operations. Save up the money to get our own." Without looking up, Clint nodded.

"Estevan, you're returning to the ranch, right?"

"Yes, ma'am. Rory's returning, too. Him and Jackson are talking partnership."

"Ma'am?" She tried to laugh, but it sounded stiff. "When did I become a ma'am?"

They all went back to staring at their food. Half of her family was leaving her.

The rooster crowed again, and the men picked up their plates and walked away from the table, away from her. She stood to follow them.

Estevan shook his head. "Stay here, *mija*. We are going to check on the horses."

With that, they turned their backs to her, leaving her alone.

A few men from different drives sat at other tables.

Many curious stares drifted her way, but as soon as she made eye contact they darted away. She had become an oddity.

Cook patted her hand. "Cowboys don't cry."

"Good morning." Jackson's smooth voice washed over her. Focusing on him, she found a smile. Sitting at a table next to her, he dug into a plate piled high with eggs, bacon and biscuits all smothered in gravy. "Where are the boys going?"

"To sort the horses."

"Good. We'll take the ones we're selling across first, in front of the steers."

Rory sat and invited her to join them. With his mouth full of food, he wiggled his eyebrows at her.

Now her smile was real. "What is wrong with you?"

Despite the whole biscuit he had shoved in his mouth, Rory managed to swallow and looked at Jackson. "Have you told her?"

A glare from Jackson was the only reply they got.

"Tell me what? Is everything all right? Has that pirate changed the rules on us?"

Free of his breakfast, Rory laughed. "Oh, yeah. He made a point to tell Jackson you were not allowed to cross the river. He thought it best if you stayed here at the station, nice and safe and alone."

"He doesn't have the right to tell me who can ride— Wait." She twisted to face Jackson, narrowing her gaze at him. "You told me yourself that it was too dangerous, and I needed to stay with Cook."

He rubbed the back of his neck and dropped the bacon. "Yeah. I don't like someone else telling me what my men can or can't do."

A light giddy feeling lifted her. She was still one of his men. "So I'm going to get to help cross the river?"

He growled. Again. A sound she was starting to love.

"Yes, but you have to follow my every order as soon as I give it to you. No questioning or thinking. Just do it. Can you obey me?"

"Yes!" She wanted to kiss him, but forced herself to sit on her hands instead. "So what will my job be?"

"I want to keep you in front with the horses. The farther back, the worse the mud gets. I'm going to put you with Red."

And just like that all the air left her body. Red wouldn't be happy. They made it clear she didn't belong on the trail.

Jackson picked up his plate. "Cook, follow me. There's someone you need to meet."

Rory watched her from across the old table. "What's wrong? I thought you'd be jumping over the moon."

"They don't want me to work with them any longer."

Rory's forehead puckered. "That don't make sense. They love working with you."

"That was before they found out I was a woman. What are you doing here anyway? I thought you'd be with the others, getting ready for the crossing."

He sighed as they took the plates to the water bucket. "I've been regulated to wagon duty because they think I'll be more of a hindrance with the bum arm."

"Welcome to the world of the protected and useless."

"I'm not useless." He nudged her. "You are, but I have important manly things to do."

"Like what?" She stopped and planted her fists on her hips. Making sure to lift her left eyebrow as high as she could. "Watching over me?"

"Hey, that is no easy task." He jabbed her with his elbow. "Now don't get all huffy and defensive. As it turns out, I'm not even needed for that since you will be helping at the crossing."

Sofia gave Rory an overly sweet smile before turning away from him to scan the area for Jackson. "I wouldn't put it past him to forget about me and take off."

A couple of the men at another table leered at her. Maybe she should have tucked her head and scurried away, but she was tired of hiding, of not being herself.

Head high she gave them her hardest glare, daring them to say anything to her.

"Easy with that brashness, or you're going to have us all in a fight." Rory followed her. She noticed how he put his body between her and the men.

"I can handle these yahoos." A firm hand pulled her to the right. Jackson had sneaked up on her.

"You need to stay away from the riffraff hanging around here."

She forced her jaw to stay relaxed and tried to concentrate on the herd of horses they were heading to. Defending herself was becoming redundant and, according to Rory, making her huffy.

"Rory's going to handle the sale of the horses, so I—"

"We're selling all of them?" Panic pushed her heart into her throat. Every time she spoke with someone she was losing more.

"Settle down. Not all of them. We need the mules and a few extra to get us back to the ranch. Other than Estevan, you know the horses the best. Ever trade before?"

This was a real job. She walked a little faster. "A few

times with my father and brother, but they did all the talking and money deals."

"Your dad? He was a horse trader?"

That was thoughtless. She didn't think he'd be happy if he found out her father actually owned the horses. She made herself give him a cheery smile. "Sometimes. So you want to know the ones I think we should keep?"

"Yeah, then we'll get our saddles and join the herd. You can move the horses we're selling."

Nodding, she looked at the horse area. This was coming to an end, and she would be heading home. Home to a father who thought she had been shopping and preparing for marriage. At this point he might have found her note. How was she going to be received when she arrived back at the ranch? When they arrived in San Antonio, she'd send a telegraph.

The big sorrel lunged up the muddy incline, water dripping from him. Pushing off the saddle, Jackson leaned forward over his horse's neck. The last horse climbed the slope and emerged from the river. The plan was for Red and Tiago to cross the horses, but he gave into his weaker side and followed her.

Once they got to the safety of the ranch, he would be able to relax and let her out of his sight. Without thought he had reacted to the pirate's interest in Tiago being left behind at the cattle station. He had regretted it the minute the words had left his mouth. But the subtle hint that the pirate would be aware if she was alone, would have made him useless if she wasn't in his sight. The faster they got out of the pirate's domain the better.

The faster he could drop her off somewhere safe, the better for his own sanity. He could feel his feelings for her getting stronger, and he couldn't allow that to happen.

Reacting to the pirate the way he did was pure jealousy. Which hinted that his true feelings for her were deeper than he allowed himself to even consider.

Up ahead Tiago swung her lasso over her head and guided the lead horse down the path and toward the holding pens. She sat tall and smiled when she caught him watching her.

With a dip of his chin, he acknowledged her. There was no way he would have predicted her becoming a key player on this team the day he discovered she was a woman. He thought he'd spend the whole time protecting her. She was amazing.

That was probably one of the reasons he was attracted to her. She didn't wait for someone to take care of her.

She solved her own problems. Strong and independent, Tiago was full of life, and he couldn't imagine she'd allow anyone to take it from her.

Touching his heels to the ribs of his mount, he moved him into a gallop and pulled up next to her. "Great job. The holding pens are just about a mile ahead." He twisted in the saddle. "The first of the cattle have crossed. All is looking good."

The horses walked along the worn path as she nudged the lead horse on. Other than a nod, she seemed to be ignoring him. That didn't settle well with him.

"You handled the horse and river as well as any experienced cowboy."

She tucked her head, but not before he saw red marks spotting her neck. "Thank you for allowing me to help.

I know you wanted to leave me at the cattle station, but I'm so happy I got to do this."

He cleared his throat as he swallowed a laugh. "How's the back?"

"I don't feel any pain. This has been the best day."

He sighed. "Somehow I went from wanting to leave you behind at the ranch to watching you drive the horses across like a professional. I'm still not sure bringing you along was the right thing for you in the long run."

"This has been the most exhilarating experience and confirmed what I already knew. I want to work on the ranch. If it means I never get married, it's what I want."

"You don't want your own family?"

Her small shoulders lifted in a shrugged. "If having a family means I get locked in town taking care of a house, no, thank you. If I could have both? Maybe."

She dropped back to get one of the younger horses back to the herd. The rough rope rested in her hand as she rubbed her fingers along the tattered end. "All I know is I want to work on the De Zavala land. I don't want to be anywhere else."

"Do you think he'll hire you?" He didn't know De Zavala, but the man didn't seem like the kind who hired women for ranch work. "Are you going to still pretend to be a boy?"

She sighed. Her eyes lost the spark from earlier. "No. I'm tired of being a boy, but I don't want to go back to the full dress."

"So what are you going to do?"

A full bottom lip disappeared under white teeth. She shook her head. "I'm not sure how I'll bring my two selves together. Or what I'll wear, but I don't want to go back to being a house pet."

"Darling, you're too proud and stubborn to be anyone's pet." Oh, no. He just called her darling. Not good.

To cover-up how serious that was to him, he coughed. When she glared at him, he couldn't stop chuckling, but he tried.

She was so serious and he didn't want to hurt her feelings. A couple of younger horses caused a ruckus in the back. Spinning his horse, he reluctantly left her to manage the lead horse.

Riding alongside the herd, he glanced behind him to watch the cattle following them, but most of the time he was watching her. What was he going to do about the little cook's assistant who somehow found her way into his heart?

He had wanted to stay clear of people who made him care, and already he managed to collect two. Her and Rory.

If they would pair off, that would solve his main problem. She would belong to someone. Someone who would take care of her. But Rory had said no. Maybe he didn't mean it. She'd make a great wife to a cowboy.

Pushing his hat up a bit, he rubbed his eyes with the palm of one hand. The idea of her being Rory's wife didn't make him feel any better.

And since Rory had already turned down the suggestion, his brain thought it was safe to go there. No real danger of it happening. He sighed and leaned on the saddle horn. If his thoughts kept circling around his head like this he was going to lose his good sense. If he had any to begin with. He needed to stay focused.

The horses and cattle were his job. Scanning the herd, he watched them move in order. He waved to get

Tiago's attention. "I'm going back to talk with Red and check the others."

She nodded and continued talking to the horses. There was no other woman like her. She was crazy, and he was even worse for wanting to hold her.

Red led the front of the herd and smiled through the mud on his face. "Boss, we only lost three to the waters and four ran off into the woods. A nice day for a herd this size. The profits'll be good." He lifted his chin to the horses. "How's she getting along? Everything okay?"

"She is as good as she was before you found out she was a female. Why are y'all giving her the cold shoulder?"

"It ain't so much us giving her the cold shoulder, boss. It's just different. I mean, she's a girl. All the things we said and did around her. It ain't right that you knew and didn't tell us."

He popped his jaw. Had it been about her safety or had he just wanted to keep her to himself? "We thought it best if no one knew. I didn't really know y'all that well in the beginning, and it was just easier if everyone thought she was a boy."

"Well, it does explain a great deal about the way you acted when it came to bathin' and sleepin'." Spitting to the side, Red looked up ahead. "You marrying her?"

"No!" His gut bunched. The horse tossed his head, and Jackson forced himself to relax his grip on the reins. "Why would you even think that?"

"She's been with a group of men for weeks. Without a relative or another woman." Red frowned. "I'm not the most proper fellow, but even I know that's not good. When she gets home, won't that ruin her?"

"I expect she knew the consequences when she took the job. She claims she doesn't plan to ever marry."

"She is one strange female. Her family okay with that?"

"No family." Would that have made a difference? "That's what she told me anyway." Of course it wouldn't be the first time she lied to him.

He looked behind him and scanned the herd. The long horns swaying as the hundreds of hooves covered the ground. Low bellowing drifted over the breeze. "She should be getting close to the horse pens. I'm going to check on her. I'll see you at the headquarters to disperse the money."

"Sounds like a good plan, boss." Red winked at him, leading Jackson to think it wasn't the plan to meet later that he was talking about.

As a group they rode back to the cattle station. Sofia shifted in the saddle. What did she say to the men who had become so important to her in a short time?

Jackson had passed out everyone's pay, and now over half of their team would be leaving. Red came up beside her.

"Two Bit, it's been a pleasure riding with you. If you ever need anything, you have a place in Indiana." He gave her shoulder an awkward pat and smiled.

She focused on his red mustache. Torn between stifling tears and laughter, she bit her lip. Fingers came up empty when she tried to pull on a long strand of hair. The habit had gone unnoticed until the strands were gone. She settled for rubbing her neck.

"Thank you. I'm sorry I hid the truth from you." She'd already asked him to return to Texas, but he was leaving with Clint and Sam. He said he needed to stop by Will's place to give his share to his sister and to give her their condolences. "You got the letter I wrote for his sister?"

"Yep." He tapped his chest.

Clint and Sam joined them as they stopped at the cabin where they had spent the night. Cook stood on the one-step stoop, bag at his feet. The urge to cry was harder to fight. She jumped off her horse and ran to him, not caring what the others thought.

"Are you sure you won't come back with us?" Her voice, muffled, was buried in his neck as his arms went around her. "My... Señor De Zavala would hire you. I know he would."

"*Mija*, I have to return home. It's time." His hands went to her arms. Holding her back, he kissed her forehead. "No crying. Cowboys don't cry."

She nodded and rubbed her face with her sleeve.

He smiled at her. "You could travel with me. My wife would love another daughter."

Another step back, and she was back on the ground. "I belong in Texas."

"*Sí.* You do. God has great things planned for you, so be brave and face the future with faith. Even when you don't understand. It will work out for the best."

He glanced at the men still sitting on their horses. They seemed to be looking everywhere but at the scene taking place at the door. "I need to be going if I'm getting on the stage leaving for the shipyard."

Shaking the hands of the cowboys, he said goodbye to each man before giving her one more hug. Then he turned and walked away. One of the cowboys cleared his throat, and she looked up.

Clint nodded to her. "We'll be leaving, too. Hate goodbyes, so we'll just say see you later. If we pass through the hill country, we'll stop by. You'll be at the De Zavala ranch?"

"Yes. Please visit. I will make sure you have a job there if you want one."

They all laughed. "So you plan on running the place soon?"

Heat climbed up her neck. She tried to laugh it off. "Do you have any doubt?"

Sam laughed. "I hear the old man is a widower. You're a girl who knows her way around horses and cattle, maybe you can marry him."

The others joined in and gave their suggestion to how she could become the *jefe*. Rory joined the group. "What's all the ruckus about?"

She put her hands on her hips. "They think the thought of me running a ranch is funny."

"We think she should marry the old rancher."

Rory pulled his lips in disgust. "He's old enough to be her father."

Their laughter warmed her. They were joking with her like she was one of them. She didn't want to think about their leaving or what it meant to go home and face her father.

How would he take the new Sofia? She glanced back to the path Cook had taken. Jackson was with him. He had dismounted and carried the older man's bag.

"We heard there was work in East Texas, so we're heading north." Sam was talking to Rory. "You want to join us?"

Rory put his hands in his back pockets and rocked on his boots. "East Texas? Sounds interesting."

The blood pounded in her ears. Not Rory, too. She pressed her lips together and turned her attention back to Jackson and Cook. The urge to run after Cook and beg Rory to stay tore at her insides, but she kept her feet planted and her mouth shut.

No one wanted to deal with an emotional female. She wanted them to remember her as one of them. She wanted to belong with them, but a part of her feared she never would be completely.

This time tomorrow, everyone would be on their paths to different futures. Different homes.

"I thought you were heading back with us?" She tried to keep it causal. "You're not leaving me alone with those two are you? Who would I talk to?"

They all laughed. Rory winked at her. "True. Looks as if I'm still heading back to the Hill Country for now. Maybe I'll meet you on the trail later."

With one last salute, Red, Clint and Sam turned their horses and left. A part of her heart hurt. She felt like a small child who wanted to run after them and beg them to stay with her.

Making sure to breathe, she walked to her gelding and rubbed his jaw. She was going to keep him along with Rory and Estevan. Not that the horses belonged to her, but it helped to think she was keeping a small part of family together.

She turned to the road and saw Jackson riding back to them. A deep breath filled her lungs and stopped her from crying. Jackson was taking her home. That made her happier than it should.

The idea of him standing next to her as she faced her father gave her comfort. She flipped the leather reins over Domino's neck and swung into the saddle.

For good or bad, it was time to go home and establish her new life rules. Now she knew how strong she could be, and there was no going back to being the pampered daughter of a land owner. She was a Texas cowboy.

Chapter Seventeen

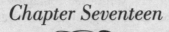

The early-morning sun was to their backs as Sofia followed the others over the hill. It seemed the closer to home they got, the longer it took. Her body was ready to call it done.

Evidence of civilization nestled in a mist that hugged the ground, breaking the endless landscape and sky. Hope surged and renewed her aching limbs. The fog might be playing a cruel trick. "Is that San Antonio?"

Jackson chuckled. "You make it sound like the city of gold. Yes. We should arrive soon."

"I'd give all my gold for a real bed, bath and hot meal."

Estevan clicked to the three mules he led on a line and urged them into a trot. Tossing their heads, they all followed, the dwindling supplies flapping against their sides.

Even the animals seemed as excited as the humans leading the way. Rory took off after him.

"Boys, don't get hurt this close in," Jackson yelled after them. Shaking his head, he moved his own mount into a faster pace. "Come on, Tiago. Don't fall behind now. Rory and Estevan are going to use up all the clean warm water in town." Over his shoulder, he gave her a wink and grinned. It felt as if her heart pounded against her breastbone as they raced down the slope in pursuit of the others.

Jackson caught up with Rory and Estevan and pulled up his mount. His smile was contagious. His strong voice rose above the sound of horse hooves. "We don't want to waste our town time with the doc."

Laughter filled the air, and the men slowed their horses.

"A bath? In a real bathtub with hot water." Joining Jackson, Sofia's knee bumped his. Even though the cattle station offered a roof and a table to eat at, there had been nowhere for her to bathe. She squinted, making sure he knew how serious she was about this topic. "You're not teasing me?"

He tipped his hat. "No, ma'am. I don't tease about warm water."

"I'm staying at my cousin's." Estevan called over his shoulder. One of the mules sat back and pulled on the lead line, so he slowed to a walk.

He came up on the other side of them. "I'd invite you, but he has thirteen kids and a wife who scares me. There is no privacy. Rory, you can join me if you want?" He laughed and nudged her. "You can thank me for saving you from that chaos."

Rory glared at him from the other side of Jackson. "But you want me to go?"

"Oh, my *tia* will love you." He leaned in close to her. "I have three cousins that are at a marriageable age. If I showed up with the three of you, she'd have you all married before we left town." He chuckled. "With you being a woman and all, it could get awkward."

Jackson snorted and Rory glared at them, leaning closer. "What is he saying? He's talking too low."

She grinned and leaned forward to see Rory. "He was saying what a great time you'll have with his family."

"After getting the horses and these beasts settled," he nodded at the mules. "I'm going straight to the bathhouse, then I'm getting a hot meal sitting at a table. Who's with me?"

"You're not leaving me behind." Rory's friendly spark was back. "What about y'all?"

Tension pushed the joy right out of her body. She wanted a real bath and was so close, but she knew going to a public bathhouse was out of the question.

Tears burned the back of her eyes, and she hated that after all she'd been through, a simple bath or lack of one would bring her to tears.

How much longer was she going to live in this caked-on dirt and grime?

"I'm going to take Tiago to a boardinghouse. It's at La Villita, close to the river. We should be able to get you a room to yourself, but you'll have to remain a boy. She doesn't allow unmarried women in the upstairs rooms. I also need to secure De Zavala's cash." He turned to her. "You'll need to be careful, but you should be safe to bath there."

Her heart picked up its rhythm. He was setting her up so she could wash without jeopardizing her disguise. Laughter bubbled up from her stomach. She might just fall in love with this man.

With a sigh, she looked at him. If he was staying on

the ranch, it would be so much easier. He'd be a perfect foreman.

How hard would it be to change his mind about buying her mother's property? She hated the idea that her father would sell the place. And having Jackson on the ranch would be beneficial to it. Keeping him around wouldn't be bad for her either.

The thought of showing up in her father's office dressed as a boy with a new foreman to hire made her chuckle.

Estevan looked at her with one eyebrow raised. "I think our little Tiago has gone loco."

"Oh, I guarantee that happened a long time ago," Jackson replied.

She could live with her secret identity a little bit longer if she could get a bath.

"What do you say, Jackson? My kingdom for a bath?"

"You already gave me your kingdom for a cup of tea. Not that it's much anyway. Your kingdom is made up of a worn-out saddle and a rifle. But I tell you what, I'll throw in a new pair of boots that fit you." Jackson's crooked half grin melted her heart into a giddy, gooey mess.

Yes, she was in trouble. But she had already done what no one thought she could do, so why couldn't she win his heart too?

What would Jackson do if he found out she actually had a kingdom.

A sharp intake of her own breath startled her.

Marriage to Jackson? Marriage was not for her. With a glance she took in Jackson's easy movements, which rolled with the gait of his horse. A man at ease in the saddle and in his life. But he had made it clear that he would never marry again, and he had too much honor to marry for land. She hated the thought of someone marrying her for the ranch. That was basically what her father's plan was. The reason she was on this drive.

"You okay?" He leaned in, trying to make eye contact.

The coolness of the morning was burned away by the rising sun. She averted her gaze and studied the braided rawhide of her reins.

He said he'd never marry again. San Antonio became more real with each step. Small shelters spotted the countryside. Soon her new life would be over, and she'd be Sofia De Zavala again.

When he found out the truth, would he laugh and see the irony or would he feel betrayed? She couldn't put off telling him any longer. It had to happen tonight, after a bath and dinner.

She was different now. Her father would never be able to make her go back to the old way of life. She closed her eyes and absorbed the power of the horse under her. She was a new person.

Lord, please go before me and soften my father's heart. Please be with me as I go back to my father's ranch. I want to be a good daughter, but I also know the desire of my heart is to work the land.

"Hey, kid." Jackson nudged her. "You're not going to sleep are you?"

She chuckled. "No, just spending some time with God. Things are about to change."

His gaze pinned her in place. The clear green had depth she'd never have the privilege to explore. Why was he so guarded? With a sigh, he turned his attention to the horizon ahead of them.

"I've been thinking about my new setup. I could use someone who's good with horses, someone I can trust. It would be a safe place to live. Room and board would be covered. Rory's joining in with me. I could use one more."

"I don't think Estevan would leave my—" She coughed to cover up her slip about her father. "Señor De Zavala pays well, and he just started there."

"Yeah, I figured that. Which was why I was thinking about asking you."

"Me!" He was offering her a job, a job working with horses. "That would be... I... I—"

"You don't have to answer now. I'll be honest, I don't think anyone else would hire you unless you keep pretending to be a boy. And I'm not sure how much longer you can keep it hidden."

Sophia licked her lips. It was time to say something, but how without Jackson getting mad?

"What if he doesn't sell his wife's land to you? Would you be his foreman? It's a large spread, one of the largest in the area. He'd let you raise your own horses and—"

"Whoa. Stop. Take a breath. First of all, I want to be my own man. You're rattling on about things you have no control over. Are you nervous about returning home? Is there someone you're afraid of seeing again?"

His green eyes cut through her. She felt as if she should be bleeding. "No..."

A couple of kids herded some long-haired goats across the narrow dirt path to the river on the other side. The horses had to stop in order to avoid stepping on any of them. A few baby goats jumped and played at the back.

Estevan and Rory were on the other side. While she

been talking to Jackson, they had fallen behind. The two cowboys waved. "We'll see you in town." They rode on, leaving a slight trail of dust.

"José!" Jackson's sudden call out caused her to jump. A boy of about ten in white baggie clothes waved at them.

"*Hola*, señor." The boy ran to Jackson's big sorrel and patted its shoulder.

"Does your mother have rooms available for me and the kid here?"

"*Sí*. You want me to run ahead and tell her to prepare a room?"

Jackson leaned down and handed José a coin. "Two rooms. It would be much appreciated."

Without another word he took off between the homes. The houses of rock and caliche became denser as they went farther into town. Some of the houses stood empty. Many of the families fled after the battle for Texas.

Chickens and pigs mingled in the yards. Women sweeping porches and hanging clothes waved as they rode by.

She would miss being Tiago, but she also missed being Sofia. There had to be a way she could merge the two. Tonight at dinner she would tell Jackson everything.

After washing the trail away and filling their stomachs with good food, she would present her problem to him. Would he look at her differently once he knew her father was the man he wanted to do business with? She should have told him sooner. She didn't know what he was going to do. That scared her. What if he never forgave her?

* * *

Jackson made sure Tiago was settled into a room, before he dumped his gear in another room and joined Rory and Estevan at the bathhouse.

Now with all the dust and grime washed away, he walked lighter. His new clothes were softer and smelled fresh. He checked his pocketwatch. He'd been gone for a couple of hours.

Estevan pushed back his dark wavy hair and put on his hat. "*Jefe*, Rory and I are heading over to El Mercado for some dinner and fun before I head to my cousin's *casa*. Want to join us?"

He shivered at the thought of being in a house with so many young females looking for a husband. "I'm going to check on the kid. Don't want to leave her alone for long. No telling what kind of trouble she'll get into."

Clicking his tongue, Estevan patted his back. "No rest for the weary when it comes to that one."

"Do you think she has anyone back at the ranch to look after her, or is she truly alone?" Rory asked.

Jackson squinted into the sun and shook his head. "I hope she has some family I can turn her over to. Not sure what to do with her."

Both men laughed. "Oh, I'm sure you'll figure something out."

Remaining silent at this point in the conversation seemed the best strategy. With a salute, they parted ways.

Whistling, Jackson walked back to the boarding-house. He paused in front of a mercantile that had a couple of pretty dresses and fancy bonnets in the window.

Would she go back to being a woman once they returned to the ranch? Did she even own a dress? It could become dangerous if she tried to continue her masquerade.

She had hinted at family a couple of times, but then would claim they were all gone.

Even if there was just one family member he could leave her in the care of, it would be the best for them all. The last thing he wanted was her in his life every day. But if he hired her, that's what would happen. Why had he offered her the job?

With a sigh, he crushed the desire to buy her a dress and forced his legs to keep walking. But then he stopped. He had promised her a new pair of boots that fit.

Going back to the store, he passed the dresses and headed straight to the leather section.

He would do this for her, then move on to his own future, no matter how much he was coming to care for her.

She was a threat to the vow he had made to Lilly. After everything else, he couldn't break that promise.

New tooled leather boots in hand, he tried to focus on his share of the profits and what he would be able to do with the property he'd buy from De Zavala.

It didn't work. He kept wondering what her real name was or what she'd look like in that dress with long hair around her shoulders. Getting back to De Zavala's place would change everything for her, and he needed to remember it wasn't his problem.

Lost in thought, he felt the rough adobe wall pressed against his back and a blade cutting into the skin at his throat.

"Where's my daughter?" The deep voice with the slight Spanish flare sounded familiar.

"De Zavala?" Without moving, Jackson glanced

down at the shorter man. "I don't know what you're talking about." The twist in his gut told him he was lying. His little orphaned Santiago wasn't an orphan at all, but the daughter of the man he needed in order to make his plans of the future work.

The Spaniard shoved a paper that smelled of roses and vanilla in his face. "She says she is going on the cattle drive. You led my drive. You're positive you don't know what I speak of?" Anger caused each word to have a sharp cut.

"If you lower the knife, we can have a civilized conversation." Jackson held his breath and waited.

De Zavala's jaw flexed a couple of times before he stepped back. "What do you know of this?" He thrust the paper in Jackson's face.

Rolling his shoulders, he checked his neck and found a line of warm blood. Taking out his bandanna, he wiped it clear. "The cook's assistant is a young woman dressed as a boy. She's going by the name Santiago." Anger rolled up from his gut. She had lied to him, used him. "Cook and I were the only ones who knew she was a female for most of the drive. I don't know if she's your daughter."

Why did he even try to protect her at this point? She may well be the reason he missed out on this perfect new start.

The wide brim of De Zavala's hat hid his face. When he lifted his chin, eyes so dark that they were black stared at him. "My son's name was Santiago. Is this boy-girl the horse thief you spoke of the night by the barn?"

"Yeah."

And just like that the fire in the older man was gone,

his shoulders fell. De Zavala looked tired. "She is good with horses. Better than most men I know."

Jackson added. "She ropes well and knows cattle, too."

He nodded. "That sounds like my Sofia. Double the stubbornness and pride any female should embrace."

"Sofia?" He had a name. Sofia. It sounded so soft and feminine. He couldn't help but whisper it one more time. "Sofia."

Straightening his spine, De Zavala narrowed his eyes. "Do you know where she is now? She survived the drive unharmed?" He closed his eyes and tilted his chin toward the sky. "My daughter was on a cattle drive."

"If she is your daughter, she is fine and locked in a room at the boardinghouse. That's where I was heading."

One step closer and the shorter man had the knife out again. "You have her locked in your room?" Rage flared in the dark eyes.

This was not good. "She has her own room. We just got in today. I went to the public bathhouse to give her some privacy."

The irate father stepped to the side, one hand on the iron weapon in his belt. "Take me to her."

Jackson walked with De Zavala close behind.

She had known how important his relationship was to De Zavala and hadn't said a thing. That didn't matter to her. She used him to get what she wanted.

As the daughter of a wealthy landowner, she had everything she wanted. He would think her a spoiled child of privilege if he hadn't seen how hard she worked. He didn't understand her.

Each step that took him closer to the little liar pulled

his nerves tighter. He was tired of playing the Good Samaritan and having people turn on him. They killed his
family, they took his dreams.

Was his brain too slow to learn a lesson the first
time?

Now his new future was in jeopardy because he felt
sorry for an orphaned boy who never even existed. He
tasted blood in his mouth. With a deep breath he re
laxed his jaw.

"Is she well? Was she hurt in any way?" Uncertainty
floated over the harsh words.

"Your daughter worked hard, and there were a few
incidents." Stopping at the door of the La Villita home,
he knocked. "But for the most part she is unharmed.
We lost Will to a stampede."

The tiny woman with flowers embroidered on her
dress and real ones in her dark hair opened the door
with a smile. "Welcome back Señor McCreed. Supper
will be served in the next half hour."

He ducked his head and entered the room. "This is
Señor De Zavala. He's just visiting."

"Oh, *si*. You'll join us at the table? There's room,
and it's a fair price."

Removing his hat, he gave her a quick nod. "*Gra-
cias*, señora." He turned to the stairs. "Which room is
she in?"

Jackson hit the stairs without pausing.

"She? There are no women here." The friendly
woman frowned. "I don't allow unmarried woman in
my *casa*. Señor Jackson?"

Her voice faded as he went to the last door on the
right. Hitting his knuckles against the wood, he waited.
The door was flung open wide, and Tiago… Sofia

smiled. "Oh, Jackson. This is the most marvelous place. Look what Señora Juana brought me— Oh! Are those boots for—"

"Sofia?"

She froze. Her eyes darted back and forth like a trapped animal looking for options.

"Sofia? That can't be you." Anger and doubt laced the older man's words together.

Jackson let the boots drop to the floor as he put his body between father and daughter. Despite her betrayal, he still followed his instinct to protect her. He was an idiot.

Her shoulders drooped, and she took two deep breaths. With the caution of a scared doe, she turned and laid a hand on Jackson's arm. "Papi, how did you find me?"

Standing so close to her, Jackson could smell the rosewater she had used to bath. Her hair, free of grease, curled around her face and brushed the top of her shoulders in uneven lengths. A clean white shirt hung to her knees over breeches he'd never seen her wear. Barefooted, she was shorter than usual.

His gut tightened at the sight. Even with pants on, she looked soft and feminine. How had she survived the cattle trail?

A fleeting thought of her being the most beautiful woman he'd ever seen was shattered by guilt. He closed his eyes and thought of his wife, Lilly. Her golden hair in long waves, her eyes as clear as a summer sky against ivory skin.

Everything about the cook's assistant was the opposite of his wife. Where Lilly was shy and gentle, Tiago... Sofia was bold and stubborn. There was nothing shy or gentle about the newly named Sofia except her name.

She stepped around him and faced her father with her hands on her hips. He cleared his throat. Hoping the right words found their way up.

Lifting that now familiar stubborn chin, Sofia glared at the man with the same dark eyes. "I did it, Papi. I not only survived the trip, but I helped. I was as good as any of the men you hired. I would dare to say better than some."

Standing behind her, he could see her rib cage expanding. Not a timid bone could be found in this woman's body.

"That may be so." The fire was back in the De Zavala's eyes. "But it is not where you belong."

Jackson had faced that glare a few times in the matching eyes of De Zavala's daughter. This would be an interesting battle of wills. But it wasn't his problem.

How to handle the business deal without getting pulled into the family drama would be the trick to seeing his future settled. She hadn't thought about his future and how her stunt would affect him, so she was on her own now.

She looked over her shoulder, at him. "Jackson, tell him what I did. Even during the stampede."

The dark skin paled. "Stampede? You allowed my daughter to ride into a stampede? The one you said killed Will?"

"Sir, she is here and unharmed. I have the payment for the cattle and horses. We only lost—"

"She is not unharmed!" His clinched fist raised, and he pointed at his daughter. "Look at you! You are ruined."

"No!" She threw her shoulders back and took a step

closer to his accusatory finger as if to challenge him. "I'm not. I'm better than ever. It was amazing and grand and scary and the most incredible adventure. Papi, I loved—"

"You stand dressed as a boy in a strange place. Your hair is gone, and your skin is as rough and dark as a field worker. No gentleman will marry you now. You. Are. Ruined." He turned to Jackson. "You ruined my daughter."

"No, Papi. You will not blame him. He didn't even know I was a woman at first. He just now learned I was your daughter. I knew he would send me home the minute he heard my name."

The angry father turned to Jackson. "Did you treat her with honor?"

Jackson tried not to be offended. The man didn't really know him. "I treat all who work with me with respect. Male or female."

"When did you know she was a female?"

"Papi, what does this have to do with anything? I wanted to prove I was as good as any man and could help you on the ranch as a partner. The way Santiago would have if he still lived."

Her father held up one finger. "Do not speak your brother's name. If he and your mother were here…"

He didn't finish the thought, but it was clear to Jackson it hit her hard. For the first time, he saw doubt shadow her expression. She bit her bottom lip, and a shine reflected off the moisture building in her eyes. He wanted to comfort her. But he had to remind himself it wasn't his problem. She had lied to him.

"You have been impulsive and irresponsible. Now you will have to suffer the consequences."

Taking a step back, she hugged herself. "What consequences?"

"You say this man treated you with respect even though you didn't behave as a lady."

"I don't understand what that has to do with anything."

Ignoring her, De Zavala turned to Jackson. "My daughter has ruined herself, and I understand it is no fault of yours."

Some of the tension left his tight muscles, and he released a breath he didn't realize he had been holding. "I have your cash and the record of sale. Estevan is the only one—"

The man held his hand up. "We will talk of that later. Now we need to talk of my daughter's future. I don't think she understands the depth of scandal if she returns home unmarried."

"Papi—"

"Hush. You are done."

She clenched her fist. "I will not marry."

Her father spoke over her as if she hadn't spoken at all.

"Are you willing to marry my daughter here in San Antonio?"

"No!" She screamed as if a snake had slipped into her boot.

De Zavala turned to the door, calm but stiff. "Mr. McCreed, I think it would be better if we spoke somewhere else while my daughter pulls herself together."

Addressing Sofia, he continued, "It would be best if you take the time to remember the etiquette your mother taught you. I will send someone up with a meal for you and to make sure you have a proper dress. You will not leave this room until you are presentable again."

He opened the door. "Mr. McCreed, you will join me now. There are two options I have for my daughter, and it will be up to you if she stays in Texas or is shipped out of state to live with cousins."

"No!" She stood alone in the center of the room. Her father looked at Jackson as if his daughter was not standing a few feet away.

"With all due respect, sir, I would like to speak with San—Sofia alone. A very short time is all I need. I'll join you downstairs."

Sofia went to the small window with her arms tight around her middle. Her father gave him a stiff nod. "No longer than a bit."

He left the door open behind him. The room was heavy with silence.

Jackson reached out and touched her shoulder, hoping to get her attention. Not only did she turn, but she also crushed herself against his chest and wrapped her arms around his middle. Sobs shook her body. "I'm so sorry." She took a breath. "Tell him no." Hiccups jerked her shoulders. "He can't make you marry me."

He caressed her hair. Silky and soft, it slipped through his fingers. He didn't think she understood the ramifications to her reputation. "You lied to me."

"I know, and it's unforgivable so I won't even ask for forgiveness, but I want you to know I'm sorry."

"We might not have much choice if we want to have a chance at the dreams we both want."

Looking at him, confusion clouded her eyes. "I don't understand. What do you mean? All I want is to work on the ranch with my father, and you want to raise your horses."

He nodded, his jaw sore from the tension. "Because of your games, your father has the power to put an end to both of our dreams. He now has all the control." He wanted to hate her for putting him in this position, but it was just as much his own fault, just like the brutal death of his family.

Shutting his lids, he closed down that part of his thoughts. He had to stay calm and solve the problem in front of him. "Despite you lying to me, we were friends, right?"

She nodded against his chest.

"We talked about you working for me."

"But that is different from getting married."

"It doesn't have to be."

That got her attention. Moving back, she wiped her face clear of the tears. "What do you mean?"

"We can treat it like a partnership. I didn't plan on ever marrying again."

"I know. My father can't force you to marry me. I don't want a husband."

"Good. Because I don't want a wife. We could just stay friends. Have our own rooms, our own lives." He shrugged. "It could work if we don't think of ourselves as married. Just friends, business partners. But I'm not going to let your father force us into this. You have to agree."

A half smile found its way to her face, and he lifted her chin. "Business partners? We don't have to marry. In time, my father will settle down and—"

A cough at the door made them both turn. Juana Alvarez stood there with a tray of food, which she placed on a stool by the bed. The smile gone, replaced by a fierce commander who had been disobeyed. "I have spoken with her father. You need to leave now Señor McCreed, and you will not be coming back until we have your bride ready for you. I'm a godly woman and do not appreciate the trick you played on her father or me." She moved to the side and waited for Jackson to leave. "Your father has sent my sons to secure the church and my daughters will fit you for a wedding dress."

One step over the threshold, he turned to reassure Sofia, but the door was slammed and the bolt slid into place.

For a moment he just stood there, not knowing what had just happened. This morning he was looking forward to a good bath, a hot meal and sleeping somewhere other than the ground. The new future he'd mapped out was giving him hope and a purpose. He should have known it would end in disaster.

Now because of his habit of playing Good Samaritan, his life was not his own. He headed to the stairs. She had said her father couldn't force them, but it appeared he already had set their new wagon in motion and it was heading downhill.

Gritting his teeth, he knew they were out of options.

She was naive about going back to the normal life she wanted on the ranch. As for him, her father had the power to make him start all over again.

Job's story fluttered across his mind. Why couldn't he just live in peace? He wasn't as faithful or understanding as Job had been, so maybe bad things would keep happening to him until he learned some big lesson. He stopped on the narrow steps.

What is it, God? What do You want from me? You took my family now You're taking my freedom. Back in motion, he ran his hands along the rough adobe wall. To be fair, it wasn't God who made the decision to help stranded travelers or take an unknown orphan on a cattle drive.

He found De Zavala sitting at a large table, eating. He waved Jackson to the chair next to him. "Sit. Sit. We have much to talk about." He slid a bowl of *carne guisada* across the table and the basket full of warm tortillas.

"My daughter has gotten herself in trouble. You are a good man, so you will help me decide. Does she get sent out of state to live far from Texas, or do you marry her and live on the ranch?" He dipped a torn piece of tortilla into his bowl and scooped up a chunk of meat.

Jackson had lost his appetite. His stomach rebelled at the thought of taking another bride. He had vowed to never marry again. But if there was one thing he knew about Sofia De Zavala, she would wither away if taken out of Texas. She was as much a part of the land as the cypress that dug its roots deep into the rocky riverbed.

"I hear you already set our nuptials in motion."

The man shrugged as if there wasn't a big drama taking place in their lives. "I figure you or one of the other vaqueros will step in and take the payment I offer. Which Americans returned with you? Any of them good husband material?"

Okay, that knocked the wind out of his gut. He shook his head. "Just the Irishman. I'm not sure he's an American citizen. Why an American?" Were they really sitting here having this conversation as if they were talking about the weather?

"Our new Congress has yet to vote on the status of the old Spanish land grants. The man who marries my daughter would receive that grant to ensure it stayed with the family."

"The whole ranch?"

"It's all very complicated. But we are in uncertain times, and no decision has been made yet. I do not want to lose my legacy. The land needs to stay in my family, and Sofia is all the family I have left, so an American husband is needed."

"So the man that marries your daughter will get all of the land, and all he has to be is American?" Jackson was a little sick in his stomach.

De Zavala paused and looked Jackson straight in the eye. *"Sí."* After holding eye contact for a few breaths, he went back to eating. "So do you know a good man? You, perhaps?"

"You'd trade your daughter in marriage to keep the ranch in your family?" He pushed the bowl away and leaned back in his chair. Staring past De Zavala, he watched a small group of children play outside.

If De Zavala was talking, Jackson didn't hear him. His mind had him standing on the edge of darkness.

The day he buried the bloody bodies of his wife and babies he made a vow. He would never stand at that place again. He would stay true to her memory for the rest of his days. Never again would he throw dirt over someone else he loved, someone he should have protected. Someone he married.

But then again he didn't love Sofia. But could he walk away from her and leave her to someone who just wanted the land?

Everything in him screamed for him to get up from

the table and walk out the door. She had lied to him. Why would he even consider betraying his vow to Lilly for her?

Then he thought about her face as they drove across the last river. She deserved to be free to work the land she loved.

"I'll do it." He broke out in a cold sweat. There would be no going back now. What had he done?

Chapter Eighteen

Sofia smoothed her hands over the silk skirt of the wedding gown Juana's daughters had brought up to her. The most daring, adventurous time in her life was being cut short by her own wedding.

It wasn't lost on her that in trying to avoid getting married she forced the issue. Poor Jackson was paying the price. So was she. She would be married to a man that loved his dead wife more than he would ever love her.

The women, several generations of Juana's family, fluttered around her. They bounced from giggling to whispering to tear-producing laughter. These women she didn't even know were excited for her.

Her father had charged them with getting her ready for the wedding. Juana had organized her troops as if Texas freedom was at stake again. Currently their hands tried to fix her short hair.

"Your hair is so short. Why?"

"It's not polite to ask why." An older aunt glared at the youngest girl in the room. It was the same look her own mother had bestowed on her the times Sofia had broken social protocol.

Juana's oldest daughter, Veronica, worked with her hair. "She was dressed as a boy when she came in with her vaquero."

A need to explain rushed in, but then the words lodged in her throat. He wasn't hers. Chills creeped over her skin. By the time the sun settled, he would be hers and she would be his.

The few women who didn't know the story gasped. The one telling the story nodded with a knowing look and stuck another pin in Sofia's hair. "She went all the way to New Orleans on a cattle drive with him."

The younger women turned to her with awe in their eyes. "You rode on a cattle drive dressed as a *nino*?"

She would have nodded, but now her head was being twisted in order to make her hair look presentable.

Juana moved in front of her, blocking the view of the younger girls who had gathered on the floor.

"She is blessed to be alive and that he is willing to honor her by giving her his name and protection." She looked down at the younger girls. "Imagine what could have happened to her in the wild. No woman wants to be alone and shunned by good people. Would you want your friends to turn their backs on you because of an impulsive action?"

"Real friends wouldn't do that." Sofia's voice sounded hoarse to her own ears.

The boardinghouse owner slowly brought her gaze back to her, and everyone leaned back.

Mouth dry, Sofia cleared her throat. Her own mother would be horrified that she spoke up in such a way. "Señora, I apologize. I meant no disrespect. I just would hope that if I had friends they would be loyal enough to stay my friends when I needed them most."

Juana narrowed her eyes and stared at her. "Yes, this is true also. Our God is forgiving when you repent. I understand this has to be a stressful day for you. Your father, God bless him, said you had lost your mother and brother recently. And now you are being rushed to the altar without your mother's guidance."

She pulled a large silver comb from her pocket. "This has been worn by all the women in my family. The doves represent love, peace and faith. All the things you will need for a good marriage."

The doors opened, and one of the cousins entered carrying a vase full of red, pink and yellow roses.

Finally, the attention was off Sofia, and Juana made her way to the newest arrival. "These are beautiful. Good job, *mija*." She turned to Sofia. "No bride should enter her new life without the color and beauty of the roses. Soft and silky but strong and steady. Even a few thorns for protection." She laughed at her own joke, and all the other women giggled. The full blooms were clipped and pinned into her hair. Then the women placed the two yellow rosebuds between the large open pink and red flowers.

"And now for the final piece. Mercedes, bring the veil." Juana's younger sister draped the delicate lace over her arms and presented it to Juana. The exquisite material was whisper thin, and the scalloped edging created the most beautiful cloth Sofia had ever seen. The soft gold color was accented with ivory lace and embroidered roses. Her mother had loved roses.

Tears burned her eyes again.

"Oh, *mija*. No more tears. We are here for you. Your

handsome groom will arrive soon to take you to the chapel. Everything will be right in the eyes of God."

Sofia took a step back. "I can't wear that. It's too precious. You've done too much already."

"*De nada.* This is a special day, and it needs to be treated as such." She touched the one short curl that had escaped the pins. "And your groom needs to be reminded that he is marrying a woman."

Oh, no. The tears were building again. She blinked, hoping they would go back where they came from. Stupid tears, they served no purpose and only complicated things, making her look weak.

The cross-country cattle drive had pushed and tested her, but she survived and flourished. So why was she falling apart now? This was something almost every woman in history had gone through, some in much worse circumstances.

Lowering her head, she nodded to Juana. "I'm honored by your gift and blessings." The women surrounded her, fussing over the final details. They giggled as they talked in a mix of Spanish and English.

Smiling, Sofia thought of her mother and almost started crying again. She would have loved the gown and roses. What would she think of Jackson?

Her mother put a great deal of stock in bloodlines and social standings. Jackson McCreed might have been a disappointment. She wasn't sure he even wanted to marry her.

She knew most men wouldn't have allowed a woman to stay on the cattle drive or respect the skills she brought to the trail. Would he still after she became his wife, or would it all change?

On the trail, she proved she could rope and ride. She

didn't want to use the good wife skills her mother had taught her. Could she make Jackson happy by being herself?

Finished, they turned her to the oval mirror in the room. The woman staring back at her was a stranger. The trail had changed her, but in ways she liked.

Her skin was darker, her hair easier to deal with and her posture stronger. She lifted her chin and studied the new Sofia De Zavala. She approved.

Gently touching the veil that fell from the roses and cascaded over her shoulders, she wondered what Jackson would think.

He'd seen her only as a boy. Dirty and dressed in ill fitted clothes. Would he like this side of her? What if he didn't want her back in the breeches? What if seeing her like this changed the way he thought of her?

Pressing her hands against her stomach, she closed her eyes and took a deep breath. Calming her stampeding nerves, she opened her eyes and rolled her shoulders back.

He was a good man who loved horses and the land. She loved those things, too. It was a good place to start a marriage, right? What if it wasn't enough?

This was one of the worst days of his life. The one thing he vowed never to do again, and here he was taking a spruced-up fancy horse to retrieve a bride he didn't want.

A glance down the road reminded him that he could just keep walking. The other direction was the church.

If he left, no one would blame him. Let her deal with the fallout. She was the one who had lied. Never would he have allowed De Zavala's daughter and his only living child to work a cattle drive.

Which of course was the reason she never told him.

He thought of all the times she had been in danger, and his stomach tightened. He didn't want to be responsible for someone else's life again.

But with this marriage, he would have more land and horses than he ever dreamed. So he'd give her his name, but that was it. Was it wrong to profit from her predicament?

She'd get what she wanted, too. What other husband would let his wife run all over the ranch in pants?

The warm breath of the horse he led tickled his neck, and he reached up and rubbed the big mare's muzzle. Who knew his decision to come to Texas would end up with him becoming a major landowner? He took a deep breath. All he had to do was marry the cook's assistant.

He was sure that if he was in a better mood, he'd find that funny.

If he walked out of town, not only would Sofia lose everything she loved, but he would leave with nothing but his stallion. Back to the beginning. He'd have to start over again somewhere new.

He didn't have anywhere to go.

West was the chapel, where her father, Estevan and Rory were waiting to serve as witnesses.

Earlier in the day he found the two cowboys and told them the name of her father. They were both speechless. A rarity for the Irishman. When he shared his doubt about marrying her, Rory grinned and offered himself up without hesitation.

It took a world of strength to not smash his fist into

his charming face. The cowboy was too pretty for his own good anyway. Someone needed to break that perfect nose and knock a few teeth out of his perfect smile.

He had the gall to laugh at him. "Yeah, that's what I thought, hombre. You won't let anyone else marry our girl."

Estevan chimed in. "It's like one of those fairy tales where the hero goes on a journey and wins the princess and a kingdom." They kept giggling like a pair of old ladies.

"Didn't she offer you her kingdom for some tea and a warm bath?" They thought they were so humorous.

"Be in the church at six." He growled and stomped off.

He didn't deserve a happy ending. Lilly and his babies were in a grave, and he should be with them. No way should he be getting married again and gaining more land than he knew what to do with.

He stopped in front of the boardinghouse, one step away from the small covered porch.

The dappled gray horse he had brought for Sofia dropped his head looking for grass. He thought about bringing her Domino, but that cow pony was too impatient and hot. This job needed a calm steady horse. It would be carrying…his bride, in full wedding attire. A cold sweat covered his skin.

Once he knocked on the door, it would be over. For the second time in his life, he would be taking a bride.

The road to the left would take him back to Galveston, but he'd have to get his horse. Galveston was out. Shaking his head, he lifted his hat and pushed his newly cut hair back.

Just do it. One, two, three steps and he was at the door. On the other side, his new unplanned future waited. He lifted his fisted hand and knocked on the dark wood.

He wasn't sure what he expected, but an army of women covering every age was not it.

Juana stood in the center of the doorway, arms crossed and the look of a stern schoolteacher firmly in place. Behind her, a sea of faces stared at him. Some were full of glee, others stared in curiosity and a few with censure.

"Señor McCreed, state your business." Despite her small stature, she managed to look down her nose at him.

"I've come to collect Miss Sofia De Zavala." He pulled on the edge of his new gray overcoat. He forced himself to stand still under her scrutiny.

"Have you officially asked her to join you in marriage?"

The urge to rub the back of his neck ate at his gut. "Um… I'm not sure what you mean. Her father—"

"Yes. Her father did the right thing and arranged all this, but have you asked her?"

This morning when he left Tiago in the room, he never imagined he would be arriving at the door before dinner to pick up his bride. "I'm not sure what you want."

She took a deep breath. A stern look of disappointment had him shifting from one boot to the other. "We will present the beautiful bride to you. You will go down on one knee and ask for her hand in marriage. Every woman deserves to be asked. Is this agreeable?"

The stiff collar of his starched shirt tightened around his neck. "Yes, ma'am."

With a nod she waved her hand. Two girls around Sofia's age ran off.

Breathe, Jackson, breathe. It was just words. He wasn't replacing Lilly. His heart was not involved.

The women parted. Juana moved from the door and stood to the side of the porch. His gaze darted from her to the horse to the direction of Galveston.

He closed his eyes and counted his breaths, slowing the blood that pounded hard through his veins.

Feet shuffled followed by silence. When he opened his eyes, the new Sofia would be standing in front of him. His scalp prickled, and his stomach quivered.

Why was he so nervous? He knew her. He'd ridden with her for weeks now. At this point in his life, she probably knew him better than anyone else. She knew about his past but didn't look at him with pity or blame. He could live with that. Deep breath. He lifted his eyes.

The blood left his body, and he felt numb. In front of him stood a vision of feminine beauty. This was not his Tiago.

This woman was new and exotic. What did he do with her? She was unnaturally quiet and still. Her enormous ebony eyes blinked in rapid motion. How had he ever mistaken her for a boy?

A few lose curls framed her heart-shaped face. A veil fell over her shoulders. In her hand, she crushed a small bouquet of flowers.

A guttural throat clearing pulled his attention to Juana. "Oh, yes."

His own throat suddenly needed to be cleared. Licking his lips, he went down on one knee and took her hand. He used a little more force than intended, and her stiff body stumbled.

To stop her forward movement, he planted his open palm on her hip until she was steady again. Dropping his free hand, he looked up and gave her a friendly smile, at least he hoped it was friendly.

"Sorry." Her voice was so low he had to lean in closer.

"It's fine. Being in such a big dress has to be awkward after running around in breeches."

Moisture beaded on her bottom lashes. He wanted to hit himself in the head. *Idiot.*

No woman wanted to be told she was awkward. Words weren't as easy now that he'd lost his Tiago. He swallowed. "I'm the one who needs to apologize. You're beautiful."

He shifted his weight off his knee, which was starting to hurt. Clearing his throat didn't help. He patted her small hand and gulped in air, feeling like a fish flopping on the riverbank.

He could do this. They were just words. They didn't mean anything. "Sofia De Zavala, would you do me the honor of taking my name?"

Cooing and sniffing happened around them. He kept his gaze fixed on the woman standing before him, the now crushed flowers pressed against her chest with her free hand.

A slight nod from her, and his life took a new path. A path he didn't want to take.

He made sure to smile, hoping it didn't look as tight as it felt. An image of Lilly on her parents' porch as he asked her to marry him flashed across his mind. Closing his eyes, he forced it away. He should be running, but he couldn't humiliate Sofia and leave her abandoned like that.

For better or worse, he would soon have another wife.

I'm so sorry, Lilly.

Chapter Nineteen

Sofia studied the contrast of their hands. Her hand seemed so much smaller in his. Her heart pounded. It had been rushing in her ears since he dropped to one knee in front of everyone.

This was happening. They were getting married. "Where's my father?"

"Waiting at the chapel along with Estevan and Rory." His voice sounded like he had swallowed river rocks.

She gasped and pressed her hands flat against her chest. "They'll be in attendance? That is so sweet of them to be there for us." Why did that make her feel so happy?

He glanced to the side of the porch. "You haven't said yes yet. Do you agree to join with me in marriage?"

"What if I don't say yes?" Taking the time to study him, she saw the tightness of his smile. The green in his eyes lacked life.

"Then this is all over."

"Do you want to marry me?"

He sighed and shifted his knee. "Yes."

"Okay. Then I'll say yes, too."

He nodded as if glad that chore was over and done. Rising from his knee, he pulled her into the yard.

They stopped in front of a beautiful dappled gray with black muzzle and legs. She had been so focused on Jackson and his neatly cut suit and hair she hadn't noticed the beauty of the horse he brought to her. The soft hair was warm under her touch.

"She's not one of ours. Where did you get her?"

"Your father knows a man who had some horses. She's your wedding gift." He didn't make eye contact with her but stared at the horse, his hand resting on the black mane.

Sofia traced the black leather of the saddle skirt, engraved silver decorating the edge. The large horn was made for a woman to sit sidesaddle. "This is not a working saddle."

A lopsided grin pulled on a corner of his mouth. "No. Your father wanted you to ride in a proper lady's saddle. It's his gift to you."

One of Juana's sons brought a wood box to her. "Here is a block for mounting."

Gathering the front of her full skirt, she looked up to the stirrup. "Life is so much easier in pants." They placed the box on the ground. A couple of the girls who had come to help giggled.

She sighed.

He took her hand and helped her up to the block, and from there he lifted her and guided her into the saddle.

She'd never felt so helpless. It took him and three of the girls to get her settled in the saddle and her large dress arranged.

The tip of her delicate laced boots peeked out from the front of her dress. The full skirt flared out behind her, covering the back of the mare and cascading down the sides.

Jackson stood at her side looking up. The warmth of his hand was so strong she could feel it through all the layers of fine material.

"Do I look okay?" Her mother taught her to never ask how she looked. It either sounded that you lacked confidence or you were asking to be complimented. She bit her lip, but she couldn't suck the words back down her throat.

"You're majestic. A real life princess." The rough edge to his voice made her feel strange. He looked like he wanted to say something else.

She leaned down, anticipating his next words. Her lungs refused to work while her heart waited.

It needed him to say something, but she didn't know what. In silence they seemed frozen in time. His expression closed, and he moved away from her.

He patted her leg. "Are you ready?"

Was she ready? She was completely turning her life over to him. Would he change now that she was his wife? She wanted to make him promise they would still be friends even if he didn't want her heart, but all she managed was a nod.

There was time to make this marriage work. She wouldn't rush him.

He nodded back before turning away from her and taking the mare's lead rope. One step and they were on their way to the church. The sway of the horse calmed her.

Her finger itched to take control, but she didn't even know where they were going. Would this be her life from now on, him taking the lead and her following without a word or question?

As they started walking, she noticed the women followed. She twisted and looked over her shoulder. "You're joining us?"

"It is your special day, and we all want to celebrate with you." A few of the younger girls ran along the side of the dirt road gathering flowers. People came out of their yards and houses and waved.

Some joined them. Jackson looked over his shoulder. "Do you know any of these people?"

Joy caused her heart to grow and push at her chest. "No. I thought you did." She tried to suppress a giggle. It was so girly, but an odd sound ended up escaping. Leaning over the large saddle horn, she spoke quietly to him. "We have become the talk of the town. They just want to join the wedding parade."

He chuckled. "I guess this means there is no changing our minds." He winked. For a brief moment she saw the man she could love.

Her heart melted. Yes, she was falling in love with her soon-to-be husband. Maybe he wasn't so set against the marriage. What did he have to gain from marrying her other than helping her?

He faced forward again, nodding to people who waved and congratulated them. More flowers were handed up to her, some put on her dress.

As they walked through the dirt-packed streets of San Antonio, they made their way to the large cathedral. Standing in front of the giant wood doors, her father waited with Rory and Estevan. The last two had foolish grins plastered on their faces, stretching from ear to ear. She could already hear the teasing.

She braved a glance at her father. Her only family member left in the world. There was no joy or laughter on his face. A stern disapproving line pulled his mouth taut.

A smile had not touched his lips since the moment the storm hit and his wife and son were late returning home.

Jackson stopped the horse and moved to her side. The mare twisted her neck and nudged her boot. It was time to get off, but she realized without Jackson's help she was stuck.

"What's wrong?"

Heat climbed her neck, and she knew she was blushing. "I hate being encased in all this material. I can't even move on my own."

"Here, I'll help you." Before he could even touch her, her father was calling out to them as he approached.

"Stay on the horse. I have paid a photographer to take a picture so we can make the announcement of your wedding in all the papers." Standing next to Jackson, her father looked smaller. She always thought of him as tall. Music drifted through the air.

"You have mariachis here?" From the opposite end of the road, a group of men with string instruments, horns and large sombreros strolled toward them.

"Of course. My daughter will have a real wedding done properly. Everything your mother wanted for you and your brother."

His firm jaw clenched and a sheen in his eyes reflected the fading light of the west.

A man set up a large black camera in the middle of the street and started giving orders. Her father moved to the other side of Jackson. Everyone was ordered to close in around the bride and groom.

The musicians continued to play somewhere in the background. It seemed to take hours of everyone being still for the man with the camera to get what he wanted.

Her legs had gone numb, and her back hurt from sitting in the awkward position on the sidesaddle. After today, she was never riding on one again. Would her father get offended if she traded this one in for a working saddle, one that fit her?

Finally, Jackson reached for her, but her legs were useless. His strong hands encircled her waist; she felt so small next to him as he set her on the ground.

He didn't let go. Looking up at him, she held her breath. The warmth of his fingers caused her skin to tingle. All the times he had almost kissed her but had pulled back because he was a man of honor.

Soon she would be his wife. And they would have their first kiss in front of everyone.

Without any warning, he turned and left.

"Mija." Her father's hand slipped into hers, and she tucked her fingers into the crook of his arm. A boy she had seen earlier in the day took her horse, slipping the coin her father gave him into a leather pouch.

Together they stood in front of the large cathedral doors and watched, as what seemed to be everyone in San Antonio crossed the threshold.

"Your mother would love that you are marrying in the same church as us. Married. We could not have planned it better. God surely has His hand in this union." His profile was stark in the fading light.

"You and Momma married here?"

He gave two quick nods. *"Si.* She was a breathtaking bride who stole my heart." He turned to her, his lips in a tight smile. His rough hand cupped her face. "She wore roses as you do. Jackson McCreed is a fortunate man to get the honor of your hand."

She blinked, not wanting to cry. "You said I was a burden."

His head went back as if she had hit him. "I have never told you such a thing. You are my most precious treasure. Worth more than all the land in Texas."

She forced down the lump stuck between her heart and throat. "Before the cattle drive, I heard you tell Jackson that I was a burden. I didn't want to be a burden. I wanted to prove to you I could help with the ranch. I can help build a future here on our land just like you wanted with Santiago." Her voice broke as she said her brother's name.

"Oh, *mija*." He pulled her against him. "You are not the burden. My worry over your future is heavy on my shoulders. You are all I have left. When I discovered you had not gone shopping but had joined the cattle drive, I died a thousand deaths. You are my future. Without you, I have nothing of value."

He leaned back and tucked away a loose curl. "Look at you all grown up and about to become a wife."

He sighed and cupped her face again. "I was protecting you the only way I knew how. Now you will live on the ranch. Jackson will make a good husband. He cares for you and the land. Saving it for my grandsons. Everyone says he is a good man."

"He is."

"If you say so, that is all that matters. I had a plan, but in my faith I have to believe God's plan is better."

She placed her hand over his. "I'm sorry I worried

you, but does Jackson want this marriage? I don't want him forced, Papi."

"What man would not want to marry you?" He stepped back and once again placed her hand on his arm, ready for the wedding march into the church. "Your mother wanted a man of good family and education for your husband. Jackson is a man of honor and integrity who speaks well and stands tall. I think she would approve."

"If she didn't, Jackson would charm her until she thought he could rope the moon." She smiled.

He patted her hand. "Are you ready daughter of mine?"

In a few minutes she would be Mrs. McCreed, after a lifetime of being a De Zavala, she wasn't sure how she felt about that change.

With a nod and one foot forward, and she was heading into the church. Two of the young girls carried her train, lifting it off the dirt. It had the weight of a million stones. As soon as this was over, she was changing back into her pants.

Her own eyes burned as she reached for his hand. "Thank you, Papi. It's more beautiful than I ever imagined." She took one of the yellow rosebuds from her bouquet and placed it in the buttonhole of his jacket.

"That's your mother's favorite color of rose."

"I know." She patted his chest.

With a stiff jaw, he looked forward again. Light gleamed off the moisture gathered in his dark eyes. "I wish you the love I had for your mother and the love your mother had for me." Then he gave her a quick wink. "And that you are blessed with children as we were." He gave her a hard quick jerk of his head and patted her hand.

Together they walked through the open doors of the church, the pews filled with people she had just met.

At the end of the long aisle stood her trail boss. He was the most handsome man she had ever seen, and he was going to be her husband.

From there everything was a blur, the words and vows she couldn't remember. Her hand stayed in Jackson's once her father handed her over to him. His voice was strong and steady even though she couldn't recall any words.

They were proclaimed husband and wife. Jackson was given permission to kiss his bride. Stomach muscles quivered. This was it. She tilted her head and closed her eyes.

His lips briefly touched hers and then vanished. Just as fast as he came, he was gone. Confused, she opened her eyes and found him facing all the happy people who witnessed the exchange of vows. That was it? That was her first kiss as his wife?

His hand slipped into hers, and he pulled her back down the aisle. Petals covered the floor. Focused on Jackson, she had missed them earlier.

The edge of her skirt caused her to stumble. Jackson's pace was too fast for her finery. He stopped and looked down at her. "Are you all right?"

She blushed, suddenly embarrassed, but not sure why. "I can't keep up in this dress."

"Oh, sorry."

Now they stood in front of the cathedral and everyone hugged them with congratulations as they stood at the doors. Once most of the people disappeared down the road, her father hugged Juana.

"I can't thank you enough Señora Juana for the epic job of organizing a wedding at such short notice. Are you sure you don't want to come work for me?"

"Within a matter of weeks you would be working for me, old man." Her warm smile contradicted her words.

Rory, Estevan and a few of Juana's relatives erupted into laughter.

Head high, Rafael De Zavala glared at them. "I have secured a dinner party for a small group at the hotel. It's late, and we need to eat and celebrate this new day and new family." He turned to the people left standing around them. "Come, join us."

As a group, they headed to the hotel. Jackson had dropped her hand, but walked next to her as they followed along. She hated that now she didn't know how to talk to him. "That was so fast. It's a bit strange to think a few words and now we are joined forever."

He grunted, which made her heart lighten. That was her Jackson. She wrapped her fingers around his arm, loving the strength she felt under her hand. "Will we stay in the hotel today or at Juana's boardinghouse?" She knew red spots crawled up her neck, and she looked at her hand gripping the light gray sleeve of his coat. The skin was cut, rough and callused. Not the hands of the Sofia De Zavala that left home all those weeks ago.

"I'm going back to the boardinghouse. Your father has a room for you at the hotel."

"What? But we're—"

"Business partners.

"Yes, but I—"

"Sofia, we have a business arrangement. We have not even courted." He never once looked at her.

Dread wormed its way through her limbs. "Do you already regret marrying me?"

"No." The muscle in his tight jaw told her otherwise.

What did she say to that? Rory laughed at something Juana's daughter said. Estevan punched him in the arm.

The people walking and laughing in front of her started to blur. She bit the inside of her cheek until she tasted blood. "If you didn't want to be married to me, why did you agree to this?" She kept her voice low. Humiliated if someone found out her husband was already leaving her and it was their wedding night. "Could we at least stay in the same building?"

"We talked about this." A doorman opened the entrance to the hotel, giving them a nod as the boisterous group headed to the dining room, Jackson and her father both looking more like they were going to another funeral.

She knew it was a business arrangement, but she didn't think it would exclude any chance of a real marriage. Why couldn't they have both?

On the walk to the cathedral she had started dreaming about a real marriage with Jackson. Seeing him standing at the end of the aisle, repeating the vows of husband and wife shifted something in her. She was in love with her husband.

She wanted to cry and scream at him. It wasn't his fault. He had been clear. The mistake was hers. There had to be a way to fix this.

As they sat around the long wood table, several courses were placed before them. Each bite she took hit her stomach like heavy metal.

Jackson sat next to her. He didn't even pretend to

eat. Finally, with the cake on the table, he put down his napkin and leaned toward her ear.

She closed her eyes and thought of things that would take her mind off the way she felt when she was close to him.

"I have a few errands I need to take care of before I leave for the ranch. I will meet up with you and your father soon. Should be about a week."

Her spine stiffened. He was leaving their wedding dinner before it was even over.

Rory called out to him. "Hey, boss man, you're not going to kiss your beautiful bride?"

Sofia held her breath as Jackson paused. He leaned over her and kissed her forehead. The way you would kiss a child. She would not cry. She smiled. "I'll see you soon?"

He straightened and nodded. "Soon."

It had been a week. All of Jackson's business was done. It had actually been done four day ago, but he couldn't bring himself to leave for the ranch.

She was there. His wife.

Her dark eyes looked into the heart of him, and he knew she wanted more than he could give her, more than he was willing to give.

What he feared was she'd get it. He would give his love to her, but it wasn't his to give. It should have been buried with Lilly.

He looked down at the letter he had started days ago. All his mistakes and guilt poured into the words.

Maybe if he explained it to Lilly's parents he would re-member. He would stay strong in the face of his new wife.

The union with Sofia was a business arrangement.

Not a real marriage. She was land. Work that would keep him busy until he joined his family.

He reclaimed his vow to Lilly in the letter. Promised his in-laws that he would stay true to their daughter, his first love and true wife.

A few drops smeared the ink. He wiped his face and went back to writing. Finishing it, he knew it was time.

He had stalled enough. With his resolve replanted, he would send the letter off tomorrow and make plans to go back to the ranch.

There was a wedding reception to attend. For now, he'd go to El Mercado and forget he was married, but he had responsibilities and duties he had to honor.

It wasn't fair to Sofia for him to abandon her. He needed a plan. Something to do once he got there so he wouldn't have to spent time with her. The idea of moving into De Zavala's house didn't sit well with him either. If he was going to live on the ranch, he wanted his own house. One big enough so that he wouldn't be close to his bride. That gave him another excuse to stretch his stay in San Antonio. He needed to have supplies sent to the ranch.

He dug his fingers into his scalp. How was he going to see Sofia and not have feelings for her? He didn't deserve the land or the beautiful wife that came along with it.

Chapter Twenty

It had been two weeks since she had become Mrs. Jackson McCreed. Now Sofia stood next to her father in the receiving line without her husband. Her hand hurt from all the shaking, and her muscles on her face were stiff from all the fake smiling.

Every single person cast a glance to the empty spot on the other side of her. The side where her new husband should be standing.

The photo of their wedding had hit the newspapers. Seeing it for the first time had been startling.

The picture was beautiful, the horse, her dress, the limestone church and all the people made it look as if it had been a well-planned wedding. When she focused on her groom, she saw a stern, unhappy man.

Shaking the useless thoughts out of her mind, she glanced at her father as he shook the hand of Sheriff Ballinger. Once again he explained why the groom was not at his own reception.

A couple of days ago she asked him if he had forced Jackson to marry her, and he denied it, assuring her

Jackson was willing and just needed the time to take care of business.

They had expected him four days ago.

Her mind went to dark places—accidents, bandits or illness could have claimed him or held him up. His stallion was still here, so she knew he would come back even if it was just to get his horse.

The sheriff moved to her next. "I hear you already need to put out wanted posters looking for your husband. That didn't take long."

With the best impression of her mother, she gave the man a stern look. "I'm sure my father told you about his business in San Antonio." She never had liked the new sheriff. He held her hand a little too long, she tugged at it, but his grip tightened.

"If you need anything, Mrs. McCreed, please let me know and I will be there."

"I'm sure she won't be needing your services, Sheriff, but we'll keep that in mind."

She spun. "Jackson!" She clasped her hands in front of her so she wouldn't throw her arms around his neck and make a spectacle for everyone in town.

His head was bare and his hair tousled. A shadow of a beard coated his jawline.

Mud from his boots left parts of the trail behind him. He shook her father's hand and apologized for arriving late. He had the look of a cowboy who had been riding for days and just got off his horse. She scanned him from head to boots. Other than needing a bath, he looked healthy. He was here and safe.

Turning back to the sheriff, he wrapped his arm around her, pulling her close. He offered his other hand to the lawman. Both men did a bit of narrow eye surveying before Sheriff Ballinger moved on to join the others drinking punch and eating whatever the church ladies had set up on the tables.

He stepped away from her. "Sorry I'm late and I look like something the cat dragged in. I was afraid if I stopped to clean up I'd miss the whole thing."

"I've been worried." She had so much to ask him, but this was not the place. "Are you hungry?"

His strong chin tilted down toward her and his deep green eyes squinted. "That's all you got to say to me? I'm about a week late and almost missed the reception and you just want to feed me?"

"Well, Mr. McCreed, you do look hungry, and I figured anything I have to say can wait until we are alone." She gave him her best hostess smile. "My mother's training wasn't completely wasted. I know where and how to plan my battles."

With those words she took his hand and led him to the food tables. People she knew, some all her life, others just a few months, watched as they left the receiving line and cut across the community hall.

One of her mother's best friends, Pastor Phillips's wife, Mable, handed them each a plate with peach cobbler.

"Thank you, ma'am." Jackson's baritone voice slipped along her spine. She needed to keep it together. If their marriage was going to work, they had a great deal to talk about, but this was not the time or place.

She laid a hand on his arm and leaned in closer to Mable. "He's been riding hard all day to get here."

The older woman nodded and smiled, her eyes softening. "What a heroic thing to do."

"I'll go get you something to drink, darling." She

smiled at him, and he returned the look with skepticism. She could hear her mother's voice telling her to let them wonder what was behind the smile. "Is lemonade okay?"

He took a slow bite of the cobbler and nodded.

Mable started talking to him as Sofia turned and went to the other side of the room where they had set up the drinks. She was having a hard time breathing. And the nasty eye burning had started.

She couldn't cry here. Whatever was going on with her marriage had to be settled in private.

A moment alone to gather herself was what she needed. All the doors had been opened to catch the cool breeze of the night. The moon was bright, as if God was holding up a lantern to check on them. She smiled.

Maybe her momma was watching over her, too. Giggling came from behind the building. "Did you see him? He's as handsome as they say."

"It's not fair that Sofia got him before he met us. He could have made a better choice in town."

"It's not fair. I heard her father had to offer him the whole De Zavala ranch to marry her because she was ruined. The marriage is a sham."

"What?"

"How?"

"Annie, this is just mean gossip. We should be happy for Sofia." The others shushed Laura, her one true friend apparently.

"It's not gossip. It's the truth." Annie, the banker's daughter, continued. "I heard my parents talking. Señor De Zavala came to the bank and sent papers off for everything to be put in Mr. McCreed's name. That's the only reason he married her."

"I guess if my father was willing to hand over all his possessions, I'd have any husband I wanted also."

"Did you see the way he looks? He didn't even bother to clean up for her. What do you think she did to be ruined?"

Sofia couldn't listen to another word and ran inside, ducking behind a wall, into a space they stored boxes.

People were saying she was ruined? Her father's plan to make everyone think they had been married didn't work.

Annie had to be lying about the land. She was mean and loved gossiping. The rest of the girls were just jealous. Eyes closed, she pressed her hands against her middle.

Was the only reason Jackson married her for ownership of the land? Would her father make that kind of offer? Give over all their land to him?

Stepping out of the storage room, she scanned the reception area. She needed to talk to her father.

He would tell her the truth. The butterflies in her stomach that started fluttering when she saw Jackson now had claws and fangs.

Lilly had made the best peach cobbler. It had been his favorite. Jackson took the last bite of the warm dessert and forced it down his dry throat, smiling at the nice woman talking to him. He didn't hear a word. The image of his new bride filled his head.

He had hoped when he saw her again the feminine allure that had hit him in the gut at the boardinghouse had been a fluke. He'd chalked it up to the surprise of seeing her in a dress for the first time.

He'd wanted to believe the stunning bride was a trick

of his memory. He'd spent the days apart hoping she wasn't as beautiful as his imagination kept telling him.

When he came in and saw the sheriff holding her hand, he had been knocked to his knees again.

Riding into town he had been starving, but after seeing his new wife, he didn't feel so well.

A couple of older women joined him and introduced themselves as friends of Sofia's mother. "We were devastated when we lost her. Sofia's been so lost without a mother's guidance."

The other continued where the first one left off. "When she disappeared for all those weeks, we were so worried. And to think she was with you the whole time." They both nodded and looked at him waiting for his response.

He had no clue what to say to that statement. What had De Zavala told everyone? "I know losing her mother was hard. I'm happy to know she has had women like you in her life." Looking over the crowd, he couldn't find her. "Speaking of Sofia, I've seemed to have lost her. Do you ladies happen to know where she has gone?"

They tittered. "Oh, newlyweds. I remember when William used to get anxious when I was out of his sight."

"Now they slip away as soon as possible. Oh, there she is!" They pointed to the back wall by a large open door.

What was she doing in the corner by herself? "Excuse me, ladies."

"Of course." They smiled and waved him on.

As he walked across the crowded floor, music started to play. People he had never met smiled at him, a few tried to stop him, but he explained he was trying to get to his bride.

His bride. The churning in his stomach went up a notch. *I'm so sorry, Lilly.*

Everyone nodded with a twinkle of understanding in their eyes. They thought they understood anyway. How could they when he didn't understand himself? There was not one clear thought in his head or maybe it was his heart.

Either way he was not happy.

As he got closer to her, he noticed she had a panicked look in her eyes as she searched the room. Had she been crying?

"Sofia?" He reached for her shoulder.

She jumped. "Jackson. I thought you were eating."

"I was until I saw you were hiding back here. Who are you looking for?"

"My father. I need to talk to him."

"What's wrong?" he asked.

"Nothing."

He raised an eyebrow. Being married before had taught him one thing—he knew when a woman said nothing was wrong he needed to back off, because something was most certainly wrong.

He scanned the room. "How long is this reception going to last?"

Rory walked up behind him and gave his shoulder two solid hits. "Good to see you, old man. We were starting to think you weren't coming back." He laughed.

Sofia clasped her hands in front of her. He hated the uncertainty he saw in her eyes. Knowing he put it there tore at his gut. Why didn't he realize earlier that he wouldn't be able to keep his vow to Lilly and not hurt Sofia in the process. He was going to have to pick one.

"We are looking for Señor De Zavala. Have you seen him?" The last thing he wanted to talk about was the reason he was late. He was a coward.

"I see him. Excuse me, gentlemen." She turned to leave.

"Do you want me to go with you?" He started to follow her.

"No. Stay here and talk with Rory. I need to speak with him alone." With her shoulders back and chin up, she left.

Rory gave him a side look. "Trouble already?"

He pushed his hair off his forehead. "I'm not sure. It should be a simple arrangement. I'm not sure what is going on anymore."

A chuckle was his answer. "Our Tiago put on a dress, and everything got complicated."

That was it. It was all this wedding and reception happenings. Once he got Sofia back on the ranch and on a horse, they would go back to being friends and business partners.

It would go back to normal. "Thanks, Rory."

Confusion marred the Irishman's face. "Um…sure. Anytime?"

People had started dancing, so he had to skirt the edge of the room to find his new father-in-law. He saw the man heading straight to him. Unfortunately, alone.

"Where's Sofia? She went to find—"

"She found out about the trade I made with you for the land. I think she took off to the ranch. I would follow, but I think she needs to hear from you. You need to make this right."

There wasn't a thing on this Earth that could make this right. He'd miscalculated, and they were both paying the price.

"I'll make an excuse for your early departure. You're newlyweds who have just reunited. Everyone will understand."

There was no avoiding it. He had to talk to her, alone. He gave De Zavala a nod and shouldered through the happy crowd. Many of the men patted him on the back, and he smiled and nodded.

Acid burned his gut. He tried not to run to the barn. He wouldn't put it past her to take off on her own across the hills at night.

Her impulsive nature left his world on wobbly ground. His stallion had been brought into town. Was she saddling him now?

Stepping into the doorway, he found the light from behind him made it easy to see her. She was next to Domino.

The relief vanished just as fast when he saw the saddle. She threw a man's work saddle on the horse's back. A heart-wrenching sob followed the horse's grunt. "Sofia. Stop."

She spun, the twirling of her skirts causing the Appaloosa to sidestep away from her.

Sofia grabbed the reins and calmed the horse. "Did you?"

"Sofia, you can't ride out to the ranch this late. In that dress you're asking to get hurt."

"Did you marry me for the ranch?"

Jackson rubbed his eyes. He wanted to lie, to give her the answer that would take away the hurt. But in the long run, a lie now would just hurt her more.

He wanted to reassure her, to apologize, to tell her everything would be all right. He flexed his jaw.

The ugly truth sat between them, growing in the dark silence. His gut, his heart wanted to be the hero she needed. Wanted to hold her and kiss—

No! He slammed the door on that thought. He was not the hero, for Lilly or Sofia. All he managed to bring to their doors was death and pain.

He should have stayed away. Being with her just made everything more complicated.

"It's true isn't it?" The last word was lost in a sob.

"I married you to save your reputation. I had made a vow over my dead wife's grave to stay true to her. To never marry again. I broke part of my vow to her. I can't break it all. I can't. Yes, your father signed over the land to me. It was to protect your future."

No. No. No. She was not going to cry in front of him. Sofia tightened the girth with one last pull and tied off the cinch on the old working saddle she found in the tack room. She was not going to ride in the dark in that one-sided death trap. She was finished with being a lady.

Men acted as if women were weak and couldn't think for themselves. When in reality, they had to work twice as hard and be twice as smart.

Encased in layers of material, she was forced to balance on the side of the horse. The act of giving birth alone should prove how strong women really were.

The soft green-and-pink material was in her way, so she twisted it and tried to figure out the best way to mount without killing herself.

Perhaps she could just rip the top layers away. It was

dark, and she was going straight to the ranch. Air lodged in her throat, not able to move up or down.

The ranch her father gave to Jackson in exchange for her reputation. With one hand on the saddle horn and the other on the back ridge, she pressed her forehead against the side of her horse and cried.

Her father gave away the ranch.

Jackson married her for the ranch.

"Sofia. What are you doing?" At her back, the low and steady baritone voice was less than an arm's length away now.

He had no reason to be emotional. His world was not falling apart.

"Darling, you need to stop. You're going to get yourself killed riding at night."

Wiping her face with one hand, she threw her shoulders back. With a lift to her chin, she turned to face him. The light from the community hall created an outline of his tall frame.

"Don't call me that and don't come any closer. You lied to me! Did you know the whole time?" Taking a deep breath, she tried to calm her breathing. "Did you know who I was? Was this all part of your plan? Ruin me, then force my father to hand over the ranch to you?"

"Whoa!" A harsh expression seized his face. His mouth opened as if he wanted to say something else. He gently wrapped his warm fingers around the exposed flesh on her arm, then he stepped back.

Swallowing hard, she didn't give in to the urge to close her eyes and lean into him. Why had he betrayed her? "I thought we were friends?"

"We were friends, but you lied to me first. You

dressed as a boy. Pretended you didn't know English. Told me you were an orphan."

She wiped at her face again. That seemed a lifetime ago. "I told you I lost my mother and brother. That was not a lie."

He snorted and put some distance between them, turning his back. Good. She didn't want to look at him. Her brain worked better when she didn't see him. She focused on adjusting the stirrup.

He started pacing. Maybe he wasn't as calm as he appeared. "Sofia, I never misled you or lied. You're the one who brought this on yourself."

"Uh." If she had something in hand, she would be tempted to throw it at him. "This is my fault?"

"What did you think would happen when you returned to the ranch? You didn't think anyone would question what you were doing alone with a group of men? Did you really think you'd just be able to waltz back in and your dad would let you run the ranch?"

A sob escaped. She squeezed her eyes shut and turned back to Domino. Jackson stopped in front of her horse and rubbed the flat spot between its eyes. Before she realized what he was doing, he took the reins from her hand.

"Give those back to me." She refused to reach for them. Her brother used to play "keep away" with her. He would laugh every time she jumped to get her item back, but he'd move it out of her reach. She bit down hard on her teeth. *Santiago, why aren't you here?*

"Sofia, you can't ride out alone, in the dark. I wouldn't let Rory, either. It's dangerous."

"I just want to go home." She wanted to ask him if

he even liked her or if it was just about the land. But she was afraid to ask for the truth. She had fallen in love.

Once again her impulsive nature had her jumping in, then dealing with the consequences. With her back to him, she had to ask. "Jackson?" Her throat burned. Silence gripped the night.

"What is it, Sofia?" His voice almost sounded like he cared. Maybe he did. Maybe she overreacted. "I want a real marriage and family. Can we find our way to make this work? If not now, sometime in the future."

"Oh, Sofia." For the first time, she heard a crack in his voice. "I told you this would be a business deal. We're partners in the ranch and raising the horses. But I... I can't be a real husband to you. I buried anything left of my heart with my wife and babies. I don't have anything to give you. The thought of bringing more children into this world. Into a world where I can't protect them? I won't do it."

Her body went agonizingly numb, and she clung to the saddle. She was married to a man who couldn't love her or ever want a family with her.

The irony was not lost on her that future generations were the reason her father wanted her to marry. There would be no grandchildren, ever.

"Let me take you to the house in town. You can stay there for the night, and then we can talk in the morning." He went to a stall and got his stallion. "Right now you're too upset."

"My mother's house. Did you get that in the marriage agreement too?" She bit the inside of her cheek. Now she just sounded petty. *Please, God, don't allow me to become a bitter woman.* "I want to go home."

"It is your home. If nothing else, think about your

horse and your father." He threw a saddle over the large black horse. The animal turned and pressed his muzzle into Jackson's arm.

She hated his calm voice. Her world was collapsing all over again, and he just carried on like everything was fine. "I'm done talking to you."

Great. Now she sounded like an ill-tempered five-year-old. All she needed to do now was stomp her foot.

Reins in hand, he walked over. Stopping next to her, he frowned at the saddle. "How are you going to ride astride in that dress?"

"It's dark, and I didn't think anyone would see me anyway. I'm not getting back in that sidesaddle ever again." She lifted her skirt and put the delicate silk shoe in the worn leather stirrup. When she went to put her weight into it, her foot slipped. Even her shoes were against her.

"Here let me at least help." The warmth of his hands circled her waist.

She wanted to protest and tell him to move away, but she needed him. She hated needing help. Without even a grunt, he lifted her into the saddle.

The monster butterflies in her stomach had run out of room and were looking for an escape.

"I'll take you to your mother's house." With one jump, he was in the saddle.

"Easy when you're allowed to wear pants." She muttered the words under her breath, but the way he looked at her told her he had heard her.

"You know I don't have a problem with you in pants," he said. After turning in a circle, his horse leaped to the door, eager to go.

She pressed her heels into the Appaloosa's ribs. "What did you tell everyone?"

"Now you're worried about how leaving early looks? We're newlyweds who were just reunited. They don't expect us to stay long."

Now the heat climbed her neck. How could she walk into church on Sunday knowing her marriage was a complete lie?

Chapter Twenty-One

Rafael De Zavala filled the stall door. "Sofia, it has been a month. You need to talk to your husband."

Without looking at him, she continued brushing the mare. She paused when she felt a kick against the horse's extended ribs. The unborn foal was active today.

"Sofia, look at me." She pushed her flat wide-rimmed hat off her head, and it hung against her short braid. Maybe if she ignored him he'd leave.

It had worked with Jackson. After their reception four weeks ago, she decided to go about her business on the ranch. If he wanted to talk to her, he knew where to find her.

She had new clothes made. Split skirts and cropped jackets made it easier to work on the ranch.

Hand on the mare, she checked her pulse. The foal would be coming soon. It was the last baby of the season.

"There was a... What is happening between you?" Her father didn't seem to get the hint that she didn't want to talk about her marriage. "You never eat meals together. He sleeps in the bunkhouse. How will I get any grandchildren if you don't even talk to one another?"

Snorting, she shook her head. "He's not a prized stallion that will just do your bidding. No matter how much you paid him."

"Sofia de Zavala! That is inappropriate speech for a young lady."

She gave the pregnant mare one last pat before pushing her way past her father. "Well, I'm a wedded woman now. You saw to that."

"But I don't understand. When I spoke to him, and the men riding with you, he liked you. I thought he'd treat you well. What happened?"

It felt good to slam the brush into the bucket. She spun to face her father. "You offered a man a ranch to marry me. Who would turn that down?" This was why she had avoided her father. The anger had been simmering, and now it boiled over. "So now that we aren't following your orders, you're upset?"

"I'm not upset. I'm concerned. Don't you want a real marriage and a family? You will not get that by living apart."

Hands on her hips, she stood in the middle of the stall and stared at her father. The only family she had left. This was it. Because of her marriage, the De Zavala family would come to an end.

"He doesn't want to be my husband." A sob tore from her throat. She buried her face in her hands. "He won't—" a deep painful hiccup "—have children with me."

Arms pulled her into a tight hug. *"Mija."* His hand stroked her hair. "Shhh."

She shook her head. He didn't understand. Her husband blamed her for breaking his vow to the woman he loved. He hated her.

"We will fix this. Do you want to end the marriage?"

The gossips would love that. "What about the ranch?"

"Congress voted to protect the land rights of any grants held by men loyal to the new Texas. The ranch remains safe. He can be paid off. We don't need him anymore if you want to be free."

"Shouldn't I be included in this conversation?" Jackson stood a step outside the door. His big stallion was next to him.

Her heart fell to the bottom of her stomach. They hadn't talked since the night he made sure she was safe at her mother's house. She pulled at the edge of her cropped jacket, and took a deep breath. There was no reason for her to feel guilty.

She wasn't the one who misled him. Okay, she did, but that was before she realized what he actually meant.

Her father shifted to the side, blocking her view of Jackson. "My daughter is upset. You didn't tell me you would not even make an attempt at being a real husband. I—"

"Papi." Resting her hand on his shoulder, she moved to face her husband. "I think Jackson and I need to work this out."

The men held a hard stare for several heartbeats. "Please, Papi."

He jerked his stubborn chin down. "*Sí*. Don't mistake this. She is my daughter and my most precious treasure. I will see her happy. Whatever it takes." With that her father left the barn.

"Jackson, I—"

"Sofia, I have to apologize. I shouldn't have married

you. I thought we could… I don't know what I thought." He closed the space between them but left enough that it might as well have been a canyon. "Do you want an annulment?"

She wanted to yell no, but her throat closed out any words or air. All she could do was look at him. She was married to this gorgeous man who had treated her with respect on the trail, but he wasn't hers. She wanted him to be her husband. She wanted him to love her. It wasn't fair to him that her feelings changed. She wanted more than he had offered.

No! But that word had to be swallowed down. "I don't know." His green eyes penetrated right through her heart. She held her breath.

A nod was the only response she got. After a few minutes that felt like hours of silence, he cleared his throat. "I like your new clothes. They fit better than the boy's garb, but they are more practical than the dress."

She nodded. "The boots you gave me are a perfect fit."

His head bobbed up and down, mirroring hers. Silence lingered, filling the space. The stallion took a step toward her, lowering his neck.

"Hey, big boy." She rubbed his jaw as he nudged her in the chest with his wide forehead.

"He always liked you. Heard you rode him while I was in San Antonio." Low and rough, his voice tickled her spine.

"We got to know each other. He's a fine boy. Aren't you?" She rubbed his favorite spot under his jaw.

"Will you be staying here?"

"If you want me to." He led Dughall to the post and

cross tied him. "Sofia, I'm not sure how to make this work."

"We could start by talking to each other." She carried the bucket full of grooming supplies to him as he removed the saddle and blanket.

"What you want? A normal marriage? I can't do that."

"I want to live on the ranch and work with you as a partner. I want a family. Not necessarily today, but I need to know it will be a possibility one day."

"How can I forgive myself or ever forget the vow I made to Lilly? How can I go on and…" He turned away from her.

She wanted to reach out and touch him, to reassure him, but everything in his tense muscles screamed *stay away.*

"Sofia, how can I go on with another family while they are dead?" His voice was so jagged it hurt to listen.

"Do you think they are still in those graves or free with God?" She bit her lip.

Talking to him about his loss wasn't fair. How could she understand? "I'm sorry. I just hate that you can't forgive yourself when God has already taken care of them. They aren't here with you. God has them." Tears hung in her eyelashes. "You're punishing yourself by not allowing me to love you. What if I'm part of the plan God has for you?"

"My job was to protect them. My family was killed by men I brought into our home. I went off to the field, and they came back to steal everything we had. While I was thinking how hot and hungry I was, they were being murdered for things we owned." He turned to her, the green in his eyes burning. "I tracked those men down and turned them over to the law, but it didn't help. It didn't take away the nightmares of my children crying out for me."

His hand gripped the top of Dughall's neck as if it were a lifeline. "Tell me, how can I go on and live a happy life with a new family? I don't deserve it." His breath came in hard. "You do deserve a husband who can give that to you, so maybe ending this marriage is the right thing to do."

Placing her hand on his stiff back, she swallowed down her tears.

"No." Words played in her head, which ones would help him understand? "I do deserve a real husband, but I think God can free you. It doesn't mean you don't love Lilly and the children. I'm not asking you to forget them. They will always be a part of you. They will always be your family."

"I know we had a business agreement, but I didn't really understand what that meant for my future. I just want to have a chance at a real connection with you as a wife. But I don't think God wants you to stop living."

He shook his head. "The more time I spend with you, the more the memories start to fade. I don't want them to fade."

"I don't want to replace them, but why can't I be your future?"

He narrowed his gaze. "That might be the problem. I don't see a future. How can I when they don't have one?"

Tears fell from her lashes. "I can't believe God has abandoned you with no plans for a full life."

He started to rub down Dughall. The birds outside called out to each other. The horse shifted his weight and flicked his tail at a fly. Jackson rested his hand on the powerful rump.

"Do you think my purpose is to love you?"

Blood rushed her ears and her heart went still. "I don't know. That would have to be between you and God."

"He doesn't talk to me anymore. Or maybe I quit listening." With a pat to his stallion, he turned to her, his wife. "I know I can't live this way anymore. I'm torn up inside. Sofia, there is a part of me that wants what you offer, but the guilt won't just go away. I can't just toss out my promise to Lilly because something better came along. How do I have both? How do I know what God wants from me?"

She shrugged. "I wish I knew. You could meet with Pastor Phillips. He helped me many times. Sometimes just praying and being still. I think God talks to us in so many ways that we miss." Not able to hold back any longer, she moved closer to him and took his hand. "If you need to end the marriage—" *do not cry* "—we can look at that."

"Do you want to?" His eyes searched for answers she didn't have at the moment.

"How do we end something that never started?"

A half snort was followed by a lopsided grin. "If I'm ever going to marry again and have another family, you're the only one I would want to do it with. You're the reason this is so difficult."

"I'm sorry to cause you stress, but maybe it will move us in the right direction. My father always said that the things you have to fight the hardest for have the most value."

She could fight for this marriage if there was hope. "How do we move forward?"

"Slowly." He untied Dughall and led him to the far back stall. "How about I escort you to church Sunday?"

"So now that we're married you want to court me?" She followed him and waited outside the stall as he settled the stallion in for the night.

"We need to start somewhere, might as well be at church." Stepping out of the stall, he put his hands in his pockets. His eyes darted around the barn. The evening light softened his face.

"Will you join us for dinner?" Was she just extending the pain by thinking they could be more than two strangers working on the ranch together?

"Not sure if your father wants me in the house tonight." He put his hand on the center of her back and guided her out the barn doors. The urge to lean into him tightened her nerves.

Jackson seemed to realize he was touching her, and pulled his hand back as if fire had lapped at him. She bit her lip to ensure that she didn't cry.

He turned and slid the barn door closed. Hands back in his pockets, out of her reach, they walked into the setting sun.

It seemed a lifetime ago that she was sneaking in to ride his horse. "There are days I really miss Tiago." As they headed toward the house, she wanted to reach for him, any touch to reassure her that he was here.

"I rode out to the five hundred yesterday, and you weren't there. Have you been going to the east pasture?" Great, their first evening together and she was nagging him about where he was.

"I was riding over the area. I want to get a good grasp

of the land and what kind of improvements we can implement." He picked up a lose rock on the path to the house and threw it out into the tree line. "I do take the management of the ranch seriously."

Not knowing what else to say she nodded. *God, please give me the wisdom to know what to say and do to make this relationship be what You want.*

She knew what she wanted, but what if God or even Jackson wanted something else?

Chapter Twenty-Two

Hammering echoed throughout the small valley. The roof on the new house would be finished today. Jackson stepped through the door he just hung. The front room was open and large. A rock fireplace dominated one of the outside walls. Later he would add more walls if she wanted to separate the rooms.

The house he was building for this bride he didn't want was almost ready to live in.

For weeks now the cowboys had been taking shifts to help build the two-story farmhouse. The German builder in town had helped a great deal. It was different from the Spanish ranchero, but he had modeled it after a house in San Antonio she had liked.

He stepped onto the deep porch.

Rory jumped from the low roof over the porch. "Boss, the house is looking great. Sofia is going to love it. Any woman would." He took a scoop of water from the bucket and poured it over his sweaty face.

Jackson looked at the two-story farmhouse they had been working on in secret. Sofia might not have a real husband, but she deserved a home. It was the least he could do for her.

There was stonework and details in the extra rooms that needed to be finished, but overall it was ready. It was time to start ordering furniture, but he wasn't sure if she would want to do that for herself.

He pushed a small rock around with his boot. "Do you think I should let her order the furniture?"

"You know I thought you should have told her about the house from day one. Doesn't she question all this time away? You're working the ranch and building a house. Does she even get to see you?"

The plan was to spend as little time with her as possible. The more time he spent with her, the harder it was to keep his vow to Lilly and their children. "She's fine."

Just a few days ago they had gone to church together and sitting next to her had felt so right, the guilt came back with a vengeance. The hole in his stomach grew. This back and forth was killing him, and he was sure she was just as confused.

He pulled out the worn envelope from the inside pocket of his vest. Lilly's parents had replied to his letter. It arrived four days ago.

Unopened, it stayed in his thoughts. Would they be angry? Heartbroken all over again because of his lack of faithfulness?

In the days following his wedding to Sofia, he had written them with heavy guilt. Hoping that restating his vow to stay true to Lilly's memory would help him keep Sofia out of his heart and head.

But the pastor had preached about God's forgiveness and the arrogance of not accepting it. Was it some warped sense of self-importance and pride that kept him from God's forgiveness and peace?

His heart was still a battleground.

"Boss?" Rory said his name like he'd said it a few times already.

Jackson nodded without a clue to what he was agreeing to. He should open the letter and read it. Take the hit. Accept their disappointment and grief.

He had let them down. He had let Lilly down.

A touch on his shoulder startled him. Rory stood just inches away. "You okay?"

No. "Yeah."

"Me and the boys are heading back to the ranch. It's about time for dinner. Are you coming?"

"I'll be there in a bit." With a narrow gaze, Rory studied him for a moment, then with a nod turned and followed the others out.

The envelope sat heavy in his hands. The past twisted his gut. He had to read the letter that was covered in the blood of his own mistakes. It's what he needed to put his world back on a balanced scale.

"Jackson?" The voice was so soft he looked up, expecting to see Lilly. Sitting on Domino, Sofia stared at the house. Raw and bare, it wasn't ready for her yet.

Past her, the retreating backs of the cowboys meant they had no one to buffer. It was just the two of them. How had he missed her riding into the yard?

So young and small, she sat on the horse with confidence. It was easy to believe she thrived on the cattle drive. The ragtagged boy was gone. So was the princess bride. She wore a fitted cropped jacket that matched some kind of flared pants that hit her at midboot.

The boots he had given her the day they had arrived

in San Antonio. She had found a way to merge her two halves. Why couldn't his heart keep her as a friend?

Sofia had his world so off-kilter he didn't know what was up. "What are you doing out here alone?"

"Looking for my husband. I went out to the five hundred again. When I asked about you, they all stopped talking."

Her gaze moved over the house, then came back to him. "You're building a house?"

"How did you know where to find me?" He sat still, trying to determine the best plan of action. That was the problem; he didn't have one.

"I cornered Diego. Since he is the youngest, I was able to threaten him within an inch of his life, and he believed me. But all I could get out of him was that you had a secret project he wasn't allowed to talk about."

His gut clenched at the sight of tears rolling down her face.

"You're building us a house?" A few rapid blinks, and she brought her focus back to his face. "My brain has been going crazy trying to figure out what you would be doing over here in secret. A house, for us?"

Standing, he dusted off his pants. He didn't want her to read more into this project than he meant. "I'm trying to figure out how to give you what you need while keeping my vow to Lilly and her parents. You deserve a home of your own at the least."

She swung her leg over the saddle and hopped to the ground. Her movement was natural and light.

He could watch her forever. He shook his head. Not helping. He started to move toward her but stopped. He slipped the letter back inside his vest. Now was not the time to read it.

"It's beautiful." Eyes on the house, she walked past him and stopped on the top step.

"Remember the house you saw in San Antonio? The one on the corner you liked so much?"

"Yes. I see it."

"There is still a great deal of details that need to be worked out, but it's almost ready." He followed her but stopped on the bottom step. It almost put them eye to eye. She was slightly above him.

Turned her back to him, she faced the house. The sun hung low in the sky, highlighting the red in her dark hair. Her braid was finally getting a little longer. Lying flat against her neck, it barely touched her back. His fingers moved to trace the silky strands, but she spun back to him.

Eyes wide, she looked at his hand hanging in midair. "What are you doing?"

Keeping silent, he crossed his arms over his chest.

Her eyes searched his face. How could he love someone so different from Lilly?

Love. He couldn't love her. But he did and it was a problem. His heart was faithless.

She reached up to him. Gentle fingers brushed the stubble on his jaw. He took her hand in his, lowering it away from his skin, and looked down at the small hand lost in his. They weren't as beat up as they had been on the drive, when she was Tiago, but they still had the evidence of ranch work.

He caressed her skin. Her hands were so unlike his, unlike Lilly's. Everything about her was different from Lilly.

With a couple of steps, she was on the very edge of the porch. "Can I kiss you?" Her voice was small.

It made his heart hurt that he had done that to her. He needed to fix this.

He gave her a smile. "A kiss would be nice."

She looked at him as though she'd already walked the twisted canyon of his heart and found the way to its center. As she leaned in, he closed his eyes. He needed to hide from her, but he feared it was too late.

She was inside him, trying to bring life to a dried-out heart.

The gentleness of her first touch rattled his walls. His fist clenched at his side, not touching her. Needing to keep some sort of distance.

Tentative at first, her fingers slid into the hair at the base of his neck. He couldn't hold back any longer and wrapped his hands around her small waist. He was careful not to pull her closer as her lips explored his.

The need to be loved burned slow and deep in both of them. She deserved to be loved, completely and honestly.

He didn't.

Maybe he did. She believed he did. He relaxed his hands.

The world slipped away, and he gave in to the kiss, gave in to her. Time ceased to exist.

Not able to breathe, he had to pull back. Her hands slipped away and regret he shouldn't feel took hold. What he needed to feel was guilt for enjoying it, not regret that it was coming to an end.

The inky lashes surrounding her eyes fluttered briefly before she closed them. She took a step away from him. He clenched his traitorous fists again. He should be reaching for her.

She cleared her throat and walked to the door, caressing the stained-glass inlay as if touching a newborn.

"The German craftsman in town made this door, and when I saw it, I thought of you in the early mornings on the cattle drive."

Her fingers traced the rays of yellow, orange and red surrounded by the cool blues of an endless Texas sky.

"It's stunning." She faced him. "I've been trying to avoid it, but I think we need to stay honest, so I'm going to ask about the letter you were staring at when I rode up. You put it away. Is it from family?"

"Yes."

"What's the letter?"

"Nothing."

"You didn't even hear me you were staring at it so hard." She moved to him again, placing her small hand over his heart, over the letter. "Please, no more secrets. I'd rather deal straight on with the truth."

Slipping his hand under hers, he pulled out the letter. "It's from my in-laws, Lilly's parents. I wrote them after we got married." His jaw popped a couple of times. "They had been asking me to return home. We grew up next to each other."

"Is that why you wrote them?"

He shook his head. "I wanted to let them know I had married. To reassure them I had not forgotten my vows to Lilly. Even though I had to marry, I would be faithful to her memory." He looked at the letter, not able to meet Sofia's gaze.

"Then I'll head home and let you read it in private." She passed him going down the steps.

He caught her hand. "Do you want to see the house?

There's still a lot of work to do. But it's close to being able to move in."

"Are you moving in with me?"

"I don't know. I don't seem to know my own mind right now."

The light in her eyes died. "I think there are too many people in this house for me to move in." Her hand came up and caressed his jaw. Standing on her toes, she reached up and gently pressed her lips against his. A slight shift, and a cold empty space separated them.

Sofia's smile was slight and sad. He never thought of a smile as being sad.

With a nod, she pointed to his letter. "Read what they have to say to you. Staring at an unopened envelope won't help. I'll be at my father's when you're ready."

The confident stride that took her back to her horse reminded him of Tiago. She had found her place in the world, and now he was the loose end in her life.

God, what is Your plan for me? Will this guilt ever go away? Should it? Pastor Phillips said forgiveness was his as soon as he asked for it. And without it? His life would remain stagnant. Missing out on the fulfillment of God's promise.

God would forgive him, but how did he forgive himself? Would Lilly's parents ever forgive him? Holding one end of letter, he slit the other end open. He forced his breath out. Sucked it back in until his lungs and nostrils burned.

With great care he pulled out the folded sheets of paper. Three pages. They had filled three pages.

Dearest Jackson…

Chapter Twenty-Three

Two days and not a word from Jackson. Now that everyone knew that the secret was out and she had seen the house, they gave her hourly updates.

He was getting the house ready before he came for her. How long was she going to lie to herself? He knew where she was and that she was waiting for him.

The fanged butterflies had started a colony in her stomach when she thought of possible words and advice he might have read in the letter. The letter from Lilly's parents. The fluttering rolled into a stampede.

Unable to sleep, she threw on a pair of pants and an old shirt that had belonged to her brother and made her way to the barn by the light of the moon. Clouds were passing over, and shadows stretched out the darkness.

Rena would be the last mare to foal this season. Thunder rolled far off into the distance, so they might miss it.

With the full moon and the change in weather, tonight was probably the night. Mares loved picking the worse time to foal. Walking through the barn, she looked in on the few that were boarded for the night, mares with babies by their side. There were no wranglers on watch, which was odd given they still had a mare in foal.

Who had been assigned to watch tonight?

This was Rena's first foal. Entering the stall, Sofia talked in a low soft voice. The young mare tossed her head and flicked her tail as she turned in a circle. One direction, then another.

Stepping up against her, she ran her hand along the mare's extended ribs. She focused on the mare and locked away all of the personal worries that had been clogging her thoughts.

The smell of fresh hay and the feel of the silky damp coat anchored her in the moment. The palomino mare snorted and dropped down to the ground. She rolled her body into a sitting position then moved back to her side stretching her neck and groaning.

She was definitely having contractions. Another gripped her large body. The soft nostrils flared with each heavy breath.

Looking at the straw on the floor, it looked as if she had been up and down several times. The mare tried to stand again, but struggled and fell back.

"Easy girl, we'll figure out what's wrong. I'm right here." A muffled snort and gentle nicker seemed to Sofia as equine gratitude. Stroking the quivering muscles, she thought about the best plan of action. Her father and Estevan were in town.

She didn't know where Jackson stayed at night, and even if she did, there was not enough time to get him.

And whoever was on duty had left his post. Not good. When she found out, they would no longer have a job with De Zavala.

The mare grunted again and pawed at the straw with her front hooves. The labor wasn't moving along like it should. Even for a mare's first foal, something was off. Sofia's forehead wrinkled when she checked the mare. "How long have you been like this, girl?"

Horses went through the final stage of labor pretty fast, twenty minutes at the most. An hour would be an eternity for a laboring horse and dangerous. She glanced at the stall door.

At the moment she was alone. In years past, she had helped with foaling until her mother put a stop to it. Checking the mare, she took a deep breath.

This momma and baby needed her to think and act quickly. There was no time to go get help. She sighed, pushing the fear away.

So silly to feel helpless after all she'd been through. Hand on the mare's tight belly, she soothed Rena as she moved in to check the position of the foal.

The mare kicked out. Sofia's heart skipped a beat, aching for the animal.

"Sorry, Rena," she whispered. After a few seconds of deep breaths, the mare's ribs mirrored her action, calming them both. "I think we're running out of time." Talking to the horse was better than talking to herself.

Easing her hands toward the mare's braided tail, Sofia checked the progress of the unborn foal. What she found confirmed her fears. She needed a knife.

She rushed into the tack room. There should be an emergency bag somewhere. She found the bag buried behind extra pieces of leather.

Returning to the mare's stall, Sofia kept calm, not wanting to stress the mare any more than she was already.

The wind banged against the siding outside. The storm had arrived. One last deep inhale, and she started cutting through the red mass that blocked the foal from being born.

Rain started to tap on the roof. Any light from the moon was gone. The only light was her lantern.

The door slammed, and wind rushed into the building. Someone had entered the barn. The wrangler must have finally returned.

She bit back the ugly words she wanted to yell at him. Right now she needed to focus as she made the cut, waiting for success or failure. Pulling the mass free, the tip of a tiny black hoof appeared.

Sofia bit her lip and leaned forward, resisting the urge to pull on the small hoof. A tiny black muzzle followed. "Good girl, come on, one more push."

"Sofia, what's wrong?" Jackson kneeled next to her. A small shoulder slipped out, and suddenly a dark long-legged baby lay in the straw. The wet, dark coat was covered in a thin layer of white. Steam rose from its warm body as it met the cool air.

"The foal was blocked. I don't know how long she was in labor." She kept her focus on the foal, willing it to breathe.

Jackson gently placed his hand over the tiny rib cage. The biggest smile spread across his face. He nodded. "There's a racing heartbeat."

She had done it, helped deliver a breathing baby. She checked the mare. Rena was now sitting up. Arching her neck, she nudged at her foal.

Giving the mare a pat, Jackson stood and held out his hand to Sofia. "Come on, the mare looks alert. We can watch from the corridor so momma here can take care of her baby."

Sofia watched as the little one shook its head and tried to stand. "It's a filly. A little girl." Why was she crying?

Taking his hand, she stood. Her legs gave out, and he caught her as she stumbled. "Sorry. I didn't realize I had no feeling in my—"

"No need to apologize. You just single-handedly saved a foal and mare. Where's Diego? He had mare watch tonight."

He held her against him maybe a little longer than needed. The warmth in his hands supported her, comforted her.

"No one was in the barn or even close by." Taking a breath, she straightened. A little separation was wise, not what her heart wanted but what her head needed. "Thank you."

His arms tightened before completely releasing her. His rumbling chuckle filled the quiet stall. "What are you thanking me for? You did all the work."

A loud grunt from the stall brought their attention back to the mare. With her front legs extended, she heaved her body up, followed by her back legs, breaking the connection from her young one. Standing on all fours, she shook off the straw and turned to her foal. With a soft nicker she licked his face. Mimicking his dam, his long front legs pulled him up in an effort to stand. His back legs pushed but wobbled, and he collapsed back down. Spindle legs spread as the filly shook her head.

The desire to help the foal stand had Sofia moving to the baby. Jackson caught her arm. "We should give them a little bit of time before we interfere. If she can get up and feed on her own, it'll make her stronger."

She nodded and followed him out.

They stood next to each other on the other side of the half door as they silently watched the foal struggle to stand. After a few attempts she made it, and went to her mother for her first meal.

"Look, she's got it." Jackson's hushed voice was full of awe. His gaze stayed on the mother and baby.

She studied his profile. Her stomach rolled. Would she ever have her own child with green eyes? Her arms ached to hold a baby, but it wasn't fair to put that burden on him if he didn't want any more children. She couldn't imagine the pain of losing a whole family, babies that were just learning about life.

"Jackson—"

"Sofia—"

They spoke at the same time. He looked at her, then turned away. She touched his arm. "I'm sorry. What did you want to say?"

He pulled a splinter from the corner of the worn half door. She loved his hands, capable of so much strength but gentle enough to handle a newborn.

She bit her lip. She needed to stop her thoughts from going in the direction of babies. She wanted to soothe his hurts, but they were beyond her abilities. That had to be between God and him.

Wrapping her arms around her middle, she turned her attention back to the scene in the stall. If she stayed married to Jackson, this might be the closest she ever got to motherhood. Could she be happy with this?

Closing her eyes, she prayed in the silence. A peace

washed through her, taking the fear and sadness. God had this.

The mare licked at the wobbly foal. After getting the first meal down, she started getting curious about her new world.

Walking over to them, she raised her soft muzzle, trying to reach Sofia. "I think she wants to tell you hi. Maybe she thinks you're her family."

The soft nose nudged her hand. Giggling, she rubbed the filly behind the ears. Jackson ran his hand along her back. "She is going to be a beauty. Good thing you were here. I might have been too late."

He left her and went to the tack room. In short order he was back with supplies to clean out the stall.

Opening the door, he greeted the mare. She sniffed at him and the tools he carried, then nickered to her baby. Sofia stepped in and gently kept the filly out of Jackson's way as he cleared all the evidence of the difficult birth.

"Why were you here at this hour?"

A shrug warned her that he was hiding something important. He shrugged when he didn't want her to ask questions.

Should she honor his wish or push him? At this point, she deserved some sort of answer, but she didn't want to upset him if he wasn't ready.

He eased out of the stall, and the tiny horse on her new legs tried to follow him. Sofia gently held her. "Rena, we might have a go-getter on our hands."

Jackson came back empty-handed. "She's going to be smart. We'll have to stay one step ahead of her."

Together they checked her legs and eyes. "Thank you for being here. When you walked in, I knew it was going to be okay." She smiled to reassure him. His eyes were heavy with sadness, but he gave her a smile, a smile that didn't reach his eyes.

He went back to checking the newest addition to the ranch, his head down. "I couldn't sleep. I was working on the house when I heard the storm in the distance. Mares like foaling in the worst weather, so I thought I'd ride over and check on her."

He took off his hat and pushed his hair back. "I couldn't get you off my mind, either."

Dread rolled over her heart. This was it. They were over, not that there was ever a "them." How could it hurt so much to lose something she never truly possessed?

"I read the letter." He stroked the foal's neck, and the little ears flicked back and forth. "Several times. And I have done a lot of praying. More than I have in all of my life up till now."

He cleared his throat. "There was so much guilt. I love you but... I hated myself for loving you."

Her heart stopped.

He looked up, right into her eyes. "I've been fighting this since the beginning of the cattle drive, but I was hanging on to Lilly and our babies. Not from love but from guilt. The night of the stampede, when I thought I lost you, I knew it was more, but couldn't deal with it."

"Jackson." Her heart burned, heat searing her throat. "I don't—"

He cupped her face, his callused thumb wiping at a tear she didn't even realize had fallen. "Shhh. It's going to be all right."

The foal moved to her mother, looking for another meal. "Come outside with me. Remember the first time we met? It was right here." Dughall was standing in the large reinforced stall. He stuck his head over the half door. "Want to go for a midnight ride? We'll go slow." He looked out the doors. "The storm was loud, but it's gone."

She laughed as she rubbed the stallion's soft muzzle. "I told you I would ride him one day." He still had the saddle on from when Jackson had ridden him to the barn.

"You did. You didn't wait for me."

She looked back over her shoulder and gave him her best shrug. "We were married, so he was mine. Maybe that's why I agreed to marry you. I like winning." She didn't know what he wanted to say, but if this was the last night of their marriage, she wanted to make the most of it, of being with him.

He opened the door and pulled the leather reins from the hook. "So you want to ride with me?"

He swung up into the saddle and held his hand out to her. Taking it, she let him pull her up.

"You know I saw him before I saw you, and I have to confess it was love at first sight. He stole my heart."

"Yeah, he does that." They stepped out into the night. They carefully plodded along the path that had been beaten down with all the activity around the house he was building.

They rode in silence. She laid her cheek against his broad back. The beating of his heart seemed to follow the rhythm of Dughall's steps.

"Want to see the house?" The sky had already cleared, and the large moon lit their way. "I have several lamps there."

She nodded, enjoying being so close to him.

They came to a stop in front of a simple two stalled

shelter behind the house. He held out his arm for her to dismount, and he followed. This time he took the saddle off the stallion and turned him loose in the paddock.

His hand slipped down and took hers, their fingers entwined.

"I'm not always good with words, and I've been working on what to say to make it right."

She swallowed as they made their way to the back porch. Her heart raced, and a part of her wanted to tell him not to say anything. She wanted to enjoy this night and not worry about tomorrow.

He got a lantern off the post. "Mary, Lilly's mother, wrote a long letter." On the porch he had a bench. It was crude, really two cedar stumps with a wide board sitting on top of them. It offered a place to rest, a place to sit and talk with Jackson.

"She opened the letter with, 'It is well!' I expected her to rebuke me for marrying again. So that confused me, until she told me about the Shulamite woman in 2 Kings. She had lost her family, but she put her faith that God was good and all was well. No matter how bad life got, as long as she was with God all was well."

Shivering, she wasn't sure it was the air, but the feeling of her prayers from earlier being answered.

He took her hand. "Are you cold?"

Even though she didn't respond, he stood and took off his long duster. He wrapped it around her, and she inhaled, surrounded by his scent.

She looked up at him. "That's an incredible faith."

He turned from her gaze and looked out over the moonlit hills. The smell of fresh rain filled the air. "In the letter, she wrote that Lilly and our children are well and loved. She was sure that Lilly would be upset with me for punishing myself."

He shoved his hands in his pockets and lowered his head. "She gave her blessing and said that I should not just live, but laugh and love and…" He rubbed his face before turning back to Sofia.

"The only way I can explain it is that a heavy weight has been lifted from my shoulders. God… God has this. He has Lilly and the children. He has me if I'm willing to turn it all over to Him."

"And I have you. If you still want me." He walked past her to the edge of the porch. She wasn't sure what to say, but the need to reach out to him was overwhelming. She needed to let him know she was here for him.

"Love is…" Without turning back to her, he tossed his hat onto the bench and he ran his fingers through his hair. "I don't have the words."

He spun on his heels in an almost angry energy. He braced his hands on her upper arms. A warmth burned in his green eyes, causing gold sparks to dance. His gaze searched her face. "I feel whole again. I don't understand, but somehow love gets bigger."

In front of her, he went down on one knee. "Sofia de Zavala McCreed—" he smiled at the end of her name "—you make life worth living again." He licked his lips. "I love you."

She gasped, one hand covering her mouth. Not a single body part worked. He had actually said the words to her. Words she thought she could live without.

Tears burned her eyes.

"It doesn't take away from the love I have for others. It just grows." He gave her a lopsided grin.

"I don't even know what I'm rambling about now." He took one small hand in both of his.

"What I want to say is… Sofia De Zavala McCreed, will you marry me again?"

Pausing, he took a deep breath. "Marry me not because of a ruined reputation but because I love you. Not to save your ranch, but because I need your love to save my heart. Not to be your business partner but to be your husband, a real husband. Not even for Dughall, but he's yours."

His green eyes sparkled with love. "Everything of mine is yours, including my heart. Marry me so we can have a future of love together with a family to share that love with. A future God intended for us."

She fell to her knees in front of him and cupped his stubbled jaw. "I will marry you today and every day for the rest of this life we have together. I love you, Jackson McCreed. I think I started loving you the minute I saw you working that big stallion of yours."

Now the tears fell without hesitation, without apologies or regrets. "My heart was completely yours since the day I walked back into camp after the stampede. When I was being washed down the river, I had one thought—to get back to you."

He stood and lifted her off her knees. Leaning in, he took possession of her lips, otherwise she might not have stopped talking.

After he completely took her breath away, he rested his forehead on hers.

"God has freed me to love you, and I want it all. Will you give me your all?"

Her mouth widened, and her heart pushed against its limits. "If you give me your all. I want all of you, your children, your future, your past, all of it. I love you, Jackson McCreed. God knew what He was doing when He put us on that cattle drive together."

"I'm not sure that was God, little rebel, but He definitely had us. Now we have each other."

Forever and more.

Epilogue

Jackson pulled on the reins. A bucket lay on its side at the well. Water soaked the grass. His heart slammed against his chest.

Kicking his horse, he charged up the hill to their home. Rory followed close behind.

"Jackson?"

He didn't want to think about why the bucket would be down here. He'd told her to stay in the house. Jackson needed to see Sofia. In a few weeks, she would be delivering their child.

Fear made thought impossible. Cresting the hill, he saw her. She looked at him and tried to smile. Lying across the steps, she had something bundled in her apron. Her hair was a mess, and dirt streaked her dress.

Dismounting Dughall, Jackson rushed to her. "Rory! Get Rosita."

He didn't bother to check if the cowboy had left. His whole world was in front of him on the steps.

He fell to his knees. "Are you hurt?" He searched her body for signs of injury. "What were you doing down the hill?"

"Hello." She pushed her hair back with a trembling hand. "I tried to get in the house before you came back, but…"

Not letting her explain, he picked her up and forced the door open. "You weren't to leave the house. You promised."

"I never promised. You just got all bossy. I needed some water, but your son decided he couldn't wait any longer."

His gut twisted. Gently, he laid her on the bed. Leaning forward, he pressed his lips to her forehead.

She was so strong. Closing his eyes, he started breathing again. A soft cry came from the apron.

Shifting a little, she lowered the blue material wrapped around the baby. Not just a baby, their son.

"Your son was in a hurry to get into the world." She looked back at the tiny bundle in her arms. "Rafael De Zavala McCreed, this is your papi."

He was a father again. Instead of fear, he was filled with peace and awe. Carefully, he touched the newborn. "Papi. I like it." It would be easier. "He's already taking after his mother. I think I'm in trouble."

With a mess of thick black hair, his son smiled at him. Yes, his heart was gone. "He's beautiful, Sofia. As beautiful as his momma." He pressed his lips to her forehead. This woman amazed him.

"You're not mad at me for going to the well?"

He laughed. "Would it make a difference? You keep me wondering what's going to happen next. The old bull in the pasture is more predictable than you."

"That bull is loco. No one ever knows what… Oh."

He laughed, pressing his forehead to hers. With their baby boy in their arms, the world was right. He wanted to live in this moment forever. God had gifted him with more blessings than he could count. Blessings he still wasn't sure he deserved, but he would treasure them. His wife and son were a part of this great land that he now belonged to.

"Mija!"

"Sofia?"

She chuckled. "The calvary has arrived." Her soft voice was close to his ear. He didn't want to move.

A small group crowded around the bedroom door. Rosita turned on the men standing behind her and pushed Rafael, Rory and Estevan back into the hallway. She ordered Maria to get sheets and blankets from the cedar chest. "Out. Out. I will call you when she and the little one are ready for visitors."

She marched to the bed and shooed him away. "You, too."

"But…" He didn't want to leave her side. "I brought them…"

"Yes. Yes. Now go." She started moving things around. "I need water. Go."

"I'm going, but I won't be far." One last kiss and he was pushed out the door. He turned to get another look at his family. "I love you."

She smiled. "I know. I love you, too."

The door closed. He just stood there.

"Is she well?" Her father's voice had a raw edge.

Jackson faced the men standing in the room, each looking a little lost. Somewhere along the trail in Texas, he had gathered a family.

God had plans for him, even when he'd thought there was nothing left to live for.

"She's Sofia." Jackson grinned at them. Joy was his

again, because of that headstrong rancher's daughter. "Apparently giving birth alone at the well didn't cause her any problems."

They laughed. Estevan slapped him on the back. "Of course. Your woman took on a pirate's challenge and won. Something so ordinary as giving birth would not phase our Two Bit."

De Zavala gasped. Jackson needed to change the topic of discussion. Some of the details on the trail they'd never shared with her father. Some things a father was better off not knowing for the sake of his heart. "Maria needs water."

Without hesitation, Rory and Estevan rushed out the door.

"Your daughter is a strong woman. Stronger than many men I know."

Her father walked up to him and threw his arms around Jackson. "I'm proud to call you *son*. I couldn't have found a better man for my Sofia if I had searched all of America and Mexico."

He hugged him tighter. "When my plan was to marry her to an American in Galveston, she fought me. I told her she would thank me when she held her first son. It seemed God had better plans and now I find I'm the one that must thank you and her for the gift of my grandson."

Jackson swallowed hard, pushing down the burn that hung in his throat. The urge to cry was a bit unmanning, but then his father-in-law stepped back and the stoic man had tears trailing down his cheeks.

That was it. Jackson's own tears spilled over. He looked around the room. He needed something to do.

The door behind him opened.

Rosita smiled. "She is ready to show off your son."

Jackson measured his steps so he wouldn't rush to her side and scare the baby.

Sofia sat up in the bed. Scrubbed and cleaned, she had her hair pulled back in a neat braid. Her face shone with joy. In her arms, wrapped in the blanket the church ladies had given her, lay his son.

She looked as if it was just another day to visit. He went to his knees once he reached the side of the bed.

Her long black lashes hid her eyes as she looked at their son. "Do you want to hold him?"

He had no words, but somehow managed a nod. She shifted and slid the precious little body into his arms.

"Hi, Rafael. I'm your papi. I promise to…" He choked back the tears. "I promise to always love you and be here for you. I'm going to teach you how great God is."

Big brown eyes as dark as his momma's looked up at Jackson. The black-as-coal lashes fluttered. Turning his face to Jackson's heartbeat, he closed his eyes and went back to sleep. "I could stare at him all day."

Sofia held her hand out to her father. "Papi, come meet your grandson."

Jackson turned to find his father-in-law standing in the doorway.

Slowly he walked across the room and went to the other side of his daughter. Gently, he touched her brow with trembling hands. "I thank God and you for this precious gift. Your mother would be over the moon with love for this little man." He studied her face. "Are you well?"

She nodded, but he looked over his shoulder at Rosita for confirmation.

She nodded. "They are all healthy."

Jackson stood. He held his son out to the older Rafael.

Tears welled up again in his dark eyes. "God has blessed us." Taking his namesake, he pulled him close to his chest. "He looks just like you and your brother."

Rory and Estevan entered the room. Estevan sat the water on top of a dresser, and Rory stood at the foot of the bed. "So, we have a new Two Bit to teach how to ride?"

"Let's give him time to learn to walk first." Jackson shook his head.

Estevan joined them. Rafael showed off his grandson. Estevan nodded. "Good work, little momma."

She smiled at them. "He'll have the best teachers."

"It is all good." Her father tucked the baby back into Sofia's arms. "You need rest. We will leave for now to let you and Jackson get to know your son, but we will be back."

"I don't have a doubt."

As everyone left, Jackson sat on the edge of the bed next to her. He kissed the side of her head. "Do you have to do everything the hard way?"

She giggled. "I didn't mean to, I promise. But don't complain too much. I'm sure that is one of the reasons you love me. You know I'm capable of taking care of myself."

"Yes, ma'am. I do. But you have to know I love taking care of you, too. I love you more than words or gifts from this world could ever express."

"I love you, too, Jackson McCreed."

* * * * *

Dear Reader,

Thank you so much for joining me on this trip back in time. My family settled in Texas in about 1825, so my roots run deep and this story has been a passion of mine for several years.

To see Sofia and Jackson's story in print is a dream come true.

Some of the events in *Lone Star Bride* are part of my own family history, including what happens in the epilogue! Can you imagine? If you haven't read it yet, I won't spoil it for you. But really, the women in my family are remarkable. The women that settled the wild land of Texas had an independent life force.

I love research, and the little facts of people going through their everyday lives made this project so much fun, and when I discovered that cowboys and pirates crossed paths along the Texas-Louisiana border, well, it was a romance writer's dream.

I love talking with readers, so look me up on Facebook at Jolene Navarro, Author or jolenenavarrowriter.com.

Happy Trails,
Jolene Navarro

COMING NEXT MONTH FROM
Love Inspired® Historical

Available August 8, 2017

WEDDED FOR THE BABY
Stand-in Brides • by Dorothy Clark

To fulfill a mail-order bride's dying wish, Katherine Fleming brings the woman's baby to the man who promised to raise him. And when she learns Trace Warren needs to marry to keep his business, Katherine agrees to become his wife—temporarily—for the baby's sake.

FRONTIER WANT AD BRIDE
Wilderness Brides • by Lyn Cote

What starts as a marriage of convenience between a mail-order bride and a war-weary army captain grows into something more when Judith Jones's compassion and faith—and two orphaned children—bring solace to Asa Brant's heart.

AN AMISH COURTSHIP
Amish Country Brides • by Jan Drexler

Samuel Lapp is content in his estrangement from his Amish community—until Mary Hochstetter moves in next door to take care of her elderly aunt, whom he often helps with chores. As he and Mary grow close, can Samuel face his painful past and find the peace he needs to build a home with her?

INHERITED: UNEXPECTED FAMILY
Little Falls Legacy • by Gabrielle Meyer

As sole owner of his hotel, Jude Allen is free to run it however he chooses—until his late business partner's daughter, Elizabeth Bell, arrives to claim the hotel as her inheritance. As he and Elizabeth find a way to work together, can their professional relationship turn into love?

LIHCNM0717

Get 2 Free Books,
Plus 2 Free Gifts—
just for trying the Reader Service!

Love Inspired HISTORICAL

LIHI7R2

*When the wrong mail-order bride arrives with another
woman's baby, Trace Warren's marriage of convenience
brings back the memory of the wife and baby he lost.
Can Katherine help him love again?*

Read on for a sneak preview of
WEDDED FOR THE BABY by *Dorothy Clark*,
part of her STAND-IN BRIDES miniseries.

"I'm sorry I've gotten you into this uncomfortable position, Katherine. I never meant for you to be embarrassed
or—"

The baby let out a squall. Katherine rose, then lifted
Howard into her arms. "You owe me no apology, Trace.
I chose to stay to help you keep your home and shop for
Howard's sake. I'm not sorry." She looked over at him
and met his gaze. Tears glistened in her beautiful eyes. "I
may be hurt by my choice, but I'll never be sorry." Her
whisper was fierce. She bent her head and kissed Howard's cheek. The baby nuzzled at her neck, searching for
something to eat. It was the perfect picture of what he had
longed for, prayed for and lost.

His chest tightened; his stomach knotted. He looked
down at his plate, picked up his fork and forced himself
to take a bite of salmon loaf.

"Trace..."

He braced himself and looked up.

"Please hold Howard while I warm his bottle." She handed the baby to him.

He looked at Katherine standing by the stove, holding a towel while she waited for the bottle to warm. Her lips curved in the suggestion of a smile. His heart lurched. She was so beautiful, so kind and softhearted, so brave to take on the care of an infant of a woman she didn't even know. Katherine Fleming was an amazing young woman.

He jerked his gaze away and stared down at his plate. He had to think of an acceptable excuse to leave as soon as the baby's bottle was ready. It was far too dangerous for him to be here alone with Katherine every day.

She set the baby's bottle on the table. "I'm sorry. I just realized I forgot to pour our coffee. I'll get it now. Would you please start feeding Howard before he begins to cry?" Her skirts flared out as she turned back toward the stove.

He swallowed his protest, clenched his jaw and shifted the infant to the crook of his arm. The baby's lips closed on the offered bottle; his tiny fingers brushed his hand and clung, their touch as light as a feather. Pain ripped through him. The pain of a broken heart vibrating to life again. It was his greatest fear coming true.

Don't miss
WEDDED FOR THE BABY by Dorothy Clark,
available August 2017 wherever
Love Inspired® Historical books and ebooks are sold.

www.LoveInspired.com

LIHEXP0717